ALL
FUDGED UP

Nancy Coco

KENSINGTON PUBLISHING CORP.

http://www.kensingtonbooks.com

Praise for *All Fudged Up*

"A sweet treat with memorable characters, a charming locale, and satisfying mystery."

——**Barbara Allan**, author of the Trash 'n' Treasures mysteries

"A fun book with a lively plot, and it's set in one of America's most interesting resorts. All this plus fudge!"

——**JoAnna Carl**, author of the Chocoholoc mysteries

"A sweet confection of a book. Charming setting, clever protagonist, and creamy fudge—a yummy recipe for a great read."

——**Joanna Campbell Slan**, author of *The Scrap-N-Craft Mysteries* and *The Jane Eyre Chronicles*

"A delightful mystery delivering suspense and surprise in equal measure. Allie McMurphy, owner of the historic McMurphy Hotel and Fudge Shoppe, has a wry narrative voice that never falters. Add that to the charm of the setting, Michigan's famed Mackinac Island, and you have a recipe for enjoyment. As an added bonus, mouth-watering fudge recipes are included. A must-read for all lovers of amateur sleuth classic mysteries."

——**Carole Bugge**, author of the Claire Rawlings mysteries

"You won't have to 'fudge' your enthusiasm for Nancy Parra's first Mackinac Island Fudge Shop Mystery. Indulge your sweet tooth as you settle in and meet Allie McMurphy, Mal the bichon/poodle mix, and the rest of the motley crew in this entertaining series debut."

—**Miranda James**, author of the Cat in the Stacks mysteries

*To Thomas who, when asked what his mother did,
replied, "She types." Now, as you write stories of
your own, you know what I really do.
Remember always, dreams do come true,
and I know yours will, too.*

Chapter 1

I figured that, after ninety-two years of living, Papa Liam probably had some skeletons in his closet. I had no idea they were real.

Not that Joe Jessop was a skeleton . . . yet. But the man was definitely dead and lying in my second-floor utility closet.

I don't think I screamed when I found him. You know how they always scream on television when they find a dead body. I was certainly startled when I turned on the light. I'll admit that. Who wouldn't be when they walked in on a person lying against the shelves with dried blood all over his face and looking, well, lifeless.

It took me a minute to figure out what to do. Should I rush to him and feel for a pulse and try to give him CPR? The idea made me gag since the guy was a funny color and puffier than the last time I saw him. Mostly I stood there thinking about what the right thing to do was. It was only for a few seconds. I was in shock. I'm certain.

My next thought was I should probably run out screaming, but that seemed silly since I hadn't screamed at first glance and I was the only person in the building. I would have to run the length of the hall, down two flights of stairs, and out the building screaming and waving my hands. Yeah, I'm not really that kind of person.

I always thought of myself as more practical. After all, when Papa had died suddenly, I'd managed to step into his shoes with only a few bumps in the road.

After his funeral, it'd taken me two weeks to sublease my Chicago apartment, put my car in storage, and pack up my stuff. The plan all along had been for me to arrive on Mackinac Island in late April to help Papa Liam open the McMurphy Hotel and Fudge Shoppe for the season. This was to be the summer when my papa would give me all his best advice, see me through the day-to-day handling of the property, and turn over the keys to the family business.

Unfortunately, I was now on my own to figure out how to keep the family business going. Papa'd been at the senior center playing pinochle, drinking whiskey, and laughing when he'd suddenly fallen face-first into the table. Just like that. He was gone.

Sort of like Joe Jessop. One minute he was doing who-knows-what in my closet, and the next moment

I was not screaming at the sight of his dead body. Life was a mystery that way.

I took my cell phone out of my pocket.

"9-1-1, this is Charlene, what is your emergency?"

"Um, I opened my closet and there's a guy on the floor. Well, not really on the floor, but mostly on the floor." I inhaled. "I think he's dead."

"Is this Sarah Jane? I'm not taking any more of your practical jokes, girl. You're wasting the taxpayer's money."

"Wait—" The phone went dead in my hand. Well, not as dead as Joe, but dead.

Joe stared at me accusingly. I noted that his eyes were bloodshot and his pupils pinpoints. Don't the crime shows say strangulation causes bloodshot eyes—or was that poison? I wasn't about to step farther into the scene and contaminate it to find out.

"9-1-1, this is Charlene, what is your emergency?"

"Hi, yes, Charlene." I tried to be reasonable. "This is Allie McMurphy over at the historic McMurphy Hotel and Fudge Shoppe."

"Pleased to make your acquaintance, Allie. I'm a big fan of your papa's fudge, but, you should know that this line is for emergencies only. If you want to talk to me, you need to call dispatch at 906.555.6600. Bye now."

"Wait!" Charlene hung up on me again. "I'm trying, Joe," I muttered to the dead guy. He didn't answer, but then I would have run screaming if he had . . . Which would take care of the whole "proper way to act when discovering a body" thing.

For the third time, I punched numbers into my phone. This time I called the dispatch number. At least I hoped it was the dispatch number. I was a bit rattled and wouldn't be surprised if I accidently called my mother instead.

"Dispatch, this is Charlene, how can I help you?"

There was a moment of relief that it wasn't my mother on the line, although she might have been a bigger help. Except for the part where the cops ask why I didn't call 9-1-1.

"Yes, Charlene." I tried again. "This is Allie McMurphy."

"Hi Allie, how are you? I was sorry to hear about your Papa Liam passing suddenly like that. At least he went doing what he loved to do best."

Did she mean cheat at cards? I sighed and glanced at the dead guy. Did Joe wink? Okay, that thought creeped me out a little. I took a step back. "Thanks, Charlene, listen, I want to report a dead body in my utility closet. Well, at least I think he's dead."

There was a long moment of silence on the other end of the phone.

"Charlene?"

"Allie, why didn't you call 9-1-1? Everyone knows if they find someone hurt or, God help us, dead, they call 9-1-1. They don't waste time on the dispatch number."

Was it worth pointing out that I had called 9-1-1? No. "I promise to do that next time. Can you get someone over here?"

I turned my back on the "crime scene" out of respect for the old guy. I mean, he might have been Papa Liam's oldest rival, but that didn't mean his death didn't affect his family.

"I can indeed," Charlene said. "Stay on the line." I could hear her searching through drawers. "Hold on, one second. I need a pen."

A pen? Didn't they have some kind of computer database? Or was Mackinac Island that backward? I didn't think of the place as backward. Touristy maybe. Purposely laid-back in an island sort of way, certainly. But not backward.

"Found it." I heard Charlene click a pen. "Okay, now let's start with your name."

Really? "Charlene, it's Allie. Remember?"

"Yes, of course, I remember . . ." It sounded like she was writing something. "Allie McMurphy called at nine PM to report a possible DB. Allie, where are you?"

I glanced back at Joe. Was he laughing? Was I laughing? Someone was giggling like a crazy person.

"Allie," Charlene shouted. "Get ahold of yourself."

That straightened me up. If this call was being taped, I'm sure everyone would be wondering why I was laughing when faced with a dead man in my closet. "I'm sorry." I tried to breathe in and out and pretend I wasn't hysterical. "What did you ask? Oh, right. I'm at the McMurphy Hotel and Fudge Shoppe on the second floor in the utility closet."

"All right," Charlene said as her pen scratched away. "Stay on the line. I'll send Officer Manning over along with the EMTs."

I swallowed the laughter that threatened to spill out again. "Okay, um, should I go downstairs and let them in?"

"That's probably a good idea," Charlene said. "Unless the guy's not dead. Did you check for a pulse?"

That sobered me up. I turned to the puffy, blue/white, blood-encrusted face. "I, um, didn't touch anything."

Charlene made a sound very close to a snort. "Then how do you know he's dead? For goodness' sakes, you scared the devil out of me and all for no good reason."

"Oh, no, he's dead."

"How can you tell?" Her tone sounded impatient.

"He looks dead." Now I was getting impatient back.

"Have you ever seen a dead body before?"

I suppose that was a good question, but it didn't make me happy. I wanted to lie. I really did. "No." I tried not to sigh too loudly. Then a thought occurred to me. "Wait! I have seen a dead body." Papa Liam, of course.

She harrumphed. "One that wasn't prepped by the mortuary?"

Crap. "Give it up, Charlene. I'm not touching

him. In fact, I'm going downstairs right now to wait at the door for the police."

"Fine." Charlene huffed. "But Officer Manning'll be pretty upset if this turns out to be a drunk asleep in your closet."

Wait, isn't that as bad or worse than a dead body? It would mean that some strange man was sleeping it off in my closet. There was a lock on my third-floor apartment door, but still. I'm the only one in the hotel before the season opens. I could have been attacked or worse. The dead body could have been me. That thought made shivers go down my spine as I scrambled down the stairs.

"Please tell me someone's really on their way over here." I'm afraid my voice was a tad breathless by the time I reached the bottom of the flower-patterned carpeted stairs.

There was a knock on the glass front door of the shop, and I screamed . . . a little.

Charlene snickered in my ear. "He's there," she said. "You can hang up now."

"Great." I practically ran to the door. "You've been a big help, Charlene. Thanks."

"You're welcome, dear."

So much for sarcasm, I thought as I answered the door.

The man outside had all the right gear on, a complete blue officer outfit. It was dark out, but I could see in the lamplight behind him the official police bicycle complete with flashing light and siren. I had a sudden thought that the local police ought to have a flashing light on the top of their hats. A giggle slipped out.

"Are you all right, Miss?" The officer narrowed what could only be described as pretty blue eyes. They were that soft baby blue and ringed with thick long eyelashes that curled. "Miss?"

"Right." I opened the door wide and waved for him to come inside. "I may be in a bit of shock. I'm Allie McMurphy."

He took off his hat and uncovered a wide bald pate that was attractive in that "tough-guy" way. "I'm Officer Rex Manning," he offered. "Charlene told me you might have a dead body situation."

Situation? I swallowed. "Um, upstairs, second-floor utility closet. Follow me."

He did, following me through the under-construction first-floor lobby to the twin staircases that led to the second floor.

"Is it okay if we take the stairs? The elevator repair guy is coming in the morning."

"That's fine," he said. I noted that his nice gaze took in the details of the building, including the renovations. "Is there anyone else in the building?"

"You mean besides the dead guy?" I climbed the stairs. My fingers brushed the cool, worn-smooth banister. The rubber of my athletic shoes snagged at the flowered carpet. "No, the crew working on the renovations left at six PM."

"It's a big building with lots of places to hide," he pointed out.

I stopped on the second-floor landing and drew

my brows together. "Are you thinking the killer is still inside?" Suddenly there wasn't anything funny about the situation. I'd only been on Mackinac Island for a month, but it really didn't seem like the kind of place you had to keep your doors locked for fear of a serial killer. Not like Chicago, anyway.

I mean, on an island with five hundred to six hundred year-round residents, you could spot a serial killer a mile off. Couldn't you? Weren't they usually the quiet-keep-to-themselves-neighbor? Wait, was that me?

"All I'm thinking is that it's a big building," Officer Manning said with a nonchalant tone.

I pursed my lips. His words weren't encouraging. "All the rooms are locked." I lifted the master key I had in my hand. The hotels on island still had metal keys. It was quaint and fun. The keys were locked up in a key cabinet in Papa Liam's office. Once the renovations were done, they would hang from hooks behind the reservation desk. "I'm the only one with a key."

"Okay." The word was flat and monotone. I tried not to infer anything from it. "Where's the body?"

"Over here." I walked down the hall. Somewhere in the late seventies Papa had put down a green carpet with a raised flower pattern. It was a little worn now. Okay shabby, but I had it on my to-do list to replace. In the center of the hall was a set of elevator doors. Across the hall from there was the small utility closet where Joe Jessop died. The door was still open, and the light shone into the dimmer hallway.

"Yep, that's a dead body." Officer Manning stood in the doorway, his expression serious as stone. My shock-crazed brain registered that he wore a bullet-proof vest underneath his shirt, giving his pleasant girth stiffness. Even though we stood eye to eye, he looked strong.

I was glad of that because if there was a killer in my home, I wouldn't think twice about letting Officer Manning get between me and him. I mean, that's what they paid him to do, right?

He stepped carefully into the room. I knew he was a brave man because he knelt down and checked Joe for a pulse even though we both knew that ship had sailed hours ago. Officer Manning looked around, then reached up and made a call on the two-way radio that sat on his shoulder. "Charlene, get Doc Hamlin over here. We need a coroner on site. We have a DB."

"Yes, sir."

Sure, Charlene sounded completely professional when talking with the officer.

"Did you touch anything?" He stood and took pictures with his cell phone.

"I opened the door, turned on the light, and stepped inside." I hugged my waist, trying to quell the shivering that threatened to take over my body. "He was kind of hard to miss."

"He's a big guy," Officer Manning agreed absently

as he took more pictures. "Did you touch him? Check for a pulse?"

"No."

All he did was nod at that. His cell phone clicked away. My teeth chattered. I clamped down hard trying to stop them, but the sound caught the officer's attention.

"Sit down!" He said it sharp and tight, and I obeyed without thought; my knees gave way, dropping me to the hall floor. He moved lightning fast because the next thing I knew he was beside me. "Put your head down."

"Okay," I muttered as the shivering took over. I put my forehead on the floor. He must have grabbed a blanket off the shelf in the closet because he draped one over me. I tried not to think about it too much as I worked to hold myself together. The vibrations of more footsteps reached me or it could have been my teeth rattling my bones.

"What do we have?" a new male voice asked. A shot of adrenaline went through me. The sound I made would have been a scream except my throat closed up the instant I realized that I had not locked the door behind us when we came upstairs.

Chapter 2

"Was that a squeak?" the new male said. "Or a laugh?"

"She's in shock." I heard Officer Manning reply.

Could a person die of embarrassment? Maybe if I buried my face in the carpet and drew the pale blue blanket over my head, it would all go away.

The two hunkered down beside me. Someone put a hand on my back. It was a comforting gesture. I would have said something nice about it if I weren't afraid of biting my tongue with my stupid chattering teeth. Tears filled my eyes. I'm sure it was frustration. I mean, I don't cry easy.

"Miss, can you sit up?" the second voice said gently, causing more tears to track down my cheeks. Shoot. Don't be nice to me. Don't you know that nice is the worst thing you can be to a girl on the verge of losing it?

I sat up and wiped the tears off with the sleeve of my chamois work shirt.

The second voice belonged to a guy with deep brown eyes and the high cheekbones of a true local. He wore a blue uniform as well, but this one said "EMT" on it. He was lean with broad shoulders and competent hands. My vision narrowed, and I saw stars.

Mr. EMT had me flat on my back with my feet higher than my head before I knew what was going on. Shoot, he hadn't even bought me a drink first.

"Thanks," I muttered through gritted teeth as he adjusted the blanket around me and then pulled out a blood pressure cuff. With silent movement, he pumped up the cuff, released it a little, and pumped it again as he listened. I have no idea what he heard as all I could hear was my heart pounding in my head. He put his fingers on my wrist and checked my pulse. I noted that his name tag said George Marron.

"I'm"—chatter—"fine"—chatter—"really."

"Take a deep breath. In through your nose and out through your mouth."

I did what he said and concentrated on his soulful eyes until I could talk. "Not used to finding"—breathe in, breathe out—"a dead person in my closet is all."

George's calm gaze watched me. It was kind of embarrassing getting all this attention when there was a dead man down the hall.

"Was I right?" Officer Manning asked as he stepped out of the crime scene.

The EMT nodded.

"Do you want to take her down to the clinic?" Officer Manning tipped his head and studied me as if I were a specimen in a zoo.

"No!" I tried to sit up, but George put his hands on my shoulder and kept me down.

"She'll be fine."

"See." I huddled under the blanket. "I'll be fine."

Officer Manning frowned. "Is there anyone you can call?"

"Um, why?" I had to ask. "It's only a little shock. I don't need a ba . . . ba . . . babysitter."

"You can't stay here tonight," he pointed out. "This is a crime scene."

"Oh." It was my turn to frown. "The whole hotel?" Distracted by this new development, I was able to use my elbows to hold myself up. The blanket pooled around my jean-covered lap.

"The season starts in four weeks. I'm in the middle of renovations." Not that I didn't have a backup plan. My hotel management degree had taught me how to be frugal and efficient. But I was stubborn and didn't want to use Plan B. That meant at least a three-week delay in opening, giving my competitors a significant advantage.

Wait . . . Was that why someone had killed Joe, to try to run me out of business?

I pushed the silly thought away. School had taught me that people would do the craziest things to see a competitor fail. But good sense told me most people drew the line at killing someone. What was the point of that? Right? Besides, it wouldn't take such a dramatic act to see a person fail. It was far too easy to lose money in any small business, more specifically the competitive fudge shop business here on island.

After all, Mackinac Island was known as the fudge capital of the world. Everyone here took their fudge very seriously—including my Papa Liam.

"Always have a backup plan," Papa Liam had drilled into my head growing up. "Creative thinking helps."

"We'll need you out of the hotel at least for tonight while we work," Officer Manning said. "Longer if need-be."

"What? No. There's no need-be." I sat all the way up. George checked my blood pressure again. I waited patiently for him to be done before going on. "I have a business to run."

Well, get back up and running. Papa'd let the hotel wear down a bit the last two years while I was in culinary school. I'd been shocked at the shape of the place when I'd taken over.

It's why I'd started the renovations right after Papa's death. He'd already done most of the groundwork with the Mackinac Island historical society. I knew he wouldn't want me to put my dream of running the family business aside just because he'd gone toes up, or in Papa's case nose down, unexpectedly.

"At least let me continue with the renovations in

the lobby." I tried not to beg. "If I have any delays, I'll lose my subcontractors."

I glanced at George, looking for support in my hour of need. He stood and crossed his arms over his chest, waiting, I assume, for Officer Manning to tell him what to do next.

Officer Manning narrowed his eyes. His mouth tightened slightly. "Subcontractors are the least of your worries, Ms. McMurphy. Is there someone you can call?"

"Frances Wentworth." She was a retired school teacher who'd spent the last twenty years working for Papa Liam in the summers as front-desk clerk and reservation organizer.

"Call her," he ordered. "George, come with me." With that, both men took off down the hall and disappeared into the closet.

I lay back down and blew out a long breath as I stared at the hall ceiling. It needed painting. The white color was no longer eggshell, and in fact the plaster had cracked into the most interesting of shapes.

"Call her," Officer Manning said from down the hall. The man had stuck his head out to check on me.

"Yes, sir." I did my best interpretation of a salute and pulled my phone out of my pocket. "I could stay in a motel," I muttered; then I realized that I was on an island in the off-season and—the most important thing of all—the other hotels were also my competitors. Not that they had anything to worry about at this point.

I mean, I had a crumbling ceiling, half-completed renovations, and a dead body in my closet. Everyone would be taking bets I'd even open by the start of the season.

Chapter 3

"Hello?"

"Hello, Frances. It's Allie McMurphy. I'm so sorry to bother you after nine PM."

"It's okay, Allie, are you all right?"

"Yes, I'm fine. Um, is your spare room empty?"

"Yes, why? Are you having a problem with the water heater? I told you the pilot light goes out when the wind howls. I'll walk you through relighting it if you want."

"No." I took a deep breath. "No, the water heater is fine, I think."

"Are you sure? Because I can call around and hunt down Colin if you're afraid of lighting it yourself."

Colin Ferber was the McMurphy's handyman and as old as Papa Liam. He was also known to imbibe a bit too often and hadn't been the most reliable of help. Not that it mattered right now.

"No, no." I threw my arm over my eyes so I didn't

have to look at the cracked plaster on the ceiling. "This isn't a handyman issue."

"Good, you scared me for a moment." It sounded as if she pulled out a chair and sat down. "Why do you need my spare room?"

"It's not a handyman issue, it's a policeman issue."

"What?"

"I found a dead man in the second-floor utility closet, and now Officer Manning says I can't sleep here tonight. Due to the crime scene and all that stuff."

There was a long pause on the other end of the phone.

"Frances?"

"Honey, are you okay? You aren't making any sense."

"Yes, I'm fine. The EMT checked me out."

"EMT?"

"Yes, I believe his name is George Marron."

"Allie!"

"What?"

"You are not fine. Seriously, you found a dead man?"

"Yes. In the utility closet on the second floor."

"There's a dead man in the McMurphy's second-floor utility closet . . ."

"Yes."

"Did you call 9-1-1?"

"Yes, although Charlene wasn't very helpful. I

had to call her three times before she realized I was serious."

"Now that sounds like Charlene. Were you alone?"

"When I found him or when I called? Because the answer to both is yes. I'm just glad I found him tonight and didn't spend the night sleeping a floor above a dead man." I shuddered at that thought. My stomach did a little weird roll. Maybe I did need to sleep somewhere else tonight.

"Oh, Allie." She sounded like she might be a little sick.

"Stay with me, Frances," I begged. "I'm being evicted for the night. Can I stay with you or will I need to get a room in another hotel?"

"Of course you can stay with me, honey. I'm getting dressed and coming to get you."

A wave of relief went through me. I gathered the woven cotton blanket around me. "Thank you." I drew up my knees to my chest and hugged them. "I can't figure out how it happened."

"How what happened? The dead man or how you found him?"

"I know how I found him, I was looking for a mop. The lobby toilet overflowed."

"You need a plumber."

"I know. I have one scheduled to come in to update all the fixtures and snake the pipes. What I don't understand is how Joe got into the McMurphy and how he died. Why didn't I hear anything?"

"I don't understand." Frances's voice moved in and out as she clearly prepared to come get me.

"Who is it who died and did he fall? Or maybe something fell on him? Will there be an insurance claim?"

"Gosh, I hadn't even thought about insurance. Do you think this will raise my rates?"

"Maybe if it's a liability issue."

I banged my forehead on my knees. "Why don't they talk about these things on crime shows?"

"Because insurance is not as interesting as solving a crime, I imagine," Frances replied. "It's like paying your taxes. Everybody does it, but no one wants to see a show about it on television."

"But no one was supposed to be in the building," I lamented. "Will I still be liable if they were trespassing and died?"

"First off, who was it? Did you say 'Joe'?"

"Yes, it's Joe Jessop."

Frances was once again silent. I waited three whole heartbeats. "Hello?"

"Are you sure it's Joe Jessop?" she asked.

"As sure as Officer Manning," I replied.

"Well, hell." It was the first time I'd ever heard Frances curse. Not that I blamed her. I mean, Joe was a pretty important member of the community. There was bound to be a lot of press. "Don't say anything to anyone, dear," Frances said. "I'll call my cousin William."

"Why?"

"He's a lawyer, dear, and you're going to need one."

Easy Tropical Spiced-Rum Fudge

4 cups white chocolate chips (Ghirardelli are
    best.)
1 can sweetened condensed milk
2 tablespoons coconut milk
4 tablespoons butter
Juice from ½ of a fresh lime or 1 tablespoon
    lime juice
½ teaspoon orange extract
2 tablespoons spiced rum
¾ cup shredded coconut

Using a double boiler fill ⅓ of the bottom pan
with water and heat on medium high until the
water is boiling. Then you can turn the heat down
to low and in the top section, mix sweetened condensed milk, coconut milk, white chocolate chips,
and butter. Stir constantly until chips and butter are
melted. Remove from heat. Add lime juice and
rum, and stir until combined. Add coconut. Mix
well. Pour into 8" x 8" x 2" pan prepared before-
hand (by buttering pan and placing waxed paper
in the bottom). Cool completely. Cut and serve.
Store in covered container.

For party fun, place in paper or foil candy
cups and add a maraschino cherry on top. Garnish
with small drink umbrella or pirate flag.

*Invest in a double boiler for making fudge.
Using a water bath (fudge pan inside a larger and

with steam/boiling water) to heat the fudge keeps
the chocolate from scorching and or sugaring.

Also, a good candy thermometer is necessary
if you choose to make the kind without sweetened
condensed milk.

Chapter 4

"Are you positive it's Joe Jessop?" Frances craned her neck to try to see around the crime-scene tape.

"I'm positive." I hitched the handle of my pink overnight case up onto my shoulder. "Officer Manning confirmed his identity."

"Well, I'd like to know what Joe was doing in the utility closet." Frances put her hands on her hips. She wore a maxi skirt made out of a crazy swirling pattern consisting of orange and blue and yellow and red. Over that was a lovely pale blue wool peacoat, and a matching hat covered her gray-brown hair. She drew herself up to her full five-foot-two-inch height. "I know that man and your grandpa had some kind of long-standing feud, but Liam is dead. There was no reason for Joe to continue to come here and play pranks."

"Wait, what? Did Joe Jessop make a habit of sneaking into the McMurphy?"

"Only once a year. And only in the spring, but

each time he'd start a few weeks before the tourist season. It was an annual ritual. Joe would sneak in and play a prank on Liam. Liam would set up cameras and all kinds of traps for Joe. But Liam never caught him. In their old age it became a game of pride."

"What did?"

"Why, who could prank the other first, of course." Frances grabbed me by the arm and pulled me toward the stairs. "Come on. I called my cousin William."

"Yes, I know, the lawyer."

"He said you're to stay with me for the night. But first we're to tell the police that they can't search any other floor without a proper warrant."

"Right." I hadn't thought about the fact that they could go through Papa's apartment. I suppose I should call it my apartment since I lived there now. "They can't go through the McMurphy, can they? I mean, my apartment has nothing to do with Joe's murder."

"We won't know that until we check it out," Officer Manning said from the bottom of the stairs. "For that matter, we don't know if Joe's death was accidental or not."

"The apartment is a mess." I stopped on the bottom stair and stood a head taller than the handsome officer. "I'm in the middle of packing Papa and unpacking me."

"We don't judge housekeeping, we're simply going to ensure everyone is safe."

"From what? Killer box tape? Because I have a few rolls of that lying around."

"Where there are boxes there's usually a box knife or two." A second police officer walked in and adjusted his gun belt. His jacket covered his name tag.

"But Joe wasn't stabbed," I protested.

"How do you know that?" The younger officer looked me in the eye. He had dark green eyes and light brown hair. His hat was tucked under his arm.

"Don't say anything more." Frances grabbed my arm. "If you want to ask Allie any questions, you'll have to wait for her attorney."

"You have an attorney already?" Officer Manning asked.

"Yes, I called my cousin William," Frances said. "He's flying over from St. Ignace. In the meantime I'm taking her to my house."

"Before you go, are you sure you're the only one with a key to the building?"

"There's only one master key and I have it." I dug the keys out of my pocket.

"Don't you have a maintenance guy?" the younger officer asked. "A place this old takes regular maintenance."

"Colin Ferber," I said. "Papa was always here when he worked so there was no need for him to have a copy of the keys."

"We'll want to speak to Colin," Officer Manning said to the younger officer who nodded and wrote a note in his notebook.

"It's hard to tell where Colin may be at any given moment. He generally shows up when he needs money. But I did hear a rumor that you might find him at the Mare's Head Pub." Frances pulled me down from the stairs. "He's a bit of a recluse and I know he's still mourning Liam's passing."

"Right," Officer Manning stated. "I'll be calling on you in the morning, Ms. McMurphy."

"No worries," I said as Frances dragged me toward the door. "I'll be back at first light. I've got contractors to let inside."

"Great."

"Good," I said.

"Fine," the young officer said.

Frances opened the door, and I grabbed my coat from the wrought-iron hall tree next to the door. "If you see Colin, please let him know I need to see him. He can find me in my office by eight."

"Come on." Frances tugged me out the door.

"They aren't going to go through my boxes, are they?" I asked as I tugged on my coat.

I had most of my things shipped to the McMurphy because I planned on spending the rest of my life here and didn't see any need for storage. Unfortunately my grandparents had lived on the top floor of the McMurphy their entire married lives. After Grammy'd died, Papa'd created a place all his own up there, filling the space with "stuff."

In fact, the apartment still held so many of his things even his scent haunted it. I found it comforting and difficult to box up and remove Papa's things. My own stuff was in a crate stored at the dock. I even slept in the guest room. I hadn't had the time or the desire to clear Papa out of the apartment. Now I wish I had. The last thing he'd ever want was for the police to go through his things.

"They have to have cause to search the rest of the building, right?" I chewed on my bottom lip as we moved past the ambulance. The vehicle was so out of place on an island without any automobiles, and yet we were all grateful for the convenience when an EMT in a horse-drawn carriage seemed more terrifying than quaint. It was the first time I'd ever seen it used.

The sight of it had drawn a small crowd.

"What's going on?"

"Is everything all right?"

"I heard a contractor shot himself with a nail gun. Is that true?"

"Are you a McMurphy?"

"I heard Colin Ferber fell down the stairs. Is that true?"

People talked all at once when we stepped toward the ambulance. "What?" I asked, trying to make sense of the questions.

"Don't say anything," Frances reminded me and pulled me through the group. George Marron stepped out after us, and my neighbors mobbed him instead, looking for answers to their questions.

Frances hadn't answered mine. "They can't go through my boxes, can they?"

"The neighbors? No, the police will keep them out."

"No, the police," I clarified. "They aren't going to go through my drawers, are they?" Drawers made me think of lingerie and the fact that I hadn't done laundry so there was a large pile of dirty clothes in the corner of my room. Mom always told me to keep up with my laundry. You never knew who would be going through your room. Who knew she was right?

"They can if they have cause." Frances flashed her perfect teeth. "I think a dead man is good cause." Her flawless skin barely held a wrinkle, which was a trick considering she was seventy years old. Age didn't matter for some people. Besides her perfect skin, Frances was smart as a whip. When she said she thought something was true, I believed her.

"But only if he was murdered," I stated. "And even then, if I'm a murder suspect, would I be stupid enough to call in the body? And then hide the murder weapon in my underwear drawer?" I was not about to let go of the idea of handsome Officer Manning rummaging through my dirty clothes.

"People have been known to do sillier things."

I blew out a long breath. "Do you really think so little of me?"

"Oh, goodness no." She patted my hand. "I don't, but even though you are Liam's granddaughter, many people feel you are far from a local."

"What? I practically grew up here. I spent almost every summer of my childhood on island."

"That's not living here full-time. Don't worry, if you stick it out, maybe in twenty years or so you'll be a local too . . . maybe."

Trouble was, I didn't have twenty or thirty years to fit in. If I was to keep up appearances, I needed to be a local now. "Wait, do you think Joe was playing a prank on me when he died?" A cold wind blew in off Lake Huron. It hit me like a slap in the face. I walked the gaslit street, leaving my home because there was a dead man inside. My teeth chattered a bit.

"No telling." Frances shrugged. "Guess the final prank was on him."

"I suppose," I muttered as I huddled into my down jacket and walked along the darkened sidewalk. I kept my head down against the cold and nearly ran smack into a solid, warm male figure who smelled good. My shoulder bounced off his chest, sending me sideways.

"Hey!" He grabbed me by the forearm until I was steady. His dark eyes were shadowed by the streetlight. "Are you okay?"

"Yes, sorry," I muttered.

"Slow down," he offered. "People'll think you're late for a funeral."

"Right." I know it was a common saying, but his words could not be much closer to the truth. Only I wasn't running toward a dead guy, I was running away from one.

"That's Trent Jessop," Frances offered.

"As in Joe Jessop's son?" The man removed his cowboy hat and walked right into my hotel as if it were his. I turned to go back.

"His grandson." Frances put her arm through mine and dragged me toward her house. "He runs Jessop Stables. They've had horses on island for over a hundred years."

"Why's he going into my hotel?" I hitched the strap of my overnight bag higher on my shoulder. "Shouldn't I be there?"

"I imagine Rex called him to identify the body, and no, you should not be there."

"But it's my place."

"And it's in good hands." Frances patted my arm and pulled my attention back to her. "You keep your apartment locked, right?"

I lifted my keys and jingled them. "Yes." It was something Papa Liam had taught us early on. When you lived in a public venue, you always kept your door locked. Tourists seemed to have the idea that once you let them inside, the entire place was theirs.

"Then they won't search it without you there." She stepped up to the porch of the painted lady that was now split into four condos. In the dark, it looked a bit like a spooky Addam's Family house. I suppose that was part of the *Meet Me in St. Louis* feel. I loved that movie, and Frances's house always made me feel as if Judy Garland could emerge from around the corner at any moment.

She unlocked her condo door and waved me inside. "I suggest you let Rex Manning and my cousin, your lawyer, deal with Trent Jessop, my dear."

"Why? The man just lost his grandfather. I know how that feels. Are you sure I shouldn't go back and talk to him?" I stepped into the lovely golden glow of warmed dark wood and plaster walls painted in a pale gold. It was significantly warmer inside than out.

"Trent Jessop isn't going to want to talk to you." Frances made a firm line with her mouth. "Especially after he finds out that not only did his granddad die in the McMurphy, but Liam's granddaughter was the one who called it in."

"None of that was my fault." I followed her through the living room and into the spare bedroom. The condo was simple yet smart. The front held an office/den separated from the living area by pocket doors. It also had a master bedroom with a large walk-in closet. On the other side of the living space was a small spare bedroom and the kitchen, with a full bath tucked in between.

"I know that his death wasn't your fault and you know that." She flicked on the light switch, illuminating a full-sized wrought-iron bed covered with thick blankets and one of those old bumpy knotted coverlets in pale green. She faced me, her brown eyes filled with concern. "But all Trent Jessop knows is that his granddad is dead and possibly at the hands of his worst enemy."

"Wait, what? I didn't even know Joe." I slid the overnight case off my shoulder. "I mean, I met him once or twice, sure, but that's no reason to consider him my enemy or for me to do something crazy like kill him."

"Try telling a Jessop that." She shook her head and tsked her tongue. "They love a good feud. It's the Scotsman in them."

"That's ridiculous," I muttered, following her out of the bedroom and into the kitchen. "Surely everyone else on island will know better."

"My guess is they're taking sides as we speak." She took off her hat and hung it and her coat up on a coat tree in the corner. "Tea?"

"Yes, please." I hung my coat on the same tree and sat down at the round kitchenette table. "I think I'm going to need it."

"Don't worry, dear," Frances said with a serious nod. "All the best people will be on your side."

Chapter 5

You know, it's tough to pretend like everything is fine when you know that the coroner hauled a dead body out of your second-floor utility closet hours before. But I tried. Really I did. After all, Papa Liam would say, "Buck up, kid. It's just a little bump in the road."

After listening to Frances talk for hours about the seasonal pranks Joe would play on Liam, I had to wonder what Papa did in return. In fact, now that I was back home, I was sorely tempted to go into the closet and look for Papa's trap—the one that may have killed Joe.

The thought had a shiver running down my back. How often can you say someone was killed by a dead guy? My next thought was worse. What if Papa had booby traps hidden all over the McMurphy? How could I protect the subcontractors or, worse, the customers? What was that going to do to my insurance?

I sat at my office desk and dropped my forehead into my hands, then looked into Papa's smiling portrait. "You would never actually endanger a life, would you?"

Of course I wouldn't really know anything until the coroner ruled on whether Joe died accidently or if he was murdered. I didn't want to think about it. Murder wasn't exactly helpful in getting people to reserve rooms and stay the night, nor was it any good at selling fudge.

I had just dialed the security company's number when the power flickered and then went out. The window light in my office meant I could see easily. What I didn't account for was the sudden emergence of an annoying beeping.

"AlertMe Security, this is Kendall, how can I help you?" came the voice on the other side of the phone.

"Hi." I tried to ignore the incessant beeping noise. "This is Allie at the McMurphy Hotel and Fudge Shoppe. I had called last week about having a new security system installed. I was curious if there was any way I can get someone out here sooner??"

"Let me check." She tapped on some keys and clicked the mouse twice. Funny how the phone sounds didn't help me ignore the beeping. I swear it grew louder with every passing minute. "Ms. McMurphy?"

"Yes." I strummed my fingers on Papa's big old desk and looked for a source.

"The soonest we can get anyone out there will be

Saturday and there will be a five-hundred-dollar overtime fee. Do you still want it installed that early?"

I thought about Joe's dead body and my strong desire not to spend the next seven nights sleeping on Frances's guest bed. "Yes, please, let's have them out on Saturday."

"Okay." I heard her tap more keys. "The boys will be out between eight AM and noon. Will someone be there to let them in?"

"I'll be here," I said. Because I would. I lived here and only a man with a gun could pry me out. I pushed away any thought of the officer with the gorgeous blue eyes.

"Excuse me, is your power out?"

I glanced around, surprised that she knew that. "Yes, how can you tell? Is it out all over?"

"Oh, no, we have power," she replied. "It sounds like your Wi-Fi system has a battery backup."

"Is that what the beeping is?" I found the set of shelves with the Wi-Fi modem on it. Sure enough, there was a red light blinking in time with the beeping. "How did you know?"

She giggled. "It happened to my mom when she had Wi-Fi installed and the power went out. It about drove her nuts . . . Oh, and FYI, the beeps will start to get closer together as time goes by, so you might want to get that fixed."

"Thanks," I muttered, hung up, and then dialed the power company number. Unfortunately I had to go through the inane computerized menu only to be told to "please hold."

I don't know whose idea it was to have a battery backup beep. It was emotional blackmail, torture-camp stuff akin to the "Muzak-on-hold" playing in my ear.

Here I'd thought I'd been clever when I had Wi-Fi installed. At the time I'd envisioned crowds of tourists in the big lobby sitting around the fire-place, drinking specialty coffee and teas, noshing on McMurphy fudge while checking in with their buddies back home.

I hadn't anticipated the electricity going out. I wondered how often it happened. It was another question to ask Papa—if he were here. The beeping battery backup's insistent sound reminded me that Papa Liam wasn't here and if I didn't get the power problem fixed soon, not only would I lose a day of working on the hotel improvements, but I would be completely insane.

I glared at the flashing light. Beep. 1, 2, 3, 4, 5, 6, 7, 8. Beep. Was this part of Joe's prank? If so, I might have had to—

"Thank you for holding. Your call is important to us. A customer service representative will be with you shortly."

The man was already dead. No use in wishing bad things on him. For all I knew the power outage was due to a tree limb or something. I leaned my elbows on Papa Liam's old pine desk and thought that when it was my time to go, I hoped it wasn't in a powerless room listening to the maddening beep of a battery backup system.

"I'm buying a generator," I muttered and with my free hand added that task to my insanely huge to-do list. It was April 7 and, instead of being on spring break, I had three weeks to finish Papa's renovations, hire seasonal help, and make a go of the place on my own. That is, if the blue-eyed police officer let me back onto the second floor.

It took some fancy negotiation on the part of Frances's cousin William, but Officer Manning finally allowed me to continue with my renovations on the first floor as long as we kept them to the first floor. Which was fine as it meant I wouldn't lose my subcontractors to their next job.

"This is Island Electric. My name is Steve. How can I help you?"

Finally! "Hi Steve, this is Allie McMurphy. I'm at the McMurphy Hotel and Fudge Shoppe and I have no power . . . again."

"Let me look that up for you."

I could hear his fingers clacking on his keyboard as he breathed into my ear. "It looks like your power was shut off due to the certified death of Liam McMurphy. Are you saying you're the new owner?"

I rolled my eyes. "Yes, I'm the new owner. I'm Allie McMurphy. I'm the one who came down to the office, showed you guys the death certificate, and had the account moved over into my name."

"Huh." There was more clacking. "When did you come down?"

"Monday. I spoke to Heather. She said there would be no disruption in service."

"Did she give you a new account number?"

Scowling, I dug through the papers in the "done" section of my in-box. "I'm not sure. She did give me a copy of a paper I signed."

"There isn't anything I can do without an account number," Steve warned me.

"I realize that. I have the paperwork here. Hold on." I put down my cell phone and dug through the big pile of papers, with the annoying beep in the background pushing me. "Darn it," I muttered. It was right here. I know I put it here. I picked up my phone. "I'll have to get back to you as soon as I find it."

"That's fine. Our office hours are nine AM to five PM."

"Right." I glanced at the time on my laptop. It was 3:30 PM. I pressed the OFF button, grabbed the big pile of papers, and left the incessant reminder of the battery backup. The office was on the same floor as Papa Liam's apartment. I hadn't gone in the apartment yet for fear Officer Manning would see it as an opening to search the room. It's not that I had anything to hide, but I didn't know for sure if Papa did.

I took the stairs down to the lobby. The front door was currently wide-open even though it was all of forty-five degrees outside. Mackinac Island sat in the middle of Lake Huron on the northern edge of the Lower Peninsula of the state of Michigan, accessible by boat from either the Upper or Lower Peninsula. April, while lovely, wasn't exactly steamy.

The door was open because I had a painting crew working on the inside lobby walls and the exterior false front of the hotel. Papa'd left me money for repairs and general maintenance, along with scheduled subcontractors so I wasn't entirely without a plan. But even with reservations from long-standing clients, I wasn't rich by any means. If I didn't make a go of things this season, there would be precious little leftover money for next season's start-up.

Which is why I couldn't let anything—not even a dead man—stop me from opening on time. Not that I wasn't sorry for Joe and his family. It's hard when you lose a loved one. I'd gone through it last month with Papa.

I paused for a moment on the stairs. Wait, had Joe been trying to prevent me from opening? The thought crossed my mind for a second time. The idea that Joe Jessop, or anyone for that matter, might want to see me fail made me realize I would do whatever it took not to let that happen.

The lobby, where Benny Rodriquez and his crew of three worked painting fat pink-and-white stripes on the walls, was oddly quiet.

"The power's out," Benny said when he saw me come down the stairs.

"I know. I'm working on it." I took the papers

over to the fudge shop area and placed them on the long stainless-steel countertop.

"My guys don't work as fast without music," Benny called over.

"I get it." I waved my hand at him in a dismissing fashion. "I'm working on it." I carefully sorted through the papers on the wide-open counter. Water account. Phone account. Cable account. Elevator inspection . . . wait. Was the inspector still coming? I would need to check into that. I made a note on the palm of my hand, then continued through the paperwork to find the hotel inspection report. Fire inspection. Health inspector for the fudge shop. Huh, that would probably have to be redone now that they found a dead body in the building.

I made a face of disgust at the thought as I flipped through papers. There was the proof the boiler was replaced and the water was at a safe temperature for showers. Papers showing the down payment I had made on the new lobby carpet.

Let's face it. The McMurphy Hotel and Fudge Shoppe was a money pit. But it'd been in my family for one hundred and twenty years. It was important to me, as the only child of an only child, to keep the business going. If Papa Liam's father could keep the place open through the Great Depression, then I could keep it open now. I pulled over a stainless-steel stool on rollers and sat down.

It was too bad my dad didn't want anything to do with the old place. He'd moved us to Detroit and

become an architect. Growing up with Dad designing buildings and Mom teaching English at the
local high school meant that the only time I'd seen
my grandparents was in the summer. My parents
would bring me up to play on the island and help
around the shop.

It was the influence of those long-ago summers
and the stories Papa Liam would tell of the people
he would meet from around the world that made
me decide early on that I would see that the
McMurphy Hotel and Fudge Shoppe stayed in the
family.

I loved the tradition of a family-owned place and
the quaint elegance of the island. I loved the gentle
lake breezes, the sounds of summer children laughing, the clomp of the carriage horses drawing their
guests, the ring of bicycle bells. I loved the whole
Victorian feel of the island, from the colorful
painted ladies that passed as cottages to the old fort
with its limestone surface.

Mackinac Island didn't allow cars. The locals
were proud of the back-in-time feel. Tourists came
for the day or to stay a while in one of the hotels
and enjoy the ambience. They'd come to bike
around the island or take the carriage rides. They'd
come to visit the fort, but mostly they'd come for
the fudge—Mackinac's number one souvenir.

On Mackinac, the locals were proud of their
fudge, and each shop had its own private recipes.
The McMurphy recipe had been created in the tiny
cook's house of the hotel. It was a closely guarded

secret that was learned by rote memorization as no one would write it down for fear of it being stolen. Did I mention that the fudge business was highly competitive?

The fudge shops on island had seasonal recipes as well as their longtime favorites. It was why I went to school to learn candy making. So that I could develop new recipes that could compete on a national, if not world, level. My hope had been to make Papa proud and to create an enduring name for the McMurphy.

The hotel itself was smaller than the large hotels like the Grand and the Island House Hotel. It also didn't have the painted-lady architecture of some of the other bed-and-breakfasts. The appeal of the McMurphy was the fact that it sat right smack in the heart of historic downtown. People liked the charm of a small, old-fashioned hotel with a view of the harbor and the smell of fresh, homemade fudge from the shop below. My hope was that the newly remodeled lobby and the additions I planned would make the McMurphy even more appealing.

It was my love of the old building that made me vow to keep the place going, even if it meant taking another job during the winter. It was why I received degrees in both hotel management and culinary arts. I'm a planner and I planned to succeed. I also planned to spend the rest of my life on island. I wanted to raise my children here. Where they could watch the ferry boats come and go and they could play hopscotch on the sidewalk.

It was a grand plan. Unfortunately some things can't ever be planned for . . . things like Joe Jessop expiring in my closet.

Papa used to say if you wanted something, really wanted something, you'd never stop until you got it. "No matter what you do, you can't avoid the unexpected or it wouldn't be . . ."

"Unexpected," I'd say, and he'd smile at me and wink.

"You might as well problem solve toward the things you want."

And that was what I planned to do, but first I had to get the power turned on. Then I could figure out how to get everyone in town to forget that Joe Jessop died here. Not an easy thing to do if Frances was to be believed. And one thing I figured out early on—Frances was definitely a person in the know when it came to the island and the people who lived on it.

"Is it true? Did you find Joe Jessop dead in your basement last night?" Mabel Showorthy must have walked in when I was searching my papers. She'd been one of my grandmother's friends. She owned Agatha's Family Fudge Shop two blocks down. It'd been there so long no one knew who Agatha was or even if she'd ever been a real person.

"No." I kept my comments short in hopes she'd get the hint that I was super busy.

She cocked a white eyebrow with suspicion. "No, you didn't find Joe Jessop dead last night? I'm sorry but I know for a fact that man is currently in the morgue. The coroner's assistant is my sister's son-in-law."

"No, I didn't find him in the basement," I said as I continued to dig through papers.

"So, Joe is dead."

"Yes." I thumbed through another pile. This time I found a check I'd been looking for and a bill I'd forgotten to pay.

"But you didn't find him in the basement. Where did you find him?"

I liked Mabel. I did, but right now I didn't have time to play twenty questions. The clock was ticking and the power company would be closing soon. If I didn't have power, I wouldn't be able to convince Frances—let alone Officer Manning—that it was safe for me to spend the night in my own apartment.

"I found him in the second-floor utility closet," I muttered as I searched. "Ha! Got it!" I squealed with pride and waved the power contract in the air as a conquest. "I don't really have any other details, Mabel. Officer Manning kicked me out while they did their thing." I gathered up all the other papers into a neat pile and placed a crystal sugar canister on top to hold them down.

Mabel sniffed and looked around the lobby. "You're painting the lobby pink and white? Did you run the color scheme by the historical society? This is a historic building. All colors must match original time periods."

"Yes, I did, Mabel." I grabbed my purse from

behind the reception desk and my jacket from the coat tree that had been moved away from the painters. "I'll have the power back on soon," I reassured Benny and headed toward the door. Mabel shadowed me. She was small, standing only at my shoulder, and since I was five foot six that made her about four foot nothing. But she wore her purple velour jogging suit with flare and her white cross-trainer-clad feet helped her keep up with my longer stride.

"They agreed to that color and pattern?" Mabel sounded skeptical. She had fisted weights in each of her tiny hands as she powered along beside me. Her gray hair was cut close to her head in a pixie and made her big brown eyes tilt up. Like a fairy, she enjoyed being ornery.

"Who?"

"The historical committee." Her voice held a tinge of disgust.

"Yes, I showed them pictures of the interior from 1906."

"Huh." She snorted indelicately as we hurried down the street. "Those would be black-and-white photos. However could they tell color?"

"Papa Liam had a family scrapbook where they painted color samples. It was a little faded but I sent it out to the university and they analyzed the composition. Papa brought the report to the committee last fall. It was approved and I have the paperwork to prove it."

Mabel's mouth became a straight line. Her

smooth, pale skin pulled tight. "I can't believe Liam wanted to paint the place in candy stripes."

"Oh, no, that was my idea," I told her and kept my eye on the prize. The Island Electric business offices were a half a mile down and one block off Main in the Island Administration building on Market Street. "I found the scrapbook in the attic two years ago and Papa agreed that it would be fun to return the interior to the décor of yesteryear." I waved my hand through the air as if spelling out yesteryear on a straight line.

"They didn't have wall-to-wall carpeting in yesteryear," Mabel pointed out.

"What?" I glanced at her. I shouldn't have. The glint in her eyes said she knew she got me.

"Grace Gregson told me that Emily Proctor told her that you ordered new wall-to-wall carpeting from her husband Mike for your first-floor lobby. That isn't historically accurate, you know."

I stopped in my tracks. She had a point. All I'd been thinking when I ordered it was that the old carpet was too dirty and worn to clean in time for the season. Crap. "You're right."

Mabel nodded wisely. "Of course I am."

I pulled out my cell phone and dialed.

"All Things Décor, this is Emily, how can I help you?"

I kept up my pace toward the power company. "Hi Emily, this is Allie McMurphy. I need to cancel my carpeting order."

"What? Why?"

I glanced at Mabel, who had a smug look on her face. "I've been told it isn't historically accurate."

"Well, who would say a dumb thing like that?" I could hear the impatience in Emily's voice. Emily and Mike were ten years older than me and had spent their entire lives on island. They counted on knowing everyone and everything to keep their business going. Which wasn't hard when there were so few permanent residents.

"I ran into Mabel Showorthy." I turned the corner and waved Mabel good-bye as she continued power walking down the main drag. Not that you could call the street a drag since there weren't any cars. "Well, it's better to say she wandered into the McMurphy to ask about Joe and pointed out a few things about the renovation."

"What were you doing letting her in before you opened?" Emily griped.

I laughed at the absurdity of it all. It seemed everyone knew that Mabel was a troublemaker but loved her anyway. As for me, I still waited to figure out why they loved her so. So far she was merely a busybody. "The door was open. I have painters working."

Emily harrumphed. "You know that I can only refund eighty percent of your deposit. The order was already placed. Besides, you can't seriously be thinking of keeping the carpet that's in there. It's worn through in spots."

"Right. Can Mike stop by this week? I'm thinking

there has to be hardwood floors under the carpet. I want them refinished."

"Oh, good." I could hear the delight in Emily's voice and the ka'ching of a cash register going off somewhere. "I'll send him over at five tonight when the painters are done. Keep in mind that not only do we refinish floors, but we can find you some really nice vintage rugs to go over them. What circa are you decorating for?"

"I've got a 1900-era paint scheme going in." I was three buildings from the power company office.

"Wonderful, I'll collect some samples and we can talk. Can I pencil you in for Friday?"

"I'm not near my calendar."

"No worries, I've got you down for Friday at ten. I'll have Mike bring over a reminder card when he comes."

"Okay . . ."

"Now, while I have you on the phone, you have to give me the scoop."

"What scoop?" A quick glance at the time on my watch, and I sped up.

"Joe Jessop, silly! Did you really hit him over the head with a metal bucket after he made untoward advances?"

That stopped me in my tracks. "What?! No! Who said that?"

"I heard it from Julia Keystone. Her brother is Rex Manning's best friend. I assumed she got the story straight from Rex."

"Well, you assumed wrong," I said. "Joe Jessop

was dead when I found him. I definitely did not kill him and he certainly never made advances."

"Oh . . ." I could hear the disappointment in her voice. I suppose her story was more interesting than my real one.

"Look," I said. "I promise, all I did was find him and then I called 9-1-1."

"But you didn't," she pointed out. "You called Charlene direct, which was very strange since everyone knows you should have simply dialed 9-1-1."

"I did dial 9-1-1. It was Charlene who told me to call her direct."

"Why would she do that?"

"Because she . . ." I paused. Some things were best kept to oneself. "Because I confused her."

"Oh, honey," Emily clucked. "That's okay. We all have our moments. I'm sure it was the shock of finding a body in your closet."

"It was a shock." At least shock was an excuse everyone would understand.

"I know—"

"Rex Manning told you." I interrupted.

"Not Rex, Julia."

"Oh, right."

"Never fear, Allie." Emily sounded a bit like a superhero or a lawyer stating a case. "Mike and I knew you were innocent. That's why we're wearing a green ribbon."

"What?"

"A green ribbon, silly. Oh, a customer just walked

in. I've gotta go. Bye now." The phone went dead in my hand.

I didn't have time to ponder what she meant by the green ribbon thing. The heat from the power company's front office hit me in the face as I walked inside.

Everyone stopped and stared. I stood frozen to the spot, surprised to be the center of attention. I glanced down to ensure I had clothes on. Indeed I had on comfy athletic shoes, dark blue jeans, a paint smeared T-shirt, and a spring-green Windbreaker jacket. Maybe it was my hair. I tried to pat it down and make some sense out of the mop that was my dark brown hair. The stuff was wavy enough to never be flat but not curly enough to be called curly. It seemed to always be doing the wrong thing. I usually dealt with it by ignoring it, except to brush it, of course.

I stepped forward while people glared at me. One woman turned her back to me with a huff. Then I noticed Mrs. Brewster stood nearby. She gave me a smile, a wink, and put her thumb in the air. I hesitatingly smiled back. She pointed to the green ribbon on her lapel and rolled her eyes at the purple ribbon on the woman next to her.

I shook my head slightly. Wait. Most everyone in the crowded office had a purple ribbon on. What was I missing?

"Don't let them get to you." Mrs. Brewster came over to stand by me.

"Why would they get to me?" I shook my head in confusion.

"Because they aren't wearing green ribbons," Mrs. Brewster said. She wore a knit cap on unnaturally dark curls.

I leaned down to get close enough to whisper in her ear. "Why should the purple ribbons bother me?"

"Because, dear"—she wagged her finger under my nose—"the island is taking sides. Green is for the right side and purple is for the other side."

"Oh." Well, that certainly cleared things up. Not. "I'm sorry, why are we taking sides?"

"Because you killed Joe Jessop," she said loud enough that everyone stopped again and stared.

I swear you could hear my heart beating in my chest. "But I didn't kill him. When I found him in my closet, he was already dead."

"Oh course he was, dear." She patted me on the arm. "That's why I'm wearing green."

"I still don't understand."

"Why, everyone knows that purple stands for the House of Jessop, green for the McMurphys."

"The House of Jessop?"

"Yes." She leaned in closer. "With Joe's death, the feud has escalated. The general store is selling ribbons so that the community can show support for their side. I prefer green." She winked at me. "Okay, have to go. I've got other errands to run. You take care, dear." She patted me again and walked out, leaving me feeling very alone.

I looked around at the obviously hostile crowd. It was then that I noticed the most important thing of all. The clerk at the front wore a big purple ribbon and a black armband.

I had the sudden sinking feeling that getting my power turned back on was not going to be as easy as showing my account number.

Chapter 6

"Best take a number," said a Chippewa woman of indeterminable age. She wore jeans, a pale blue T-shirt, and a jean jacket. Her black hair had gray strands and hung in that lovely straight fashion that I only dreamed about. She was knitting or crocheting, I wasn't sure which. Best of all, she didn't wear a ribbon.

"Thanks." I followed her directions and pulled a number from the little machine at the end of the roped-off section. I had number 231. The machine at the front of the line displayed the number 150.

I couldn't help the sigh. I'd better settle in for the long wait.

The building held the prerequisite Victorian décor of the island. The exterior was painted white and looked as grand as a Southern plantation. The floor was old varnished wood. The walls were painted antique white with a ten-foot ceiling that was trimmed with brown woodwork. There was a picture rail, and a few old photos of the island and downtown were framed and hung from strings.

A large desk separated the hostile receptionist from the customers. It took up a full third of the room, leaving the lobby area feeling very small. I took a seat in one of the four plastic chairs that must have been green at one time but now were faded from the sun and worn to a green-tinted white.

I did a fast head count. There were fifteen of us inside—ten wearing purple ribbons.

"Next," came the call. No one moved. "Next." The woman at the desk flipped a switch. "Number one fifty-one." An elderly lady rose. Well, she tried to rise. She was bent practically in half and could barely shuffle her way to the front. I glanced at my watch. It was four-fifteen. "What number are you?" I asked the woman who had pointed out the number system.

"I don't need a number." She didn't even look at me.

"You don't?" I drew my brows together.

"I'm next." She had a bag at her feet filled with yarn and her fingers adroitly danced over the thread as if her life depended on it. She pulled extra material from the skein and continued on with the next row.

"How do you know you're next if you don't have

a number?" I settled back into my chair and crossed my arms. Did I ever remember meeting her when I was a kid? Was she teasing me?

"Numbers are for fudgies," she proclaimed.

"Fudgies?"

"Tourists."

"Wait, I'm not a tourist."

"Yes, you are, or you would have known what a fudgie was."

"I haven't heard that term used in a while. But I do live here."

"That's what they all say, trying to get out of using their number." Her fingers continued on with a cable pattern on beautiful blue wool with a hint of white mixed into the weave.

"Seriously, I spent my summers on island," I protested. "My last name is McMurphy. I own the historic McMurphy Hotel and Fudge Shoppe."

"You say that like a fudgie." She seemed unimpressed with my credentials.

"But I'm not." She was right. I sounded like a pouting five-year-old. "I'm the current owner of the McMurphy. My grandfather left it to me. See, this is the paper with my power account on it."

I waved the paper in front of her and waited a moment for her to apologize and welcome me home. She simply shrugged. "Fudgie."

Frustrated, I had to ask. "Okay, if this paper isn't enough, how do I prove I don't need a number?"

Her gaze never left her work. "Name the two men in line who are not tourists."

My eyes grew wide. I rubbed the edge of my nose and studied the five people who actually stood in what appeared to be a line. Three had numbers in their hands. I deduced that meant the bulky bald man wearing a plaid flannel shirt and jeans was a local and the middle-aged man with brown hair that grayed at the sides, who wore a blue polo shirt, Dockers, and boat shoes, was most likely the other local.

I pursed my lips.

"Don't know, do you?" The corners of her mouth went up slightly.

"I certainly do," I blustered through and prayed my brain would come up with a name. Luckily the bulky bald guy turned enough I could see his face. "That's Pete Thompson . . . and the thin guy is . . ."

"A tourist," she stated.

"Next," came the call as the old woman shuffled to the side.

The Chippewa woman stood and grabbed her tote.

"Wait!" I held out my hand as if that could stop her. Strangely, she stopped and looked at me, her brown eyes laughing. "I'm sorry, I didn't get your name. I'm Allie McMurphy."

"Susan Goodfoot."

"Next."

Susan headed for the desk. I sat back deflated. I

suppose she was right on some respects. I was a tourist. It was pretty clear I didn't know who she was and clearly she lived on island. In fact, the only people I knew on island were friends of Papa Liam or Grammy Alice. I was more likely to know everyone at the senior center than the townies standing in line.

I frowned. Why did so many of them wear a purple ribbon? Did they all see me as a stranger? A murderer? Or merely Papa Liam's silly granddaughter?

"Well, well, well." Pete Thompson stood in front of me with his hands in his pockets. "If it isn't the little McMurphy girl all grown up." He held out his hand. "Pete Thompson, I own the Oakton B and B behind the McMurphy."

"I know who you are." I remember the summer I was twelve. Pete followed me everywhere, taunting me, pulling my hair, and generally being a bully.

He barked out a laugh and pulled his hand back. "Spunky, like I remember. Well, little girl, I heard you killed Joe Jessop." He tapped the purple ribbon on his chest.

I scowled. I was not a little girl. I was thirty years old. "I am going to say this for the last time—" My voice rose loud enough to echo through the lobby. "I didn't kill anyone. I found a dead man in my closet and called the police. End of story."

"Really?" His obnoxious grin widened. "I saw the painters out front today. I figure you're sprucing up the old family place to sell. Maybe cut your losses and run. Am I right? Because I can make you a decent offer."

I raised my chin. "I'm not selling. The place has been in our family for a hundred and twenty years."

He rubbed his right earlobe. "Not selling, huh? Don't tell me you're going to try to make a go of it. . . ."

I stood. "What if I am?"

His laughter rang through the room, drawing the attention of townie and tourist alike. "Then good luck to you, little girl. That place hasn't been profitable in fifty years."

I fisted my hands, the paper crumpled. My eyebrows furrowed. I could feel the heat rising in my face. "You're wrong. I've been over the books. Papa left me enough to prove the place was profitable."

Pete's smile widened. "Oh, sweet, sweet, little girl."

Every time he called me that I swear I wanted to deck him. If he patted me on the head, I was going to take him down. Even if it meant everyone would think I really was a killer.

"Your granddad's profits didn't come from the hotel business. I suppose if he didn't tell you where they came from, then I'll let you figure that out on your own."

I narrowed my eyes. "What does that mean?"

"Next."

"That's me. Nice to see you again, little girl." He turned on his heel. "Good luck with the fudge business." His laughter took the sincerity right out of his words. I swear the other people laughed with him. What did they know that I didn't?

Chapter 7

I didn't make the cutoff. I know, frustrating, right? I suppose I should have known better when I saw how many people were there and the fact that only forty-five minutes were left until closing. Probably the purple ribbons should have also been a clue, but I was as stubborn as the locals.

My only satisfaction was the fact that I made the clerk stay thirty minutes after closing. No, she didn't help me. If I couldn't go home happy, neither would she. I argued with her about closing for so long she had to get a local cop to come and throw me out.

Officer Charles Brown was the young cop from the night before. He recognized me immediately. "Ms. McMurphy, are you having trouble?" The man was straightforward, his green eyes sincere and his light brown hair gleamed like caramel in the sun.

"Someone accidently turned off power to the McMurphy," I protested. "I have the paperwork right here authorizing it to be turned on in my name."

"The office closes at five PM. Perhaps you should have come in earlier." He was nearly a full head taller than me and he stood between me and the locked door to the utility. The gun on his hip was added incentive not to make too big a fuss.

"I came down the minute the power went out," I explained. "My contractors need power and so do I—especially if I hope to have any protection from killers."

"I'd be glad to walk you back to the McMurphy and check it out for you. But you'll have to wait until the morning to get your power turned on."

I noted that he wore a purple ribbon on his blue police jacket. "Officer Brown, is it?"

"Yes." The wind was warmed by the sun and ruffled his hair.

"Look, I get that you don't really know me." I shoved my hands in the pockets of my jacket. "But I'm a nice person. I spent the last six years of my life preparing to make a career out of the McMurphy. I can't do that without electricity."

"I understand." He pointed toward the McMurphy. "Shall we walk?"

"Fine." I let him turn me away from the utility. That battle at least was already lost. "Look, I get the purple ribbon. You probably grew up with Trent Jessop."

"He was in my class at school."

"Really?" The scent of fudge and beach blew

through the air. A horse-drawn taxi clomped by. It was empty. The pace on island was slower, more relaxed. It was one of the things I loved about it. "I thought you were younger."

"I'm thirty-three."

"Huh, okay." I felt the heat of a blush rush up my cheeks as we walked back toward the hotel. "I want you to know that I have nothing against the Jessops. The last thing I want is to cause trouble on the island."

"Good."

"But I need power and apparently having a ticket doesn't mean anything at the power office. People who came in after me were waited on first."

"If you're talking about Betty Hutchins, she has a long history of donations to the island community. In return she expects to avoid standing in line the day she gets back on island. It's a perk."

"It's ridiculous," I grumbled and shoved my hands deeper into my pockets.

"It's a tight-knit community, Ms. McMurphy. I suggest you take some time to get to know the people and the culture before you barge in. Now the utility opens at—"

"Nine. Yes, I get it."

"A word of advice, Ms. McMurphy." Officer Brown stopped walking and leaned into me. "Don't threaten the power company employees. It looks bad . . . considering."

"Considering what?" I put my hands on my hips.

"Considering they found a dead man in your hotel." He crossed his arms over his chest.

I rolled my eyes. "Please, I found a dead man. If I had killed him, do you really think I would have done something as foolish as call it in?"

"Serial killer 101, they insert themselves into an investigation."

"Seriously?" I wanted to sneer, I really did, but he looked at me with his big green eyes and his hair flopping over his forehead and I didn't have the heart. "Fine. I'll be more careful how I treat people."

"Good." We continued walking toward the McMurphy. "You know the people on island are friendly once you get to know them."

"How long does that take?"

He kept walking. "Depends."

"On what?" I asked.

"On how well you treat them."

"What? I treat them fine. It's not like I'm going to go back and stalk the clerk or anything."

"Just got to make sure that you don't."

"Oh, for Pete's sake." I shoved my hands in my pocket and kept walking. "You're walking me home, aren't you?"

"I am," he said and stood between me and the electric company office. "It's my duty to see to the safety of the community."

I wasn't sure if he was talking about my safety or the power company clerk's. Not that it mattered. I was doing my best to ignore the officer and go straight home when my eye caught the silhouette of a man in the alley behind the McMurphy. "Colin? Colin!"

Officer Brown stopped me with a hand to my arm. "Is that your maintenance man? We didn't get a chance to interview him."

"He hasn't been around," I said as whoever it was faded into the shadows of the alley.

"If it's him, let him know we want him to come down to the station, okay?"

"Okay." I strode off after the shadow in the alley.

"Be safe," Officer Brown called after me.

"No worries," I replied. "I have my cell phone and Charlene's direct number. If I get into any trouble, I'll call." I waved my phone at him.

I think I saw him shake his head. I ignored it. "Colin," I shouted as I went after my maintenance man. "Colin, I need to speak to you."

Colin must have been deaf as a post because he never even turned around. He disappeared around a corner and was gone when I reached the back of the McMurphy. For an employee, he had been MIA. If he didn't come into work by the end of the week I was going to have to fire him. Papa's old friend or not, I needed workers who worked. Not drunks who showed up when their accounts ran dry.

Easy Dark Chocolate
Rum Cherry Fudge

1 cup dried red sour cherries
4 ounces spiced rum
4 cups dark chocolate chips (2 bags)
1 can sweetened condensed milk
4 tablespoons butter
1 teaspoon vanilla
1 cup chopped walnuts

Soak dried cherries in rum for at least 1 hour—drain just before use.

Butter an 8" x 8" x 2" pan, then line with wax paper or plastic wrap. (I prefer wax paper.)

Using a double boiler fill ⅓ of the bottom pan with water and heat on medium high until the water is boiling. Then you can turn the heat down to low and in the top section, melt chocolate, sweetened condensed milk, and butter until smooth and thick.

Remove from heat. Add vanilla and stir until combined. Add drained cherries and walnuts. Pour into pan. Cool. Tip: let cool outside of the refrigerator for 30 minutes so that no condensation mars the top. Refrigerate overnight. Remove from pan. Cut into pieces. Store in a covered container.

Chapter 8

"I am not a fudgie." I tried not to pout. "I have every right to cut in line as Mrs. Hutchins."

"She donated a million dollars to the library last year," Benny said. He waited near the reception desk for me to close up for the day.

Without any power, I'd been advised to spend one more night out of the McMurphy. I'd declined of course, but I still needed supplies—like flashlights and such. Staying in a dark building with no light or power was spooky. Knowing a guy had died there the night before made it creepier. Only my stubbornness kept me from running straight to Frances and asking for another night in her guest room.

Benny and his crew worked until they could no longer see well enough to paint. He'd sent his crew home and waited for me to close up.

"If I had that kind of money to give. I would. I'm a member of the community," I insisted. "I shouldn't have to pull a number. Besides, I need power to keep you guys working. Don't you have another job in two weeks?"

"Yes, and that job is guaranteed, so we have to show up on that date."

"Then, if you don't get the McMurphy done . . ."

"It will have to wait."

I scowled at the reality of contractors. "Great."

"It's been a long day." Benny wrapped his coat around his white painter overalls. "I suggest you be first in line in the morning. I heard if you get there at eight forty-five you'll be first when the doors open at nine AM."

"Oh, I'll be there by eight forty-five AM," I said as I did a quick check of the lobby and pointed Benny toward the door. "And I'd better be first in line since I was the only person not helped by five PM tonight. I even kept my ticket."

I waved the triangle-shaped paper, stepped out, and locked the McMurphy's front door.

"Good night, Ms. Allie." Benny gave me a short nod. "Never fear. Tomorrow will be a better day. You'll see."

"I certainly hope so, Benny. I certainly hope so."

April evenings were cool on island. A few early-bird vacationers sat out on the front porch of one of the bed-and-breakfast hotels on Market Street. They had a fire going in a fire pit. The scent of wood smoke followed by their laughter blew across the street. A horse and buggy went by on its way back to the stables.

I pulled my jacket tighter around me and did my best to walk off my mad. It was something I'd learned as a teenager. When I felt threatened by injustice there was no calming me down. The only way to get through was to wear myself out. There really was nothing I could do but lodge a complaint with the electric co-op and even that wouldn't help if I was seen as an outsider.

Daffodils waved in the flower borders of the Victorian summer homes. Someone had been brave and planted purple and yellow pansies. April was a funny time. It could be cold and snowing or it could be seventy degrees and sunny. It really depended on whether winter decided to fight for a few more weeks.

This year was warmer than usual. I had flown in for Papa's funeral, then back to pack up my things for the move. By the time I returned, one of the ferry companies had started running routes, bringing in supplies and business people from St. Ignace. Most people left the island when the ferries quit running. They had homes in St. Ignace in the Upper Peninsula of Michigan or Mackinaw City on the Lower Peninsula. Some came from Chicago or Detroit and only lived on island during the season.

Papa had been an islander his entire life and refused to become a snowbird. Snowbirds, Papa used to say, left for the winter and came back in the spring. But they missed the best times on island. When the state parks were left to the wildlife and the streets, empty of horses and bicycles, held only footprints or snowmobile prints.

The general store was open along with two bars where locals gathered to check in on each other. The police force would be cut back to only a handful of men who were brave enough to live here year-round.

Market Street ended at the fort and I turned toward Main. The sound of my footfalls filled my ears and the warmth of my breath caused a mist in the cold air around me.

"Allie!"

I turned at the sound of my name and saw Frances hurrying toward me, a basket in her hands.

"Wait up."

"Hello Frances, what's up?" I asked as she came up beside me.

"I was thinking about you being all alone in the McMurphy and I was worried about you," she said, her breath puffing out. She wore a long quilted coat that shone purple in the streetlight and a purple felt fedora on her head. Her gray-brown hair stuck out from under it.

"You don't need to worry," I said. "I'll be fine. I'll do another walk through before I go to bed tonight. It's rare for a killer to return to the scene of the crime, anyway."

"Well, that may be true, but I'd still worry so I decided to bring you something for your protection." She stopped suddenly as if making up her mind.

"You didn't have to bring me anything." I was

confused. The basket was too small to hold a baseball bat and I doubted she was going to hand me a gun. Then again, this was Frances.

"I know that it's a bit presumptuous of me to bring you this, but I think it's for the best." She opened the top of the basket, pulled out a little ball of white fluff, and shoved it at me. "Allie, meet your new roommate."

The tiny puppy reached for me and I took it out of instinct rather than desire. She put her front paws on either side of my face and licked me as if to say, "Mommy! Where have you been?" and I was lost.

"Oh." Frances clasped her hands and tilted her head. "How sweet."

I couldn't help the dopey smile on my face as the puppy snuggled under my chin. "Frances, what have you done?"

"Don't worry," she said and linked her arm through mine. "She's a bichon/poodle, completely shed free. I thought she'd be perfect for greeting customers. Socialize her well and she'll never meet a stranger."

Frances handed me the basket. "Here is some puppy food. It should last you about a week. There is a pack of puppy training pads, a collar, and a leash. She'll need to be walked at least twice a day."

I took the basket as the puppy shivered in my hand. "How old is she?" I said, blowing out a long breath that I refused to believe was a sigh. I opened my jacket and wrapped it around us both.

"Three months," Frances said. "She'll need to be spayed and finish her puppy shots. There's a veterinarian who has a clinic in St. Ignace. He's on island three times a week when the horses are here." She handed me a business card. "His name is Ryan McCotter. I've already set you up an appointment time for next Wednesday."

I studied the card. "I'm in the middle of renovations," I protested. The little bundle snuggled harder against my chest and licked my collarbone. Frances simply walked me back toward the McMurphy.

"Fine." I gave up. It was clear I had no real choice. Who could resist the warm little fluff ball snuggled against their heart?

She smiled. "I knew you'd see reason. This way you won't be alone."

"I don't mind being alone," I protested as I stopped to open the door of the McMurphy. The scent of fresh paint wafted through the air. A piece of crime-scene tape flapped in the entrance. It must have gotten stuck on someone's shoe. The interior was cloaked in shadow, and I had to admit to a certain creepiness. I tried not to think about it too much.

"Do you want me to stay while you check the place out?" Frances eyed me. My expression must have given away my trepidation.

"No," I said. "Benny just helped me close up. Besides, this is my home. I'm fine." I clutched the small ball of fur inside my jacket. "Welcome to your

new home, baby." I stepped inside and closed the
door, waving Frances on.

Frances waved back and continued down Main.
I locked the doors behind me and put the puppy
down on the dropcloth–covered floor.

"I think you're going to love the McMurphy. I
know I do." I tried not to feel silly talking to a fluffy
dog the size of my fist. "Come on. Let's make sure
we're alone."

While I checked all the closets and behind the
counters of the first floor, the puppy piddled . . .
twice. "Really?" I muttered and grabbed her up. I
don't know why I thought if I held her she would
stop piddling.

Needless to say I shot out to the back door and
across the alley to a small patch of grass. I kept the
puppy at arm's length until I set her in the grass.
My jeans were wet and clung to my leg. As for the
pup, she sniffed the grass, suddenly concerned
about where she peed. I shivered while she
turned figure eights until she found just the right
spot and squatted.

The sides of the McMurphy were attached to the
Bristol T-shirt shop on one side and the Old Tyme
Photography shop on the other. Neither place
was occupied at the moment. The McMurphy was
wide. The back of each level had a prerequisite
door. The second and third floors opened up to a
black wrought-iron fire escape that had been put in
sometime during the turn of the twentieth century.

There was a light outside of each door that

turned on when the sun set. I noticed that the escape ladder was pulled down, meaning anyone could climb up to the second or third level.

"I wonder how long that's been like that," I said to myself.

"Are you talking to the dog?"

I gasped and turned to find Mr. Beecher, one of Papa's card buddies, walking down the alley. He wore a brown coat that hung open to reveal a tweed sweater, a brown vest, and a white-and-brown button-down with the collar open. His corduroy pants and brown shoes lent him an air of old-world elegance. Maybe it was the cane he used or the fedora that sat on his head as if he stepped out of a 1940s movie. "Mr. Beecher, you startled me."

His brown eyes were watery and gentle. "Your pup is wandering off." He pointed with his cane. I followed it to see the puppy, nose to the ground, following the alleyway as if she could find her way back home.

"Thanks." I scooped her up and she licked my chin. "What are you doing back here?"

"Shortcut to my place," he stated as he strolled over and stopped to look at the McMurphy. "Heard about old Joe. Darned shame." He eyed me. "It had to be difficult finding him so soon after your grandpa's death."

"It was," I admitted and hugged the puppy.

"I heard that the town is taking sides over it." He

shook his head. "Darned fools. A man is dead and they're making a game out of it."

"Thank you." It was good to finally find someone with reason. Then I noticed the purple ribbon on his coat. "Wait, you're siding with the Jessops?"

He shrugged. "Liam beat me at the last ten card games, the old cheat."

"Oh for Pete's sake . . ."

"Now don't get yourself all worked up," he said. "My black coat has a green ribbon. Old Joe was a mean bastard. Like I said, foolish to take sides."

I tried not to frown. "Just out of curiosity, how often do you walk back here?"

"Oh, once or twice a day depending on how my knees feel. I usually cut through when they're unhappy. Why?"

"Do you have any idea how long the fire-escape ladder's been down?" I pointed to the wrought-iron ladder hanging from the second-floor platform.

"Hmm, maybe two days." He shrugged. "Don't see as it's a problem. All you have to do is jump up and pull it down."

"Do you think Joe could jump up and pull it down?"

"Not likely," Mr. Beecher said. "Old Joe had hip trouble." Mr. Beecher walked over to the ladder. "Still . . ." He pushed it back up. The ladder rolled into place without so much as a squeak.

Odd, right? Considering the general condition the McMurphy was in.

Mr. Beecher took his cane and looped it around the last rung and gave it a good yank. The ladder slid down with surprising ease. "Joe had a cane."

"Right." A shiver ran through me. Could it be as easy as that?

Chapter 9

I overslept.

It was the puppy actually who woke me by kissing me. I wasn't used to wet tongue on my face or button eyes staring at me expectantly. I sat up like a shot. It was 9 AM. That meant the power company was already open and my vow to be first in line was shot.

I scrambled out of bed so fast the puppy hopped down and piddled on my rug. "Great." I picked her up and carried her over to the training papers on the floor of my bathroom. "Piddle here, please," I begged her and splashed water on my face. One glance in the mirror told me I looked like death warmed over.

Oh, well. It would have to do. I dressed in jeans and a pale blue work shirt. Pulled my hair into a ponytail and grabbed up the dog. I was going to have to name her sooner or later. Maybe when I had a moment to think.

I ran down the stairs. Benny and his crew waited outside the door.

"Good morning, sunshine." He grinned at me when I let them in. "We still don't have power."

"I'm on it," I called as I grabbed my jacket from the coat tree near the door.

"Hey, is that a puppy?" Benny asked.

"Yes, Frances gave her to me for protection."

"Kinda small for the job," Benny teased.

"She'll grow into it," I replied and put the puppy in her basket, then picked up the paperwork I'd left on the receptionist's desk the night before. "Have any of you seen Colin this morning? Do you think he's coming in to work?"

"I doubt it," Benny answered. "I heard he was on a bender last night at the Sailor's Bar and Grill. They had to kick his butt out after two-thirty. He's probably sleeping it off."

"Great," I muttered. "Well, I'm off to the second level of hell that is the power office," I told him. "My cell phone is on if you need me. Let me know if Colin comes in this morning. Okay? I need to ask him some questions."

"What do I do if the cops want back in?" Benny asked.

"Call me." I opened the door. "I want to be here before they look around."

"Got it, boss." He gave me a salute with his paint-brush to his painter's cap.

I stepped out onto the street to find that the ferry had come in with the first group of tourists and locals. The temperature had warmed to sixty degrees. The skies were blue and the lake was smooth as glass. Boxes of goods and merchandise were loaded up on horse-drawn flatbeds. The locals prepped for the season. As soon as it was warmer than fifty-five degrees, the entire island painted. With weather as rough as our winters can get, a fresh coat of paint was warranted nearly every year.

The town prided itself on attention to detail in keeping up with Victorian standards of manicured grounds and fresh paint on the painted lady homes with three colors on the siding, shutters and ginger-bread cutouts. The painting started as soon as the ferries began to run and bring in tourists. Before that the unpredicitable weather and expense of flying in workers and supplies kept them from doing much more than sweeping porches. Horses clip-clopped by as taxis ferried the summer home-owners back and forth. When the full season was up, there would be young men on bikes to porter the luggage and supplies as well as the horse-drawn flatbeds. But for now, there was only a fraction of the bustle summer would bring.

I popped into the general store to buy puppy treats and more puppy piddle pads. I placed the basket on the counter and frowned at the display of purple and green ribbons. The purple ones were nearly gone and the green board was half full.

"What's in the basket?" Mary Emry asked as she rang up the treats.

"Frances Wentworth gifted me with a puppy," I said and fingered the ribbons.

"Oh, you have a puppy in the basket? Can I see?"

I shrugged. "Sure."

She opened the basket and peered in. "Ooh," she cooed. "He's sleeping."

I glanced in the basket to see that the dog was indeed sleeping. Something I wished I could be doing as well. "It's a girl," I said. "And she loves green." I pointedly pulled all the green ribbons off the board. "And purple." I picked up the entire board. "I'll just buy them all."

"Oh." Mary had the good grace to blush. "Right. They're fifty cents each."

"Who benefits?" I asked and tilted my head.

"The proceeds go to the senior center," Mary said. "That will be forty-five dollars and fifty cents."

"Fine." I handed her my debit card. "I'm glad it's for a good cause."

"Oh, it is." Mary looked at me. "Did you really hit Joe Jessop over the head with a baseball bat?"

I rolled my eyes. "No, I didn't touch Mr. Jessop. I opened my utility-closet door and found him. Dead."

"Huh." She handed me my receipt and a paper sack. "How did he get in your closet?"

"I have no idea." I gathered up my stuff. "Hopefully Officer Manning will figure it out and I won't be seeing any more purple ribbons."

"If it helps any we were almost out," Mary called after me as I took my basket full of puppy and my bag full of supplies and headed out to the power office.

The pup woke up, pushing the top of the basket open with her nose. Two black button eyes looked at me with curiosity. "We're going to get power turned back on at the McMurphy," I told her. That seemed enough and the basket top closed. "I'm going to have to find you a name," I muttered.

I walked into the power office with yesterday's number ticket in hand. They were up to 155. I sat down with a sigh. There were only two people besides me inside. As soon as the clerk saw me she got on the phone. The manager came out of his office. He was about six foot tall with dark hair and a wrinkled suit. His potbelly looked odd on his thin frame. It was almost as if he were wearing a baby belly prosthetic.

"Miss McMurphy?" he asked and brushed his hair out of his face.

"Yes." I stood.

"I'm Adam Early. How can I help you?"

All right, I'll play along. "The power has been turned off to the McMurphy," I said. "I came in last week and changed the account out of my grandfather's name and into mine. When I called yesterday I was told that there was no proof I had done so. I was told I had to come down and bring my paperwork." I waved the paper under his nose. I bit my lip to keep from telling him that I didn't appreciate waiting what seemed like forever the day before only to be told to come back today.

He looked over my papers. "I see." I waited as patiently as possible while he studied the words off the document.

"I presume you brought in your grandfather's death certificate?"

What? "Yes, the first time I came in I brought in his death certificate. He was Liam McMurphy. Didn't you go to his funeral service?"

He turned five shades of red and adjusted his collar. "Of course, of course. Follow me." He took me back behind the big desk to his office.

I stuck out my tongue at the receptionist as I went by. Mr. Early ushered me into his glass-walled office and closed the door. "Please have a seat. This all seems to be a bit of a misunderstanding," he said as he walked around to his desk and sat down. He put the paper on his desk and clasped his hands in front of me. "It seems that when you first changed the account my employee who helped you did not check your credit rating."

"I was not told that my credit rating mattered." My back was poker straight, my chin high.

"I'm afraid it does, Miss McMurphy." He turned to his computer. "According to our records your credit score is quite low."

"I have always paid my bills on time," I protested.

"Right, well, you don't have a good credit score due to the fact that you don't currently have any credit cards or accounts in your name."

"I pay my bills on time," I said. "My parents helped

me through college, but I have always paid my rent and my utilities on time."

"Have you run a business before?" He clasped his hands in front of him on the desk.

"No, I've been studying to prepare for owning the McMurphy."

"Have you interned at a hotel or fudge shop?"

"No, I thought I would intern with Papa Liam this spring."

He sat back. "The electricity needed to run a hotel and a fudge shop is ten times what it takes to live in an apartment, Miss McMurphy. Even a Chicago apartment," he said. "How can you assure me you can pay the bill?"

"Oh, for goodness' sake . . . I have a business plan, Mr. Early." I clutched the basket to keep from showing my frustration. "I'm not doing this willy-nilly. Papa left me enough money to cover my first year of business. That includes utilities, based on the average from the previous five years."

"I see." He turned back to his computer and pulled up my account. "The utility rules state that anyone with a credit score under six hundred will need to put down a deposit not less than two months of the average bill for the business." He tapped on his computer keyboard. "For the McMurphy that means we need to have a deposit of two thousand dollars." He eyed me. "If you don't have it . . ."

"I have it," I said loud enough that I must have woke up the puppy. She started to stir in the basket.

I ignored my pup and glared at Mr. Early. "I take it the deposit is fully refundable?"

"Yes, as long as you have paid all your bills on time for the length of your account."

"Fine." I pulled my debit card out of my wallet. "Here."

"I'm sorry. We take only cashier's checks." He didn't look sorry as I stood and put my debit card in my purse.

"I'll go right down to the bank and get you that check," I said and hitched my purse over my shoulder. "I expect not to have to wait in line when I get back."

"As long as it's before lunch, you can come straight to my office and I'll help you myself."

"Thank you," I said. It took everything in me to not say what I really wanted to say. But I was an adult now and, as an adult I would do whatever it took to save the McMurphy.

"What's in the basket?" he asked as I picked up the basket and my bags.

"It's my puppy," I said. Oh how I wanted to take her out and let her piddle on his office floor, but I thought better of it. "We'll be right back."

"That's fine," he said.

I stormed out of his door and refused to look at either the purple-ribbon-wearing receptionist or the purple-ribbon-wearing customers in line. My anger helped me sail out of the building and down to the whitewashed limestone bank on Market Street.

"Good morning, Allie," Mrs. Amerson called from the art/photography gallery she ran on Market. She had a broom in her hand and was sweeping the front stoop.

"Hi, Mrs. Amerson," I said.

"You look to be in a hurry."

"I found out I need a cashier's check to get my power turned on." I blew a breath that puffed the bangs out of my eyes.

"What? That's ridiculous," she said. "The McMurphy has been in business for centuries."

"Yes, but I haven't," I said. The basket in my hands wiggled. I was afraid the puppy needed to piddle. The last thing I needed was for Spot? No, Sugar? Ugh, my puppy to piddle on the bank's floor. "Do you like dogs, Mrs. Amerson?" I asked.

"Sure, I have two pugs at home, why?"

"Frances Wentworth gifted me with a puppy. Would you mind watching her until I get back from the bank?" I lifted the squirming basket and the pup stuck her nose out.

"Ooh, sweetie," she said and took the basket out of my hands. "Go on, don't worry, I'll see to the puppy's needs. Does she have a name yet?"

"I'm still working on that," I said. "Let me know what you think." I left my puppy in good hands and power walked to the bank. Inside, the white limestone building was quiet. It was richly appointed in dark wood and brass fixtures. A huge crystal chandelier illuminated the lobby. I got into the only line open. In front of me was a man with wide shoulders and a nice bum. He wore a plaid shirt and a pair of worn Levi's. His dark hair was slightly shaggy and he smelled of horses and leather. His feet were clad in cowboy boots.

I took a deep sniff and noted his warm cologne. The man looked good and smelled good. Why hadn't I seen him around yet?

He turned away and I noted the square jaw and handsome brown eyes of Joe Jessop's grandson. "Excuse me," Trent Jessop said as he popped a cowboy hat on his head.

"No, problem," I said. "You're Joe Jessop's grandson?"

He tilted his head and studied me with male interest. "Yes, and you are?"

"I'm Allie McMurphy." I stuck out my hand. "I'm so sorry for your loss."

His face went frighteningly neutral. The silence buzzed through my ears.

I pulled my hand back and shoved it in my back pocket. "I recently lost my grandfather as well."

"I know," he said quietly. "Good day." He practically ran out of the bank.

Well, I thought, that went well. I blew out a long breath and turned to the cashier, who watched me with too much interest.

"Can I help you?" she asked.

"Yes, I need a cashier's check for two grand." I handed her my debit card and glanced over my shoulder to watch Trent stride away.

At least he wasn't wearing a purple ribbon.

Chapter 10

"Honey, what are you doing?"

"Now that the power is back on and the painters are done, I need to tackle the floors." I looked up from my position on hands and knees. Frances stared down at me through her big, round, red-framed glasses.

"I didn't realize you were a flooring expert."

I adjusted the knee pads I wore and used the crowbar to yank on the tacked-down edges of the dusty lobby carpet. "I'm only pulling up this old carpet. I'm pretty sure there's hardwood underneath. Mike Proctor told me the quote to refinish the floors would depend on the shape they're in under the carpet." I wiped the sweat from my forehead onto the sleeve of the ratty old shirt I wore. It was one of Papa's I found in his drawer and was more than a bit big on me, but it served its purpose.

The puppy played with the edge of the carpet I had freed. She pulled on it, leaning back on her haunches. When a piece ripped off, she shook it hard and brought it to me. "Wonderful," I muttered and took off the heavy gloves I wore and snagged the old carpet out of her mouth. She sat down and watched me with so much pride in her eyes. It was as if she said, "It's easy, Mommy, see?"

"Why isn't Colin doing that?" Frances took off the felt hat she wore. The hat was a lovely lilac color and matched the spring coat she had on.

I turned back to ripping up the edges of the carpet. "He hasn't come in to work yet."

"You need to fire him." Frances took off her coat and hung it on the coat rack that stood behind the receptionist desk.

"Fine, if I ever see him, I'll tell him he's fired."

"I heard that Colin's son, Freddy, was on island for a visit. You should talk to him about Colin."

"I suspect he already knows." I blew out a breath and grabbed the edge of the carpet and pulled with all my might. "But should I run into him, I'll certainly mention it."

Only about six inches of carpet budged. Whoever had laid this carpet had wanted it to stay forever. "Anyway, it means that I have to do my own carpet ripping." I picked up the crowbar and popped more staples. This was going to take me all day.

"Well, ever since Colin's wife Karen died, he's been useless. He needs firing."

I stopped and frowned. "His wife died? You didn't tell me that."

"Oh, honey, it happened years ago. I'm surprised your grandfather didn't fire him when he didn't straighten up." Frances pulled a small brush out of her pocketbook and faced the tiny mirror on the side wall and brushed out her hair until there was no sign she'd worn a hat. "If you ask me, he used his wife's passing as an excuse to drink his life away."

Frances patted her hair, fluffing it up. "As handymen go, Colin was good at plumbing but little else. Liam had too big a heart where that man was concerned. Whenever I complained about Colin, Liam'd shrug and tell me that he could do most of the work himself anyway." She put her brush away and turned to me. "Do you know who you're going to hire in his place?"

"I have no idea," I said through gritted teeth as I yanked on the eight-inch piece of carpet in my hands. This time it gave way, popping and ripping as I went from knees to a power squat to standing. Soon I had a good eight feet of carpet in my hands. My arm muscles shook but a rush of happiness filled me. I could do this.

"Well, look at that," Frances stood with her arms akimbo and peered at the floor where the carpet used to be. "Is that blood?"

"What?!" I moved the carpet out of my line of sight and could see the swatch of lobby floor that I had exposed. There was a large stain that was reddish-brown against the dark varnish of the wood. "Huh."

"Maybe you should put that carpet back over it."

"What? No." I shook my head. "Papa never said anything about anyone dying in the hotel."

"Hmm." Frances moved quickly off the carpet and onto the wood floor as I renewed my ripping. Dust flew. The air filled with the scent of decades of old dirt, even older floor varnish, and fresh paint. At least the walls were dry before I started. There wouldn't be a chance of anything currently floating in the air sticking in the paint, but I may have to wash the walls when the floors were done. Another thing for my to-do list.

I rolled the carpet as I went. It turns out it was only attached with strong tack strips around the edges. Once I wrenched the staples up, the carpet itself came up with relative ease. Of course it must have weighed one hundred or more pounds. My poor arms shook and my back strained. I had a feeling it was going to take a couple of ice packs and aspirin later tonight if I hoped to get any sleep. I was known for my candy-making skills, not my upper-body strength. But when the budget was limited, it was sweat equity that saved the day. Papa used to say I got my stubborn determination from Grammy. I'd like to think that was the truth anyway.

"This is definitely blood." Frances stood over the large spot and several smaller spots that trailed off toward the front door. "Maybe we should contact the police. You might have uncovered a crime scene."

I pursed my lips and tried to catch my breath. Sweat tickled the back of my neck. "Will it keep us from opening on time?"

"Oh, I doubt it. This carpet and padding were laid back in the fifties. It's not like this is a fresh scene. But reporting this and having it documented and tested is the responsible thing to do. There might be an open case, you know."

"Oh, right. Go ahead then." I waved her toward the desk phone. I looked at the giant roll of carpet and knew there was no way I was going to be able to carry it out to the Dumpster by myself. I eyed Frances. The woman was five foot six when she was young but age had caused her to shrink down to five foot two. While she wasn't exactly scrawny, it would be too hilarious to picture the two of us trying to muscle the carpet out of the building. I blew out a deep breath and watched the dust dance around in the sunlight.

There was nothing to do about it. I was going to have to cut the carpet up into smaller pieces. Before I could do that I'd have to go to the general store and purchase a box knife. If Papa had one, the police had custody of it. I imagined it was in a lab somewhere being swabbed for blood.

Chapter 11

"Yep, what you got here certainly looks like a crime scene." Officer Manning had come in about an hour after Frances called. He stood in full starched blues. His expression was serious as stone. I studied the breadth of his shoulders and the muscles in his arms. I bet he could have lifted the entire carpet up and carried it out for me.

Too bad I'd already got it cut into pieces.

Officer Manning took photographs of the floor. He used my crowbar to bring scale to the spots. My puppy wanted in on the pictures. She kept sitting beside the crowbar and looking up at him as if to figure out her best side for photos.

"I need the dog to not be in the crime-scene photos," he said.

"Right," I scooped her up and handed her to Frances. The puppy whined when I let her go. "You'll get a treat when he leaves," I whispered. She cocked her head, looked at me, rested her head against Frances' chest as if to say that waiting would mean suffering, but she'd do it if she had to. "Good doggie," I said.

When I turned back, Officer Manning was bent down, scrapping a bit of each stain and placing them in separate marked baggies. "I'll send these to the lab to see what they are, but it looks like it might be old blood to me."

"I've got Mike set to come in and refinish the floors tomorrow morning." I wiped the sweat and dust off my forehead with my sleeve. With Papa's thick leather gloves in my left hand, I studied the stains. "Will that be okay?"

"Yes." Officer Manning stood. "I've got the pictures and samples. If this stain is as old as you say it is—"

"That carpet was laid in the early fifties," Frances said. "We've got the documentation in the back office."

"We do?" I asked, although I suppose I shouldn't be surprised. Papa Liam documented everything. It was family tradition.

"We do." Frances tapped her toe, her sturdy shoes making a slap-slap sound on the wood. She gave me an impatient glance as if I should not be questioning her in front of the cops. Perhaps she was right.

Officer Manning wrote in his report book. "Then there's no reason not to refinish the floors." He ripped off a piece of paper and handed it to me. "Here's the case number and my card. Be careful. Feel free to call me if anything else comes up."

"Right, okay." I was caught by his baby-blue eyes. They were ringed with black lashes. Why was it when blue-eyed men wore blue it made them even more attractive? My eyes, on the contrary, were hazel, a blah mix of muddied green and brown. There wasn't really a right color to make anything in them pop.

I must have stared a second too long because he smiled and I swear gave me a tiny wink. The heat of embarrassment rushed up my cheeks and I stepped toward the door. "Thanks for coming out. We wanted to make sure we could continue with the remodel."

He stepped outside and put on his hat. "The place is looking good. When are you planning on your open house?"

"Excuse me?"

"I understand you're putting the hotel up for sale." He shrugged one broad shoulder. "As a local, I'm curious whenever a business changes hands, especially one that's been in a family this long."

"I'm not selling," I stated. "I don't know where everyone is getting that idea."

"Huh, really?"

"Really." I placed my hands on my hips. "We're opening in three weeks, like always. In fact we plan a grand reopening over Memorial Day weekend. I've got a full booking. Isn't that right, Frances?"

Frances studied the spots on the floor. "It's true."

"Well, then, best of luck to you, Ms. McMurphy." He tipped his hat.

"Thank you." I felt only slightly mollified. I wondered if he was patronizing me. "If anyone asks, tell them I'm not selling. Okay? The McMurphys are here to stay."

"Yes, Ma'am." He said it with that flat cop seriousness. It didn't make me feel any better.

"Call us with the test results," Frances demanded. "I'm dying to know what caused those stains."

"Will do." He grabbed his bike from the rack and rode off.

"Why does everyone think I'm selling?" I asked as I watched him ride off.

"Maybe because you're the first girl to inherit the place," Frances said with a shrug. She held the door for me. "Or maybe because your dad swore to everyone he wasn't coming back to the island. People have always assumed that meant your grand-dad would be the last."

"They assumed wrong." I stepped into the lobby and listened to the echo of my voice. Hardwood floors were pretty but failed to absorb the sound like wall-to-wall carpet. I glanced at the stains. "Do you really think those stains are blood?"

"It might be to our advantage if they are blood stains." Frances handed me the pup and pulled her lilac-colored coat off the rack. "Think about it. If it's blood, we could say the place is haunted."

I made a face. "Haunted?"

"It sells rooms." She set her hat on her hair and adjusted it in front of the mirror. "Our reservations are down this year. Everyone's waiting to see what

the new management does. Having the place declared haunted like the Island House might help
our business."

"We are not haunted." I put the dog down,
knelt, and pulled at the last piece of carpet, revealing 150-year-old floors that didn't need too much
refinishing if you ignored the big stains and the
trail near the door.

"How do you know?"

"Come on, all those years I spent summers here
as a kid, I'd know. Besides, Papa Liam was such a
storyteller, if there were ghosts in the hotel he'd
have told me . . . happily . . . with scary elaboration
and gusto."

"Hmm, well, I suppose there's some truth in
that. Liam loved to tell a good story." Frances
stopped in the doorway and eyed my growing pile
of oddly shaped but manageable rolls of carpet.
"What are you going to do with all that?"

"I'll haul it out to the Dumpster." I tore up another hunk of carpet and sliced it along the width,
then rolled it up. "They have to take it if it fits in the
Dumpster, right?"

Frances raised her right eyebrow and twitched
her mouth. "I guess you'll find out."

It occurred to me suddenly that Frances was a
townie and could help me identify people. "Wait!"
I said as she turned to leave. I hurried over to pick
up my cell phone from the counter. "Before you go,
I wanted to know if you can tell me who this is."

"Who what is?"

"The man in this photo I took." I thumbed through my phone's photos and found the one I surreptitiously took at the power office after Susan Goodfoot had gotten up. I had taken it of Pete Thompson and the man wearing the polo shirt. They left the power office together and stood out on the street talking. I figured I needed to start sorting out who belonged on island and who were tourists if I ever hoped to fit in around here.

Frances was my ace in the hole. She could tell me who each and every person on island was. Once I knew everyone's names, they had to accept me. Right?

"What are you doing taking pictures of strangers?" Both of Frances's eyebrows rose stiffly over her red glasses.

"I need to get to know the regulars on island." I stepped toward her and showed her the photo. "Now, I know this is Pete Thompson. Who's the man he's talking to?"

Frances took the phone from me and studied the picture through the bifocals in her glasses. "Well, look at that. That's Emerson Todd. I heard he was back on island."

"Who's Emerson Todd?" I ran the name through my mind a few times to try to memorize it for future reference.

"Why, his great-grandma and -granddad owned and ran the Shangri-La Resort. It was one of the biggest attractions here on island. That was back when rich families would come up from Chicago and Detroit to vacation here and get away from the city heat. They made a lot of money, but never really lived on island." She handed me my phone. "The Todds were RBs from Chicago. They sold the Shangri-La in the early seventies when air-conditioning became popular and family resorts went out. The family still has a cabin here. I heard tell the old lady died and Emerson lost all the family money when the real-estate bubble burst. He must be spending the summer on island."

I studied the picture as Frances left for the day. "Emerson Todd." The name sounded familiar. Maybe he'd come to the fudge shop before. I'd have to check Papa's scrapbooks.

My memories of summers on island didn't contain too many kids. I'd spent a great deal of time with my grandparents and their friends. Between helping with the McMurphy, our day-trip picnics around island, and evenings playing cards, there wasn't much time for locals my own age. In fact I'd grown up believing only old people lived here.

I knew now that keeping the island going took a lot of young people. My perceptions had been wrong. I glanced at the stains on the floor. Perhaps it didn't hurt to know the old people. They remembered things that most people forgot. I decided to schedule a trip to the library. Someone I know might remember what happened all those years ago. At the very least it might be listed in the newspaper.

Maybe Frances was right. Maybe it would help to be not only a historic hotel but a haunted one as well.

Easy Piña Colada Fudge

5 cups white chocolate chips
4 tablespoons butter
1 can sweetened condensed milk
1 8-ounce can crushed pineapple
1 tablespoon coconut milk
1 cup shredded coconut
1 ounce spiced rum (to taste)

Butter an 8" x 8" x 2" pan. Line with wax paper or plastic wrap. Drain pineapple, reserving juice. Combine pineapple juice, rum, and coconut milk—mix well. Using a double boiler fill ⅓ of the bottom pan with water and heat on medium high until the water is boiling. Then you can turn the heat down to low and in the top section, melt chocolate, butter, and sweetened condensed milk until smooth. Be careful not to burn. Add liquid 1 tablespoon at a time, stirring after each. (Use more or less to your taste.)

Remove from heat. Add crushed pineapple (I add only half the can) and coconut. Pour into pan. Cool. Tip: let cool outside of the refrigerator for 30 minutes so that no condensation mars the top. Refrigerate overnight. Remove from pan. Cut into pieces. Store in a covered container.

Chapter 12

"How can you not know how to use a microfiche?" asked the library volunteer with the cantankerous scowl and the impatient glint in his eyes. "What kind of education are they giving young people today?"

"Well, Mr. Devaney." I used the name from his name tag. "We use the Internet."

"And what happens when the Internet fails? Ignorant kids, I tell you." He was crabby, but it didn't keep him from rolling up his thick brown cardigan sleeves revealing competent strong forearms, and threading the machine with the newspaper reel. Mr. Devaney might have been six foot tall when he was young, but now he leaned forward a bit and stood five foot ten. He had a bald head with gray hair around the sides. He wore corduroy pants in a darker brown than his sweater and a nice checkered dress shirt under the sweater. I think it was his shoes that gave him away. They were well-worn brown dress shoes. The kind you slip your feet into. The kind I'd seen a million times where my mom worked.

"If I had to guess, I'd guess you're a high school teacher. Am I right, Mr. D? English, maybe?"

His mouth made a thin line of disapproval. "History."

"Ah."

"And I was a high school teacher. I'm retired now. That's why I can volunteer here on a Monday afternoon." He finished fixing the machine and hit the light button. "Now, you move the handle. Note it goes faster when you crank faster and slows down when you go slower."

"Thanks."

He grumbled and put his big hands in his pockets. "I'm at the desk if you need me. At least that's what they tell me I'm supposed to say. Don't ask me anything about the computers. I'd rather stab myself in the eye with a fork than figure out one of those plagiarism machines."

"Okay." I looked at the microfiche, and then something occurred to me. "Excuse me."

He turned toward me and narrowed his eyes, giving me a look that definitely said why-are-you-bothering-me-again. I tried not to laugh. "Listen, you've lived here on island a while."

"Now how the heck do you know that?" he asked. "I said I was retired. I could have moved here this season."

"Well, if you lived and taught here on island," I

pressed on, "you wouldn't happen to know anyone who's looking for a job, would you?"

"Now that's a stupid question. In this economy everyone's looking for a job."

He had me there. I swallowed and tried again. "I'm looking for a new handyman. You know, someone who's really good at fixing things."

"What'd you do, buy one of those fixer-upper cabins? Fool. Sell it back while you still can."

I did smile then. "No, I'm Allie McMurphy. I'm the new owner of the historic McMurphy Hotel and Fudge Shoppe downtown."

"Didn't that place have a handyman?"

"When he decides to come to work, which isn't often."

"Then it's your own fault you don't have one, now isn't it?" Mr. Delaney turned away. "Fire him and put up a sign on the library bulletin board."

"He's my Papa's friend." I had to say it. "Besides, I can't fire someone I never see." The old guy kept going. I looked around. One of the other ladies glared at me. I turned back to the microfiche. Putting a sign up was probably a good idea. I'd put one up at the grocery store as well.

Now then, searching the police blotters from the weekly newspaper in the early 1950s for any mention of our family hotel or a murder was a two-hour exercise in futility. The closest I got was a neighborhood column verifying that the hotel installed the newest in wall-to-wall carpeting straight from Georgia. I knew from experience that the cotton carpet fibers didn't hold up well. Papa had fixed that by tossing a wide variety of rugs on top.

Thank goodness whoever had had the place built had installed good hardwood floors. It wasn't always the case.

I dug deeper, searching for any news on my family. Up popped a news article about two boys finding some wine bottles washed up on shore. The picture with the story was familiar. It was Papa Liam when he was young. The story was interesting because the find occurred during the Prohibition era. The headline read: **Boys discover French wine bottles.** The article went on to say that the bottles were disposed of per protocol. After that, the trail went cold.

I got up, stretched, and carefully took the microfiche film off the machine and placed it in the box. I dropped the boxes off at the volunteer desk. Mr. Delaney was no longer there. I guess his shift was up. Too bad, I would have liked to know his first name. It would have been one more person I'd know on the street and one step closer to being a true local.

I hitched my purse up on my shoulder and stepped out into the street. It was a nice walk back to the hotel. Today I wore my favorite jeans and a white peasant blouse under my blue spring jacket. I figured Mike and his crew would be done with the refinishing by now. The wind blew cold against my back. The light jacket I wore seemed ridiculous now. I'd forgotten how far north Mackinac was.

The surrounding lake tempered the weather, but that didn't mean there'd be spring flowers in April. The scent of sea and fudge filled the air as I walked downtown.

I had competitors who were open year-round. It was something I considered. Papa had said he was fine with the May-to-September season. It gave him time to be retired. Still, I had to wonder how he could afford it. Then again, he did have a nearly seventy-year-old carpet on the lobby floor and a handyman who showed up so rarely that Papa had done most of the work himself.

I didn't have time for that. What I wanted to do was make fudge. I glanced in the window of the Hay's Candy Shoppe. There the baker wore a full white chef's suit and apron as he chopped up chocolate and nuts for the latest batch. I had to go in. I'd spent the last two years at culinary school during the day and perfecting my candy-making techniques at night, but I'd never worked in front of an audience. This was fudge making as show. I realized I had some things to learn.

Their fudge master chopped and smiled and dished up chocolate as if he were a god and the people inside were drawn to his smile and his flashing green eyes. What did it matter if he was a little chubby? With the smell of heaven around him he was every girl's dream. How was I going to compete with that?

I watched as he poured the fudge on the marble cooling table and stirred it with a sharp long-handled spatula. "The table cools the fudge and the mixing adds air to it—that way it keeps its creaminess as it cools," he said. He tossed a ribbon of fudge in the air and the crowd reacted with oohs and aahs sort of like when a pizza man tosses a pizza crust. "This is a crucial step," he went on. "A good fudge maker knows when the fudge is ready to fold by the color and texture." He scraped off the long-handled scraper with a short-handled one that was wider. Then he meticulously scraped and folded the candy, creating the long loaf in the middle of the table. It was that loaf that would eventually be sliced into pieces and placed in boxes and on trays.

I bought a pound of this year's flavor and walked out, thinking hard. I tried to remember Papa Liam as a master fudge maker. It was what he was known for after all. The smell of the candy shop reminded me of being a little girl, wearing a big cotton apron with pink-and-white stripes, a tiny chef's hat, and watching Papa work his magic on the candy he poured out onto the marble counter. He would tell stories while he shifted it with a silver blade and cooled it down before cutting it and placing the fudge ever so beautifully in the trays in the big glass counter.

Papa made fudge making an event. Could I do the same?

A tear of nostalgia came to my eyes and I blinked it away. I was usually more practical than that. I don't know what had gotten into me.

"Your grandfather would have a fit seeing you

with a Hay's Candy box in your hand." Mabel Showorthy power walked by. Today she wore a peacock-blue velour tracksuit and her trademark white shoes. Her hand weights were white to match.

"Hello, Mabel." I put my chin up. "Papa knew it was good to check out the competition."

She must have done a quick turn because suddenly she was beside me. "I heard you found blood stains under the carpet in your hotel lobby."

I knit my eyebrows together. "Where'd you hear that?"

She shrugged. Her tiny legs took two strides to every one of mine. "Word gets around. Are you going to sell the place now?"

"What? No. Why would I?"

"Well." She shrugged. "There is some implication that perhaps someone in your family murdered someone. That can't be a good thing to bring in customers."

I sped up my pace to mess with her. She now took three strides to every one of mine. "No one in my family killed anyone. In fact we don't even know if the stains are blood until the forensic tests come back."

"Huh, I heard you brought Mike Proctor and his crew in as soon as possible to refinish the floors and hide the evidence."

That stopped me. "What?"

She missed me by two strides and had to back up. "Are you saying you didn't rush to refinish the floors and hide the evidence?"

"I am not covering evidence. I have Officer Manning's permission to refinish the floors." I put my hands on my hips. The fudge box dangled in its bag on my wrist. "The season starts in a few weeks."

She peered at me thoughtfully. "No cover-up?"

"No cover-up."

"Darn." Her mouth made a thin line. "I had a hundred dollars on a cover-up. Bill'll be mad. He had a hundred that Liam killed someone."

I shook my head and took off. The old folks were betting on a murder? "Weren't you around the year that carpet was put down?"

"Certainly," Mabel said with a firm nod. "I remember the big hoopla about the cotton wall-to-wall carpet shipped up from Georgia."

"Then if someone was murdered around that time—and their murder unsolved—surely you would remember it."

"Well, now I was only in high school . . ."

"Okay, when was the last murder on island?"

"1973, I believe. Ken Sutton killed his brother Harold over a pretty tourist. Both boys were drinking at the time and Ken swore he didn't mean to do it. Do you know what the sad part was?"

"No." I shook my head.

"Neither one of those boys got the girl. She ran off with one of the RBs up from Detroit."

"RBs?" It was the second time I'd heard that reference.

"You know, Rich Bastar—it doesn't matter. The important part is she ran off with a tourist."

"Hmmm, it certainly seems to me if you remember that kind of detail from a murder that happened in 1973, then you would remember, at least vaguely, anyone being murdered the year the carpet was put down."

Mabel's fast walk took a small hitch. "You might be right."

I felt vindicated. "Which means no one in my family is a murderer or you would have figured it out by now."

Mabel pursed her lips and swung her weight-filled hands. "Maybe no one knows about the murder," she suggested. "Maybe the victim went missing and was never reported. There were a lot of tourists that season. I'd be hard-pressed to know if they all got off island."

"I checked the papers from that time period. No one reported anything more than a purse snatching and a dispute over a fence line."

"Something happened in that lobby." Mabel pointed at the McMurphy's door. "And there's a police report to prove it."

"Good-bye, Mabel." I waved my fingers at her. "Enjoy your workout."

"I always do." She lifted her chin in the air and power walked off.

I stepped into the lobby and onto a large sheet of brown paper. The room was quiet and smelled of floor finish and new paint. The first floor of the hotel consisted of a large lobby with a brick fireplace against one wall. The wide painted stripes were pale enough to barely be noticed. There was plenty of dark woodwork surrounding the front windows and the ten-foot ceilings, drawing the eye toward the receptionist desk. Behind the desk were the old wood cubbies from when the hotel was first built, one for every room. Even though we now had modern keys, the original skeleton keys still hung by the corresponding cubbies as decoration and a remembrance of simpler times.

The receptionist desk was snug against a staircase. In the center of the lobby stood the double elevators. They were the old-fashioned kind with wire metal accordion doors on the inside. To my right was a half wall that enclosed the fudge shop area, allowing the sights and smells of the shop to flow into the lobby, inviting people to stay. The hope was the longer they stayed, the more candy they would buy. I also installed a coffee bar against the matching stairway on the opposite side of the room from the receptionist desk. There would be free coffee for guests and a barista for fudge shop customers or anyone who wanted a drink.

My idea was to create a space where people would gather for free Wi-Fi, and purchase coffee and fudge. It was the candy and atmosphere that brought people to Mackinac Island. I wanted the McMurphy to become a place that made them want to linger.

The fudge shop itself continued the pale pink-

and-white color scheme. Against the wall were the old cabinets and counters where I would work. It had a galley-kitchen feel. Unlike the Hay Candy Shop, where they had two candy makers and a staff to sell the candy, I was the sole candy maker. My kitchen was smaller, my presentation would be less dramatic, but I still had the marble table in full view where I would cool and scrape the fudge and fold in amazing fresh ingredients before my customers' eyes.

In front of that was the ancient original glass cabinet that held the trays of fudge and on the edge stood the old-time cash register. Papa had spent money to put up-to-date electronics into the gleaming old machine. The outside was for looks, but the inside was pure twenty-first-century magic. We even had a card swipe for debit and credit cards. I paid a hefty fee for the privilege but it kept the customers happy.

The glass walls and front windows held shelves that also contained trays for fresh fudge. These were rotated out when the sun came in the window, and replaced with a sign that said "free smells inside."

The fudge shop floor held black and white tiles that were easy to clean. I remember mopping them every night as a teenager. How I hated them then. The thought made me smile. I appreciated their efficiency now.

Finally, I included an old-fashioned watercooler in the corner next to the door, along with paper cups. The idea was to offer tourists a free drink and a respite from the busy street, while the hope was that they would wander into the fudge shop and find they had to take at least a quarter pound home.

Mike Proctor walked on the paper carpet runner that stretched from the bathrooms behind the elevator to the front door. He was tall, over six foot two inches, with sandy-colored hair and a large nose. Today he wore painters' Dockers in khaki and a blue uniform shirt. His shoes were thick brown boots covered in multiple paint colors and a variety of stains. "There you are. What do you think of the floors?" he asked, waving toward the uncovered portion of freshly finished hardwood. "It took some sanding but I was able to polish out those stains."

"It looks great," I said. He was right. There was no sign of the reddish-brown stains left. Only the gleaming narrow-planked wood floors remained.

"You should be able to put the rugs and furniture back down in twenty-four hours."

"Good."

"Frances said to tell you that the puppy is in her crate in the office upstairs. You'll need to walk her later."

"Thanks."

Mike shoved his hands in his pockets and studied me. "You're really going to take on this monster all by yourself?"

"Yes." I gave him a firm nod. "It's been my dream since I was a little kid. Besides, I promised my Papa."

"Well." Mike shook his head. "Good luck to you. A building this old needs constant upkeep and the fudge shop business here on island can be a little cutthroat."

"I know." I raised an eyebrow and lifted the bag hanging from my wrist. "I've been scoping out the competition."

Mike gave a hardy laugh. "Call me if you need anything else. Unlike you, we're the only game on island. Besides, Emily can find practically anything you might need from antique fixtures to pictures and hat racks. She loves the thrill of the hunt."

"Thanks, Mike."

I walked him to the door and held it open. He stopped at the entrance, his brown eyes twinkling. "Don't let the ghosts drive you out."

Chapter 13

"What rugs did you decide on?" Frances asked.

"Excuse me?" I looked up from my work arranging the kitchen portion of the fudge shop.

"Did you meet with Emily Proctor this morning?"

"Oh, right," I said. "Yes, I'm getting three area rugs to define the space. One by the fireplace, one in front of your reception desk, and the final one is going in the small conversation space in front of the elevators."

"Do I get to see the color and patterns you picked out?"

"Sure." I pulled the samples out from under the cash register where I had temporarily put them down. "Here, what do you think?"

Frances took each pattern and eyed the spaces they were to create. "I like it. You and Emily have good design style."

"Thanks, it was easy. I'd been looking at Victorian

rug patterns for months and Emily had samples very close to what I was looking to buy."

"Nice," Frances said and handed me back the samples. "Just one thing. How are you going to keep the dog from chewing up your carpets?"

"She won't chew them. We'll watch her like a hawk and crate her if she ever thinks about it. I can't afford to put thousands of dollars into wool rugs and then let a puppy chew on them."

"Speaking of the puppy, have you decided on a name yet?" Frances asked as she grabbed a can of wood polish and a lintfree rag and polished the receptionist desk.

The puppy was under my feet, chewing on a toy that was a ball with a tail. The toy had a face and long ears. There were squeakers in the tail and in the ball. I wish I hadn't gotten a gray toy, I thought. It was better not to think of mice while working in the McMurphy. I made a mental note to buy only neon-colored toys from now on. Some simply were too realistic for my frame of mind.

"Not really," I said as I rearranged plastic tubs filled with the ingredients necessary to make fudge. A glass candy display separated the candy making from the rest of the lobby. It was important that people could see in, but just as important that they couldn't crowd the kitchen. Hot sugar was lethal in the wrong hands. Inside the glass counter were glass shelves that held trays of fudge.

A scale sat on the top of the counter ready to weigh the pieces as they were wrapped in wax paper and placed in long boxes. A box of fudge could carry up to five pieces and cost upwards of twenty-five dollars. The key to surviving in the fudge shop business was to put on a good show and have a large selection. The bigger your selection, the more people bought. They got caught up in the idea of tasting every variety.

It was a great business if you were good at what you did. I promised Papa Liam I would be good. All my professors thought I was, if that counted for something. Now all I had to do was convince the people of Mackinac.

"I've thought of several but they don't seem to really fit her." I walked over and got down on the floor with the puppy. "Hello, what is your name?" I drummed my fingers on the tile floor and the puppy pounced on my hand. "Ow." I laughed and wiggled my fingers in the air. The puppy tried to hold my hand with her paws and bite my fingers. "Silly little dog," I said. "Whatever should I call you? Hmmm?"

"How about Killer?" Frances came over and watched us play together. The pup decided it was so exciting she had to piddle. I grabbed her up quick and put her on one of several piddle pads that worked their way out the back door.

"How about Fudgie?"

Frances frowned. "She's too white for a name like that."

"Piddle pot?"

The pup tried to eat the pee pad. She grabbed

the plastic and paper pad between her teeth and shook her head. I tried to grab the pad and the puppy ran away with it, resulting in a mad dash around the lobby and a battle of wills. I triumphed finally by grabbing the pup, picking her up, and pulling the pad out of her mouth. "No, no!" I said and looked around for a place to confine her. "I need a playpen."

"You should get a second crate—one for down here," Frances said.

"No, I don't want to have to lock her up like that."

"It's good for pups to be crate trained. It gives them a space of their own and sets boundaries." Frances eyed me. "Part of being a grown-up is learning to set boundaries."

"Okay, I have a feeling we're not talking about the puppy anymore."

"I'm talking about Colin. Has he shown up for work yet?"

I shook my head no.

"That man needs to be fired."

"But he's worked for Papa for years," I said. "How can I fire him?"

"Easy, you hire someone else. Someone who actually shows up and does work."

I frowned and cuddled the pup, who decided she was going to sleep. "So I have two handymen?"

"No, you fire Colin when he comes in to work, if he comes in to work." She took the dog out of my hands and gave me a stern look. "The lobby bathroom fixtures are leaking again. The windows in room 206 are stuck and that's only the beginning."

I blew out a hard breath. "You're right."

"Of course I'm right. Call the newspaper and put in a classified. I'll take the pup and find you a dog crate that's the right size."

"Fine." I picked up my phone and remembered the fire escape. "Frances . . ."

"Yes?" She studied me through her thick glasses. They were round plastic frames that reminded me of that old cartoon character Mr. Magoo.

"Is there a reason the fire escape is so well oiled?"

Frances drew her brows together. "Maybe Liam told Colin to oil it so that it would be safe for you on the third floor."

"Do you really think that Colin would oil the fire escape but not fix stuck windows or leaky faucets?" I had to ask her. It bothered me that it was so easy to climb up on the back balconies of the McMurphy.

"Now that you say it like that, I suppose the answer is no. Perhaps Liam did it?"

"Can you see Papa climbing the fire escape with a WD-40 can?"

"No, not this last year."

"It's a mystery."

"Are you thinking that's how Joe Jessop got into the McMurphy?" She cuddled the sleeping dog against her chest.

"I don't know, but I think it bears looking into."

I moved up the stairs. First stop was the second-floor back door. The floor was deathly quiet. My footfalls were muffled by the dreadful carpet. The plaster on the ceiling mocked me. Benny said it could not safely be painted. My best bet was to bring in a plasterer and redo all the ceilings. I shuddered at the thought of how much that would cost.

Truth be told, the money Papa had left me disappeared at an alarming rate. If I didn't get customers in here soon I'd be more than broke. I'd be penniless in a falling-down money pit.

I checked the back door. It was properly locked. I unlocked it and stuck my head out. The fire-escape ladder was still up from when Mr. Beecher and I put it up the night before. I probably ought to have Colin or his replacement tie the ladder so that it wouldn't be so easy to scale.

I checked the doorjam. It looked a bit rough, as if someone had tried and failed to punch it open. The thought made my skin crawl. What if whoever murdered Joe had tried to come in through the fire escape? What if they had tried on the third-floor apartments?

The fact that it could have been me dead in the second-floor utility closet had not gone without notice. I tried to push the thought away, but it suddenly overwhelmed me. I braced myself on the locked door. I didn't want to die. I had only begun to lay the foundation to live.

My cell phone rang and I pulled it out of my pocket and did my best to stand up straight. "Hello?"

"Allie, it's Frances. Officer Manning is here and he has a warrant to check your apartment."

"What?" I took off toward the stairs.

"You have to stop him. He's coming up. I'll call my cousin." The phone went dead in my hand as I strode to the stairs. I caught him on the landing. The man could rock a uniform.

"Hello," I said. "Frances tells me you have a warrant?"

"Yes, I have a warrant to search the entire building—that includes your apartment." His blue gaze was sympathetic. "I will need you to unlock all the rooms and let me in upstairs."

"Wait." I took the warrant he handed me. "What is your cause? Was the stain on the floor downstairs blood? If so, what does that have to do with my apartment?" I tried to read the warrant but it looked like a bunch of legal stuff that I couldn't make heads or tails of.

"The coroner declared Joe Jessop's death a murder." His voice was as grim as his face.

"Well, I kind of figured that when I saw him lying there with blood all over his face."

"Allie, I need to search the entire building," he said in a strangely calm voice.

"So that stain was blood?"

"No, that stain is still undetermined. It is not relevant to Joe's murder and my current investigation." He tilted his head and repeated, "I need to search the entire building. The warrant gives me that power."

"Okay, fine. I'll open up the apartment." I headed up the steps and took the keys out of my pocket. "While you're searching, could you check the back doors for any evidence that they were broken into?"

"Why?"

"Because the whole place is falling apart, but the ladder to the fire escape was down and rolls silent as the day it was made. That seems fishy to me." I unlocked my apartment. "Doesn't that seem fishy to you?"

"I'll check it," he said. "Now you have to go."

"Wait, I have to go? Does that mean I don't get to watch you go through my underwear drawer?"

He paused and flashed me a look. "I don't make it a habit of going through women's underwear drawers. Officer Lasko will be looking through your drawers."

"Who's Officer Lasko and why is his going through my drawers any different than you going through my drawers?"

"Because I'm a woman." A small blond woman in a blue police uniform stepped into the apartment. She tugged on blue latex gloves.

"Oh, good," I said. "I'll tell you what I told Officer Manning. I think someone has oiled the fire escape so they could break into one of the back doors unnoticed. I don't know if it was Joe or his killer, but I'd like you to check it out."

"How do we know you didn't fake a break-in to cover your tracks?" she asked.

"Kelsey, no," Officer Manning said, his tone soft but official.

"Is she for real?" I asked, then stopped when a thought crossed my mind. "Let me guess, Joe Jessop was your grandfather."

"My relationship to Joe has no bearing on this case."

"Wait, is that a purple ribbon on your Kevlar jacket?" I turned to Officer Manning. "Yeah, I'm not leaving. I'll be here to ensure that anything you find is actually there and not planted, because I did not hurt Mr. Jessop. I only found him in my hall closet. Besides, I thought everyone was innocent until proven guilty."

"Oh, you're guilty and we'll prove it," Officer Lasko said with venom in her voice.

"I want someone else searching my place," I said. "Or I'll have my lawyer claim anything you find is not useable in court due to prejudice of the searching party."

Officer Manning crossed his arms over his chest. "Kelsey, get out."

"What? No, I'm here to search the McMurphy."

"Not anymore," he said. "Call Brown and get him down here."

"Yes," I sneered. "Call Officer Brown."

"If I were you, I'd be quiet," Officer Manning advised me. "Officer Brown is not exactly a fan of yours either."

I snapped my mouth shut and sat on the arm of Papa's old, stuffed green chair. It still smelled of his cigars. Grammy Alice would have cringed if she'd known he smoked in the chair after she was gone. I could almost hear her say that he was lucky he didn't set himself on fire.

There was a wicked silent battle of wills until Officer Lasko finally gave up and huffed out. She left the door open and I was glad. I didn't want to be alone with Officer Manning. I might confess to something I didn't do just to feel safe. The man had a gun and he knew how to use it. Besides, he had this whole action-figure, tough-guy bit going on. I think I kind of liked that.

"What do you think you'll find?" I asked, breaking the awkward silence.

"Nothing," he said softly. "But we have to check."

"Only a fool would keep a murder weapon in their apartment where you can find it," I mentioned and crossed my arms. "Please do check the doors. I have a security service coming in the morning to install a system. I'd like to feel safe until then."

"You do realize that Lasko was right," he said. "Even if we find evidence of a jimmied door, there's no proof of when it was done. For all we know your grandfather did it two months ago, or you did it last night."

I rolled my eyes.

"But we'll make sure there's a patrol in your alley every couple of hours tonight."

"Thanks," I said out loud while my brain screamed

no! How hard would it be for a killer to break in and finish me off between the first patrol and the next? "At least you'll find my dead body sooner, I suppose."

He gave me another one of his humorless cop stares and I realized I'd said that last part out loud.

"Okay then." I sat down in Papa's chair and waved my hand. "Start searching."

"If you interfere I will have you tossed out."

"I get it." I crossed my arms. "I'm kind of getting used to being tossed out." I sounded defiant but deep inside I was worried. I had not gone through Papa's things and the idea that these strangers would go through them first made me angry with both them and myself. It didn't matter that I'd been busy. It didn't matter that I didn't want to face the grief going through his stuff would cause. What mattered was that I didn't do it and now the police would.

Officer Manning put on a pair of blue gloves and started in the living room. I watched him do a thorough search moving around the room in a grid pattern. He went through Papa's bookshelf, searching behind the books. He opened box after box and searched through them.

"What exactly are you looking for?" I asked.

"Evidence." Officer Brown stepped into the apartment and pulled on a pair of gloves.

"How do you know what's evidence?" I was sincerely curious. How did they know? I'd seen plenty of newscasts in Chicago where the police came out with bags and boxes of possible evidence and I often wondered how they judged what to take and what to leave. Had they ever lost a case by leaving the wrong thing?

"We have an idea based on the crime scene and the autopsy," Officer Manning said. "We also look for anything that may be contraband from illegal activity and take that."

"Illegal activity?" I stood and shoved my hands in my back pockets. "Like drugs?"

"Or stolen goods," Officer Brown said and went into the tiny galley kitchen that opened to the living area. "Anything that might give us a motive behind the killing."

"If you find anything, will you let me know?" I leaned to talk so that Officer Manning could hear me as he moved to the bathroom. "I haven't cleaned out the place since Papa died."

"Everything we take will be cataloged and inventoried," Officer Brown said. He was suddenly in front of me. "It would be better if you went downstairs."

"I want to be here," I said. "I feel a little weird about you guys going through my bedroom."

"We're professionals." His tone was smooth. "It's business, not personal."

"It will feel personal to know one or both of you were riffling through my underwear."

Officer Brown turned a lovely shade of red. "Officer Manning will go through your drawers. He's had two wives so I'm sure he won't judge."

"Two wives? Really?" It was hard to imagine anyone leaving the calm, handsome-in-an-action-hero-sort-of-way man. "Why?"

"The island is a little isolated. It's great for vacation but it takes a certain kind of person to live here year-round."

"And Officer Manning is that kind of person?"

"He grew up here," Officer Brown said. "Now I need to ask you to step out." He took my elbow and turned me to the door, then waved his left hand and gave me a gentle push with his right.

"Fine, but I'm sending in my lawyer as soon as he gets here." I stepped out into the hall. "Let me know if you find Papa Liam's pocket watch, will you? I've been looking for it."

Officer Brown closed the door and I leaned against the wall. Were they really looking for evidence or where they simply trying to get me to give up and go back to Chicago?

Grammy used to say I could be stubborn for stubborn's sake. Is that what I was doing here? There were two policemen that I barely knew going through my stuff, and worse, they were going through Papa's stuff looking for clues to the murder of a man on the floor below the apartment. I mean, a man was murdered for crying out loud and all I cared about was continuing my remodel so that I could welcome guests back to the McMurphy. That was a little harsh. No wonder people wore purple ribbons. They didn't know me.

I'd been living as if Papa were still here. As if this

were his hotel, his fudge shop. Heck, I hadn't even bothered to get to know anyone in town who wasn't one of Papa's friends. I certainly hadn't been interested in anything the community did. No wonder they had trouble wearing a green ribbon. I couldn't even bring myself to name the puppy Frances had given me, because if I named her she would be mine. If she were mine, then that meant I was really going to stay here and make the island my home.

If I were going to make this island my home I needed to decide to do it and commit. That meant changing my driver's license. Even though there were no cars allowed on island, having a driver's license and bills naming the McMurphy my home meant it was all very real.

I'd been waiting to see if I could make a go at it. That was the wrong way to do it. From now on I would think of it differently. The McMurphy was my home and if I was lucky I'd be running it until the day I went toes up at the senior center. Preferably with a margarita in one hand and a piece of chocolate raspberry fudge in the other.

Chapter 14

"I'm in trouble." I sat down hard in a sheet-covered wing-back chair in the lobby.

"I told you to let William handle the police." Frances sat across from me in an equally paint-splattered, sheet-covered chair. The puppy slept in her lap and she randomly ran her hand over the sweet baby's soft fur.

"It's not the police," I said. "I have no friends." Frances sent me a sharp look and I pulled back. "I didn't mean it that way. What I meant to say is that I have not made any attempt to become a part of the community. I've spent the last three weeks here concerned about the McMurphy and ignoring the people who make Mackinac Island the beautiful place that it is."

"What brought on this revelation?"

"The fifty-two green ribbons I bought today." I put my elbows on my knees and my chin on my fists. "And the five remaining purple ones."

"Trent Jessop has lived on island his whole life," Frances said.

"I can't even bring myself to hire my own handyman or name my own dog." I waved my hand at the sleeping pup.

"Let me guess." Frances leaned her head back and closed her eyes. "This is where you toss up your arms, say it's no use, and slink back to Chicago."

"She can't leave until we finish our investigation," Officer Manning said behind me.

He had two bags of something in his hands. I stood and grasped the chair. "I have no plans to leave. What's in the bags?"

"Don't worry, you'll get a full inventory." His expression gave nothing away.

My heartbeat sped up. "I haven't gone through Papa's things yet. How will I know what you've taken? What if you leave something off the inventory?"

He tilted his head and looked at me as if I were a small child. "Are you accusing me of stealing?"

I hugged myself and fought back the tears. "No. I'm sad that you now know more about what Papa Liam left in the apartment than I do."

"I'm sorry about that, Allie." His tone was gruff. "I'm doing my job."

"I know, please be careful with whatever you took. It might not mean anything to you but it might mean the world to me."

Frances got up and put her hand on my shoulder.

I took the puppy from her and buried my face in its soft warm fur.

"We're done here," he said. "Officer Brown and I will see ourselves out. "One piece of advice . . ."

"Yes?"

"Get dead bolts put on your back doors."

He and Officer Brown left as respectfully as you could carrying bags of things from someone's house.

"Officer Manning sure is dedicated to his job," I said to Frances. "Doesn't his girlfriend get upset that he spends hours searching other people's homes instead of coming home for dinner?"

"He quit dating after his second wife left," Frances said and went over to the reception desk and started her computer.

"Well, I wonder why?" My sarcasm always came out when I was tired or upset. To downplay how mean I sounded I looked at Frances. "No, really, Officer Brown said he had two wives. They both left him . . . why?"

Frances looked up at me from her computer. "First off, he married his high school sweetheart. When you're 18 years-old you think you're a grown up. So you do what grown ups do. You get married." Frances's mouth was a straight line. "Then you wake up at 28 and realize that life is nothing like you thought. I think Rex would have stuck it out anyway, but Julie had enough of island life, packed up and hit the big city."

"New York?"

"Ann Arbor."

"Ann Arbor?"

Frances shrugged. "Any town is bigger than Mackinac Island in the off season."

"And his second wife?"

"Cindy left after her second winter on island."

I blew out a long breath and the puppy licked my cheek. Personally, I wasn't afraid of spending my life on the island. In fact, living on the island year round was a life-long goal of mine. I wasn't about to give up my goal because other people didn't think I belonged here. In that moment, I knew that I would do whatever it took to get Papa's things back. If that meant investigating myself, then so be it.

But first I needed help. "Come on, Mal," I said to the pup. "Let's put up a help-wanted sign."

"Mal?" Frances asked.

"Yes." I couldn't help the smile that lifted my cheeks. "She looks like a fluffy marshmallow, doesn't she? I will call her Mallow. Mal for short." The puppy waggled her tail and licked my face.

"I think she likes it." Frances grabbed up her coat and her fedora. "I'm going to go home and get some dinner. Are you going to be all right here?"

"I'll be fine." I showed her out. "Don't worry, I'm not leaving. The McMurphy has withstood two world wars and a Great Depression. A little purple ribbon is not going to get us down. Is it?" I asked the puppy, who answered by piddling down the front of me.

I laughed and found a house training pad and

set her down on it. "Good thing we haven't put in new rugs yet."

"The whole island is taking sides?" Jennifer Christensen, my best friend from Chicago, said. "That's crazy!"

"Right? I mean, when was the last time you heard of anyone doing that? Medieval times?" Jennifer and I used Skype often. My computer screen showed me that she was currently painting her toenails while I attacked the boxes in the living room. I'd ordered a pizza and beer from the Horseshoe Bar. Then I'd put my hair up in a kerchief and decided if the cops could go through Papa's things, so could I. I'd spent the last two hours unpacking and repacking boxes, with Jennifer on the other end of my computer. Thank goodness for Internet connections and laptops with cameras and speakers.

"Who is this guy anyway that everyone would pick him over you?"

I pulled a ceramic cat from a box and sat back on my heels. "Trent Jessop? He's only about the sexiest man I've seen in my life. Plus he owns the stables and wears cowboy boots. And worse . . . He smells good. You know, that kind of cologne man scent that makes you want to turn around and follow him anywhere?"

"Oh, my, God, does he wear chaps?" Jennifer stopped mid-toenail, her hands paused with bottle and applicator.

"Only in my dreams," I said and we both laughed like school girls. "Seriously, the last time I ran into him, I told him how sorry I was for his loss. I mean, Papa Liam hasn't been gone but two months now so I know how it feels."

"What'd he say to that?" She went back to toenail painting. Today's shade was a pretty peacock-blue.

"Nothing. He acted as if it wasn't the same thing." I wrapped the cat in white paper and put it in a box marked "estate sale."

"He sounds like a real ass," Jennifer said in her blunt way.

"A cute ass," I said. "No, really though, I need help here. Would you do me a favor and put up a sign for interns? I'm thinking I could use a couple this summer. I can't pay much, but they'd get free room here on island and I'd pay for a summer ferry pass."

"Sounds like a dream. When do you want me?"

I stopped. "You would come and work for a room and a ferry pass?"

"Honey, if you throw in all the fudge I can eat, I'm all yours."

"If you're serious, then yes, come. I'll take all the help I can get. And you're not put off by the fact some guy died in my utility closet?"

"Are you kidding? I love ghost stories. I had an aunt who used to talk to spirits. She was a major medium in her day. It'll be fun. Plus I'll get to see the yacht races up close and smell this guy who hates you." She winked at me. "Maybe he'll like me."

"Pack up your stuff and sublease your place," I said. "I'll clean out Papa's room and you can have the guest room. Here's to girl power." I raised up my half-empty can of warm beer. She grabbed her margarita and toasted me.

"To girl power." She tossed back her drink. "Look, I've got to go. I'll text you with all the details as soon as I get them."

"Sounds perfect." I grabbed the puppy from where she sat chewing on paper and waved her little paw. "Bye, Jennifer, see you soon."

"Bye, Mal, can't wait to see you in the real world." Jenn waved and shut off her Skype. My computer screen went dark. For the first time since Papa's death things were looking up. With Jennifer here I could get twice as much work done and have four times the fun.

Of course, I'd really have to clean out the apartment now. There was a knock on my back door. Startled, I screamed. Mal screamed. We were the perfect pair.

Chapter 15

The back door opened into the galley kitchen. It had a small square window that was head high. Too high for anyone but a monster to break the glass and open the door. I mean, it would take freakishly long arms to do it, but that didn't mean my mind wasn't afraid it could be done.

I crept into the kitchen. Mal barked furiously in my hands. With all the noise we both made there was no way to pretend I wasn't home. Who climbs a fire escape three floors and knocks on a back door anyway?

The knock sounded again. "Allie?"

I looked out to see Officer Manning standing at the back door. I didn't know if I was relieved or pissed that he scared me. I opened the door. "You only left four hours ago. I haven't had time to buy dead bolts."

He wore a flannel shirt over a T-shirt, and a work coat with shearling lining. He looked good in jeans and boots. It fit the action-hero thing he had going for him. "I promised we'd send a patrol by every couple of hours. I was off duty and thought I'd check on you myself."

I pursed my lips and eyed him curiously. "Don't you have another wife or soon-to-be ex waiting for you at home?"

He shoved his hands in his pockets. "No, not seeing anyone right now, if that's what you're asking. Do you want me to come in and do a quick check of the building?"

"Only if you promise to check under the bed for monsters." I held the door open.

"It's all part of the job." He stepped in and wiped his feet on the rug in front of the door. "Do you want me to take off my shoes?"

"No, it's okay. I'm planning on replacing the carpets in here anyway." I closed the door and discovered that the galley kitchen might be comfortable when you were alone, but a big man made it close quarters. "Come on then." I waved him forward. "Start checking."

He smelled of wood smoke and cologne. I had never seen him out of uniform and I discovered that his shoulders were broader than I imagined and his jeans fit him better than they should for a man who was divorced twice.

"Did I interrupt your dinner?" he asked, raising a dark eyebrow toward the open pizza box and four remaining cans of beer.

I had set the pizza box on a stack of three boxes

so that it would be out of Mal's reach. The puppy sniffed the air and reached for Officer Manning as if he'd take her. Surprisingly, he did.

"Hello there. What's this?" He scooped her up and held her out at eye level. Mal wiggled as if to say, "Let me in closer so I can kiss you."

"That's Mal. Frances gave her to me to help keep me safe." I had to steel myself against the image of a big strong man holding a sweet little pup. Talk about your Hallmark moments.

"Hello, Mal." He drew her close and she licked his cheek. He grinned and scratched her behind the ears. "Probably a good idea. She's small now, but in a couple of weeks she'll be big enough to warn you if anyone is in the apartment."

That was a sobering thought. "Who'd want to get into my apartment?" I took Mal from him and cuddled her to my chest.

"Joe Jessop was murdered one floor down," he said, his blue eyes darkened with concern. "If you didn't do it, then someone else did. You have to ask yourself why? And more importantly, how did they get into the McMurphy?"

"I've been asking myself those questions and I really have no idea," I said a bit defensively.

He put his hand up like a stop sign. "Whoa, look, I wasn't accusing you of anything."

"No? Then why'd you bring a warrant and go through my things?"

"I had to do it, Allie." He rubbed his big hand

over his shaved head. "It's my job. And it's the only way we could rule you out as a suspect."

"Or rule me in." I hugged the puppy, who had had enough and tried to squirm out of my hands, so I put her down. "Why else would you take those bags of things when you left?"

"It's my job." He stood there looking like an action figure who wished he wasn't.

I gave the guy a break. I was in a good mood. Jennifer was coming up to help me out and I had finally named my puppy. "Are you on duty now or off duty?"

"I'm off." He gave me a look like it was a crazy question. "I wear my uniform when I'm on duty."

"Just checking," I said, "before I offer you a beer."

"A beer sounds great."

I pulled one out of the plastic rings. "They're losing their cold. My power was out most of the day and the fridge is still warm."

"That's fine." He took it and popped open the top. "That refrigerator looks like it's twenty years old. You should probably think about replacing it with a more energy-efficient one."

I tilted my head and studied him. "I'll get right on that."

"Sorry." He stepped into the living area and sat on the arm of the old brown couch. The couch itself was covered in boxes in varying stages of fullness. I had been using it as my sorting table. "I have a bad habit of giving advice where it's not wanted."

"Good to know." I took a swallow of my beer. It

was warm. Almost too warm, but I'd been too busy with sorting and chatting to pay much attention. "Yuck." I made a face. "I didn't think it was this warm. You don't have to drink it."

"I'm good." He swallowed some to show me he was in fact fine with warm beer. He got up and wandered around, looking at what I was doing. "What are you going to do with this stuff?"

"I thought I'd have a yard sale." I shrugged. "Do you think there's a market for some of this stuff?"

"Sure, looks like Liam collected old tools and stuff."

"Yeah, some of the tools look really funky. Then there are the bits of horse tack and such. Some of it looks centuries old." I pulled a dry-rotted leather bit out of a box. "I don't suppose the police force has horses here like they do in Central Park."

"We prefer bikes," he said and took a swig of beer. "They've got less upkeep and they don't have to be housed, fed, or cleaned up after."

"I know, right? The island is great, but, man, there's a lot of manure on the streets. I wouldn't want that job."

He raised his brows.

"The street sweeper job . . ."

"No worse than mucking out the stables. I did that one summer when I was in junior high school."

"Really?" It was hard imagining Officer Manning as anything other than a well-built crime fighter.

"Really, before that summer I was a scrawny kid.

After all that shoveling and raking I became a mean, lean, fighting machine."

Oh, good Lord, he said it with a straight face. "I bet you were popular with all the island girls."

"I had my fair share of dates." He finished off his beer and put the can on the counter with the others. "You recycle, right?"

"You bet. It's a ten-cent deposit per can. I need every cent I can get if I want to make a go at running the McMurphy."

"Speaking of, let's go down and check it out."

"Right." I put my can next to his. "Come on Mal. Let's keep the nice officer company." I picked her up and she snuggled against me and closed her eyes.

"One hell of a guard dog you got there." He winked.

"I think she'll grow into her job," I said.

"Are you going to crate train her?"

"Frances got me a crate. Do you have dogs?" I followed him down to the first floor and watched as he pulled a flashlight out of his belt and walked through the dark lobby.

"I like dogs. I don't have one." He flipped on the switch and I followed him to see if he really was looking for bad guys or simply using this as an excuse to search my place again.

"Commitment issues?" I asked.

He paused and looked at me over his shoulder. "No, just ask either of my two wives."

Oh, boy. "Hmmm, maybe you commit too soon . . ."

"I see something I like, I take it. I don't see any reason to wait."

The look he gave me sent chills up my arms. I clutched the dog a little too tight and she protested with a tiny yelp. "Unless, of course, you're in the middle of a murder investigation," I quipped. At least I hoped it was a quip. It might have sounded this side of throaty.

"Unless there's that." He checked behind the receptionist area and flashed his light through the glass wall to take in the fudge kitchen. "Do you plan on making candy?"

"I do. I have a graduate degree in candy making."

He narrowed his eyes and furrowed his brow. "You can get that?"

"Yes, you can."

"So you won't need to rely on your granddad's recipes."

"Oh, I'll still offer the McMurphy specialties. But I'm creative. I like to try new flavors as well."

"That might stir things up a bit."

"What do you mean?" I followed him up the stairs to the second floor.

"Folks are used to certain ways around here. If you create too much of a stir, you might put a dent in other shops' business."

"That's the plan." I hugged my pup as he walked the hall and checked that all the doors were locked. "That's not worth killing over, though."

"You never know what's worth killing over," he said and rattled a door handle. "People kill for the darnedest reasons."

I frowned. "Have you ever worked a homicide case before?"

"Once when I did a rotation down south. I spent a year in Detroit shadowing a couple of guys. Came across a drug deal gone bad. Not a pretty sight."

"No wonder you were so cool when you saw Joe. It wasn't your first time."

He straightened and grinned. "It's been a long time since anything was my first time, but that doesn't mean I don't remember."

Oh, boy. I was not known to be good with quick, witty comebacks. The moment passed in awkwardness and he winked at me. I think I blushed. Okay, I know I blushed. It's not like I didn't date. It's just I've spent my whole life so focused on being the McMurphy's next owner/operator that I haven't done much more than have a couple of really bad affairs.

"What did that murder suspect look like?" I asked. "Big, ugly crackhead or creepy little old lady?"

"Big, ugly gangbanger," he said as he checked inside the utility closet and then moved on down to the final four rooms. "Any idea what Joe was doing in the utility closet?"

"No." I sighed. "Frances has a theory but it's a little odd."

He finished checking the four doors and raised an eyebrow. "Do I get to hear it?"

"There's no real way to prove it." I shrugged. "Unless Joe left a note or told someone he was coming over we may never know."

"He didn't leave a note," Officer Manning said. I suppose I could call him Rex now that he wasn't in uniform. "At least not one we've found. Trent is going through his things."

"You know I don't have any feud with Trent or his grandfather for that matter." I hugged Mal. The pup let out a squeak of annoyance. "I don't know why he won't talk to me."

"Trent has a lot on his mind. Joe didn't have a will and the family is squabbling. Then there's the whole bit about his granddad being murdered." Rex waved toward the steps and put his hand on my elbow when I tripped on a step that was uneven.

I made a mental note to fix that before a guest tripped on it.

"I'd steer clear of him until this whole thing blows over," Rex said sincerely.

I tilted my head. "Did you buy a purple ribbon or a green one?"

He walked up the stairs behind me. "Now you know I can't take sides. That lawyer Frances sicced on me would cry foul in a heartbeat."

I narrowed my eyes and turned at the landing. "You bought a purple ribbon."

"I did not." He crossed his arms over his chest, but his eyes twinkled.

"You liar," I teased. "You totally bought a purple ribbon."

"Now why would I do that?" He stepped toward me. "Trent's not nearly as good-looking as you are."

"Officer Manning, are you hitting on me?" I tried to look innocent and naïve.

He put his arm up on the doorway and leaned into me. "I'd be in big trouble if I were sleeping with my murder suspect. And it's Rex."

I enjoyed the pause where his face was close to mine and he was working on whether to kiss me or not. Then I ducked under his arm and through the doorway into my apartment. "I wouldn't want to scandalize the senior citizens." I put Mal down on the navy-blue pillow I'd put on the floor for her dog bed. "Besides"—I straightened—"incentive for you to find Joe's real killer."

"Who says I haven't already?"

Strawberry Daiquiri Fudge

4 cups chocolate chips or 5 cups white
  chocolate (I tried both. I like white.)
4 tablespoons butter
1 can sweetened condensed milk
½ cup crushed strawberries, reserve juice
  (Hint: 1 tablespoon sugar mixed in before
  you crush will bring out more juice.)
1 tablespoon lime juice
1 tablespoon lemon juice
2 ounces spiced rum (to taste)

Butter an 8" x 8" x 2" pan. Line with wax paper or plastic wrap. Drain strawberries, reserving juice. Combine strawberry, lime, and lemon juice with rum, mixing well.

In a double boiler fill the bottom with water and place on high until it reaches a rolling boil then turn to low. In the top pan, melt chocolate, butter, and sweetened condensed milk until smooth. Be careful not to burn. Add liquid 1 tablespoon at a time, stirring after each. (Use more or less to your taste.)

Remove from heat. Add crushed strawberries. Pour into pan. Cool. Tip: let cool outside of the refrigerator for 30 minutes so that no condensation mars the top. Refrigerate overnight. Remove from pan. Cut into pieces. Store in a covered container.

Chapter 16

Getting rid of Papa's stuff meant there was more room for Mal's crate upstairs. Two days ago, I had promised to crate train the puppy. It seems that bichons were difficult to house train even with a crate, but the crate helped. From what I read, crate-trained puppies loved their crates. It became their safe place. I liked the idea of a safe haven for Mal.

Before too long there would be strangers coming and going in the hotel. Mal would need a place she knew would be hers and hers alone.

I had stuffed a soft blanket in the back of the crate and added a water bottle that hung to the side. I squatted down and let her in and out of the crate. "Good baby," I cooed.

Mal answered by wagging her tail and licking my face. I picked her up. "Let's go get your halter. You'll need to go out and go potty."

I picked her up and got her halter and leash

from the hall tree where it hung. I liked walking her with a halter. It seemed so cruel to walk her by the neck when she had such a sturdy chest. Besides, if trouble flared I could pick her up quickly with the halter.

Maybe after we went for our walk it would be a good night to take some time off and play with a fudge recipe in my own kitchen.

My keys rested in the small bowl that sat on the antique hall table beside the door. The bowl was dark, with hand-painted roses on the border. Above it an oval mirror hung from the wall. Beside it was a carved coat rack and a small umbrella holder.

It had taken me nearly two days but I had sorted the boxes of Papa's collections in the living room. Half had gone to the Goodwill in St. Ignace. The other half currently sat at the Island Antique and Curio Shop on Market Street. Joy Gelger ran the shop and had been excited to look through Papa's stuff. If she sold anything she got 30 percent of the price. I wasn't here to make money on Papa's treasures, only to find them good homes.

Mal licked my hand as I pulled her halter and leash off the coat tree where they hung. The newly cleared floor of the apartment was covered in forty-year-old wall-to-wall carpet. It was green and textured with a pattern that must have resembled leaves at some point. Currently it was worn to nubbins and smelled of old people.

I kind of liked that the place still smelled like

Papa. I imagined the wallpaper carried the lingering scent of his "fine" cigars.

"I miss you, Papa," I whispered. "This would be so much easier if you were here. I bet you could tell me about the stains under the carpet and who, if anyone, might have died there."

I suppose I was being silly and morose. It was probably something silly like Papa and his friends butchering a deer in the lobby before Grammy came home and asked them what they thought they were doing. I smiled at that thought and put Mal's halter on her.

"So, little pup . . . back door or front?" I asked her. She blinked up at me with her black button eyes, her tail wagging. "You're right, we did close up the front . . . Back door it is."

The problem with the fire escape is that I imagined the metal flooring was difficult for her to walk on. Not to mention climbing the bottom ladder with a puppy in my hand. It worked for now, but what happened when she got a little bigger? Maybe I should have someone come out and bid on putting stairs to the back.

It was for certain that the ladder wasn't keeping anyone out.

The walk didn't take long as a chill had whipped up off the lake and the sun had grown low on the horizon. I walked her down the alley and around the block for good measure. What I discovered was that walking a dog gave people an excuse to talk to you. I met three other dog walkers and only two of them wore Jessop purple. The third was a tourist and had no idea who I was or who Joe Jessop was. It made me look forward to the start of the season.

We got back inside and I took off Mal's harness and leash. I poured her some kibble.

I had taken seven boxes to the antique store, but I knew Papa had a bunch of things stored in the basement, too. I hadn't had the courage to go down there yet. It was dark and made of stone and mortar and had never been my favorite place to go. So far I'd only gone down there with the furnace and air-conditioning guy for the season checkup. It was then that I noted the place needed to be cleaned out as well.

Maybe I should consider maintaining the May-to-September season like Papa. It would give me time to set the rest of the hotel to rights. A handful of the more successful hotels were open year-round and certainly so were the fudge shops. I had hoped to do the same to boost revenue. Still, it was a lot for one person—especially a person who had yet to work an entire season.

I imagined the off-season clientele were different. The ferries didn't run and the only way on and off island was by plane—unless Lake Huron froze. Then for a few days the locals would build an ice bridge and the brave would snowmobile back and forth to the mainland.

Mal followed me back and forth as I went from

the kitchen to my bedroom and back into the tiny kitchen. She stumbled over her own feet on the wood floor in the kitchen. I plucked a white apron from the bar of hooks I'd attached to the wall. The box of fudge sat near the sink. Today's flavor was orange walnut. I'd spent months perfecting my chocolate varieties. Today I was going to try my hand at making a more exotic fudge. Maybe white chocolate as a base and butter pecan flavor.

That was my intent anyway until a terrible noise came from downstairs. It sounded like someone tried to break down the house. Mal jumped and barked at the front door to the apartment. The sound was surprising as she had been such a quiet dog up until now. Her barking didn't stop the downstairs sounds. I grabbed the puppy in one hand and my phone in the other. I snagged Rex's card from where I'd attached it to the fridge with two magnets and dialed his number.

"Manning." his voice sounded comforting on the phone.

In the meantime, I'd grabbed the large metal bar that I used to keep hot fudge from running off the marble table. After all, I needed a bigger weapon than a six-pound puppy. I could feel her growl and cry in my hand. "Um, Rex, this is Allie McMurphy. I'm in my apartment and it sounds like someone's breaking in downstairs. Could you come over or send someone?"

"Didn't you install a security system?"

"Yes." Another loud crash sounded from below. "It hasn't gone off yet." I gripped the metal bar hard. "Can you hurry?"

"I'll be right over." I heard him rustle about as if grabbing his coat and hopefully his firearm. "Why don't you stay on the phone with me?"

"Sounds like a plan." I tiptoed to my door and put my ear to it. I didn't hear anything but the whimpers Mal made as she sniffed the door. "Are there a lot of break-ins on island?" I asked. I certainly didn't remember there being any when I was a kid.

"Not many," he admitted. "None around unopened fudge shops. You don't have any cash on the premises, do you?"

"No, nothing more than what I keep in my wallet."

"Hmm, are you sure you heard something?"

That got my chin up. "Of course I heard something. I've heard it again since we've been on the phone."

"Okay, don't get defensive. I had to check. With all the talk about town regarding the crime scene you uncovered, I wanted to make sure your imagination wasn't running away from you."

"Gee thanks," I muttered. "My imagination is pretty darn loud. Listen, I'm going to put you on speaker and go down and unlock the door for you."

"Okay," he said. "I'm on my way over. Take the

dog with you. I should get there by the time you get down."

I hit the speaker button on my cell phone. I had thought about getting a land line, but it was an expense I didn't think I needed. My cell phone generally got good reception and thank goodness. Right now a land line would have been useless. "Can you hear me?" I asked.

"Sure can."

"Good." I unlocked my door and checked the foyer. Whoever broke in had not made their way up to the office yet. Either they were looking for something specific or they didn't know the office was on the third floor. And, if they didn't know that, then they weren't local.

I twisted the handle on the office door to make sure Mal and I were alone. It was locked. "No one's in the office," I told Rex. "The door's still locked. I'm going down."

"Don't try to search the place without me," he warned. "Make your way slowly down the stairs."

"Okay." I tucked Mal into the large pocket at the base of my apron, then used my cell phone as a lamp and held it out in front of me. I gripped the steel rod like a baseball bat and made it down to the second floor before I heard another crash in the distance.

"I heard that," Officer Manning said over my phone speaker. "Don't follow it. Let's get you out of there. Okay?"

"Sure." The last thing I wanted was to be one of

those silly horror flick girls who goes into the basement alone when everyone knows the killer is down there.

My heartbeat sped up. It pounded in my ears. My hands shook a little as I hurried down the stairs. When I reached the first floor I hit the light switches at the bottom of the stairs. The lobby and fudge shop leapt into full light. It took me a moment to focus. Whoever was in the house must have frozen when the lights came on. I held my breath but couldn't hear anything other than the beating of my heart. "Officer Manning is on his way over," I shouted. "Whoever you are, I'd get the heck out now."

"Here I thought we'd catch them in the act," Rex groused from my cell phone.

"Yes, well, it's all good and well for you to catch them in the act. Not quite as good if I run into them on the way to letting you inside. It's not like Mal is big enough to deter them."

At the sound of her name, the puppy popped her head up out of the apron pocket. I hurried to the front door and felt a jolt of surprise when a large, dark shadow-figure loomed at the door. "Holy crap!" I pressed my hand against my chest.

"It's me." Rex waved his hands. He leaned into the light, exposing his face. "Open the door."

"Yeah, okay." Right, I wasn't spooked. Ha! My body felt like it had been hit with a live wire. It took careful thought and coordination to put down the metal rod and unlock the front door.

Rex stepped inside. He wore a long duster coat, and no hat. His tough-guy shaved head gleamed in the lamplight.

"Are you all right?" He stepped over the threshold.

"Yes." I maneuvered Mal and myself between him and the door. That way if someone were to run out they'd get him first. What can I say, he was the big policeman. I was only a candy maker from Chicago. "You're not in uniform."

"My shift was over for the day." He pulled out his flashlight and checked the fudge shop.

I stood in the open doorway and watched. "I'm sorry. I suppose I should have called 9-1-1 instead."

"It's all right. They would have called me anyway." He glanced at me with his piercing blue eyes. "I'm on call tonight."

"Oh, good . . . well, good for me anyway." I noticed that his duster was unbuttoned. He had on jeans and a tight-fitting dark T-shirt that showed off his chest. He wore his gun belt on his hips along with a nice-sized pistol.

I followed him like a scared puppy as he checked all the corners of the lobby, testing the windows to ensure they were locked. I clutched the metal rod in my hand. Mal rode in my pocket like a baby joey.

"Are you here by yourself?"

"Yes," I said as I followed him to the back bathrooms and walk-in utility closet. "I'm advertising for help and my friend Jennifer is coming up for the summer. But for now it's only me and the puppy."

He glanced at Mal and back at me. "The dog has some growing up to do before she counts as protection."

"I know," I muttered. "The whole staff needs growing up. I need a housekeeper, a day clerk, a handyman, and a couple of kids to work the coffee bar and cash register."

"A handyman? What happened to Colin?"

I swallowed at the curiosity in his eyes. "I fired him. He hasn't shown up to work in weeks." I stopped short. "You don't think Colin's dead, do you?"

Rex shrugged. "If he knows you've fired him, it's more likely he might be the one trying to vandalize you."

The thought made me shiver. Colin seemed like a nice guy who was down on his luck. Not the kind of psycho who might come in with a gun and kill you.

A loud screeching metal sound followed by a bang came from behind the basement door. I might have screamed a little. I'm not sure, but what I was sure of was that I had my hands full of the back of Officer Manning's duster as I was quick to leap and put him between me and the basement.

His gun was out of the belt and in his hand in the blink of an eye. "Stay here," he ordered and slashed his free hand through the air as if commanding a dog.

"I intend to." I pretended it was Mal he had barked out an order to as I worked to uncurl my fingers from his coat. Rex waited for me to take a step back and out of the line of sight from the door. Then he opened it, flipped on the light switch, and disappeared down the steep steps into the musty scent of danger below.

Chapter 17

Okay, it gets kind of scary being upstairs alone while the big strong man with the gun disappears downstairs into the darkness. I counted to thirty. Nothing.

"Hello?" I said to the darkness. To be clear, there was a lightbulb near the stairs, but the hotel was built before electricity. The basement was little more than a couple-room cellar with lightbulbs strung along the rafters. "Rex?"

I bit my bottom lip and listened intently. "Don't make me come down there."

"I said stay," echoed up the stairs in a stage whisper. The lights came on and I heard footfalls and then nothing.

Rex popped into my line of view, startling me. "It's clear."

"Now I don't believe that," I said and to prove it I went down the stairs. "I heard something and so did you."

"No one's here," he said and pointed his flashlight into the dark corners. "It might just be rats."

"I do not have rats," I insisted. I tucked Mal under my left arm and held my metal bar in my right hand. The basement was damp and smelled of age and mildew. The walls were made of stone and mortar. The floor was packed dirt. If I remembered correctly there were two rooms and a tiny coal bin. Next to the coal bin was the old oil tank that Papa had replaced with a modern boiler system that ran heat through pipes.

"How do you know you don't have rats?" Rex asked. He poked his head into the back room.

"I would know if the McMurphy had rats," I said. "They leave their droppings. Besides, it's been fifty years since we stored food down here. There's nothing for them to eat."

"Except wiring and insulation and floorboards," Rex said.

"They better not eat my wiring." I marched into the second room and yanked the light fixture pull cord, throwing the room into shadow.

"I thought you didn't have rats," he teased me. He crossed his arms over his chest and studied me.

I felt a little silly with a puppy tucked under my arm and a metal fudge turner in my hand. "I don't."

"How can you tell?" he asked as he waved his light over the stacks and rows of boxes and shelves filled with parts and gadgets.

"The same way you can tell no one is down here but us," I said.

There was a terrible scraping noise coming from the coal bin and I might have squealed a little. All I know is that I somehow flew across the room because one minute I was under the dangling light and the next I practically climbed up on Officer Manning's shoulders.

He had his arm around my waist and his gun pointed at the coal bin. "Who's there?" he shouted. "Come out with your hands up."

"Did you really say that?" I asked. It was a feat the way my hands clutched him and the puppy and the weapon without dropping anything.

"Of course, I said that." He frowned at me. "I meant it," he said to the coal bin. "Come out now or I'm coming in."

"You can't go in," I whispered.

"Why the hell not?"

"Because then I have to go in and I'm not going in there."

"Then stay out here."

"Oh, no, I'm not staying out here, either."

There was another long loud scraping sound of metal against metal or rock. Rex leapt forward, tossed the door open with his gun drawn and his flashlight filling the room. "I said, show yourself with your hands in the air."

My heart pounded in my throat. His tone was so

authoritative that I found myself raising my hands. Luckily I stopped before he saw me.

Rex hit the middle of the tiny walk-in space and turned on the light. The room had been built to hold enough coal to fuel the furnace. It had a twelve-by-twelve-inch opening in the wall where the coal wagon would pull up and slide coal down inside. That chute had been boarded up by Papa sometime in the fifties.

Now the tiny room was populated with a series of metal shelves. There was a faint aroma of grapes and yeast. Papa had been into making his own wine. The old bottles rested on their sides, dust covering the handmade labels.

"Someone was in here," Rex said. His flashlight showed where two shelves had been moved from the wall that butted up against the Old Tyme Photography shop next door.

The idea made my skin crawl. "Do you think it was Joe's killer?" I asked and peered over Rex's shoulder at the heavy shelving. "Whoever it was had to be pretty big. Those shelves look like they weigh a ton."

"It could have been more than one," Rex said as he tried to move the shelves, but they didn't budge.

Mal sniffed the air from her vantage point under my arm, and then she growled. The sound was so unexpected it had the hair on the back of my neck standing up. "Mal!"

She barked. It was a loud, ear-piercing sound

that had Rex staring at her. I put my hand over her mouth to stop her. She growled.

"What is it, girl?" Rex asked.

"I think she feels my fear," I said. "There's no one here. There's no room for them behind those shelves." There was only six inches of air between the shelves and the rock wall that was the basement.

Rex shone his flashlight behind the shelves, throwing the shadows into the light. "I don't like it," he said.

"One thing's for sure," I said. "Rats did not move those shelves."

"True," he said and holstered his gun. "Did your grandfather ever tell you about a secret passage down here?"

"No." I shook my head. "I'm sure he would have, too. He loved to tell ghost stories and such. I can't imagine he'd keep something as cool as a secret passage from me. But I tell you what, I can call my dad and see if he knows of any."

"That would be a good idea," Rex said. "In the meantime, I suggest we board up this door for tonight and check it out in the morning."

"Papa Liam kept his nails and tools near the stairs. I have no idea where I'd find boards."

"Maybe you should spend the night with Frances," he suggested.

I stopped short and sighed. "No."

"Seriously, Allie." He tugged me by the elbow until I faced him. "Someone was in your house."

"I know," I said. "But it's a hotel. I'm sort of used

to someone being in the house. I'll lock my doors. Besides, I'm the murder suspect, right? So shouldn't they be afraid of me?"

"How do you know it isn't someone looking for revenge?"

"Then I'll need police protection," I quipped. "But I know, there's little you can do if there's no evidence of a crime."

"Allie—"

"I'll keep my phone handy," I promised. "As long as you help me board up the coal bin, I'll be fine."

"Fine."

"Good," I said. "By the way, you wouldn't happen to know when Joe's memorial is, do you?"

"We released the body yesterday." He moved some boxes. "Trent said the funeral is set for tomorrow at noon. Why did you want to know?"

"I wanted to go, you know, to show my community support."

"If I were you, I'd stick to watching over your remodel." He pulled two heavy boards out from behind a stack of boxes. "The Jessops have enough grief without you there to cause a scene. Where are the nails and tools?"

"Here." I handed him a small glass jar full of nails from Papa's workbench. "I would not cause any trouble," I said and dug a hammer out of the workbench drawer. "Like I said, I don't have anything against the Jessops. What happened between Papa Liam and Joe was between them. If I go to the

funeral, then my actions speak louder than my
words. No one believes my protests anyway."

"Don't do it, Allie," he said as he set the board up
against the door and nailed it shut. "Trust me. You
at Joe's funeral is bad news."

"Let's just agree to disagree," I said and hugged
Mal to my chest. "I for one think it's important
that I go. Besides, I have a handful of purple ribbons.
It will be nice to have a place to wear them."

Rex hammered the boards across the door,
ensuring that no one could get in or out. "Why
don't you take a casserole over there while you're at
it," he muttered.

"Great idea," I said. "I may do just that."

Chapter 18

"What do you think you're doing here?" Trent Jessop scowled at me. He stood in the doorway of his family home. I could see people mingling behind him. At least they had been mingling, but Trent's raised voice made everyone stop. You could hear a pin drop. My heart beat in my ears.

"I came to pay my respects," I said. "I am so sorry for your loss. Here, I brought you a casserole." I shoved the warm dish into his hands. "It's three-meat lasagna. You can freeze it if you want."

He scowled, but took the dish. Unfortunately he didn't let me in the door, so it was rather awkward. Especially since I got my first good look at him in the daylight up close and personal. All I can say is, oh, man. Trent Jessop was one gorgeous cowboy. He had shoulders as wide as the Mackinac Bridge. Okay, that's an exaggeration, but they were nicely proportional to his body. The guy could wear a suit. It was black, of course, and the white shirt and blue tie were stunning. He even smelled good. Like warm starched linen and aftershave. You know, the kind of scent that was subtle but at the same time made a girl turn around and follow a guy. Yeah, that kind of nice.

He had black hair that curled at the edge of his collar. A strong stubborn jaw with a tick in it. Probably because I wasn't budging . . . or intimidated by his dark brown stare. The man had thick black lashes any woman would have died to have. It made a girl start to think about having babies with black lashes.

"Well, okay," I said, breaking the stare off. "I guess you get that I'm sorry for your loss. Heat the casserole at 325 degrees. Don't worry about returning the dish. It's not a family heirloom or anything."

He didn't say a word. He simply closed the door in my face. I suppose you could say he was the strong, silent type. Or maybe Rex had been right. Maybe it was stupid to come over and try to make peace. Trent was still hurting. I got that.

I stepped off the wide front porch of the painted-lady cottage that was the Jessop family retreat. It sat on a bluff overlooking Market Street and the lake. A girl in a gray maid's uniform dusted the black wrought-iron fence that enclosed the perfectly manicured lawn. A young man in work clothes trimmed bushes. I walked down the long sidewalk and took three steps before I went through the gate and onto the street. A horse-drawn taxi pulled up filled with people dressed in Sunday black. Men in suits and women in dresses. They were perfectly groomed and looked like money. It was a cultural difference, I guess. People with old money always dressed differently. They wore elegant clothes with the same comfort level as most people wore jeans and T-shirts.

They glared at me as they passed by. I took note of the purple ribbons on their lapels. I, too, wore a purple ribbon. It had been a kind of joke. A hope that they would see that I was taking the thing in stride. But lightheartedness was not in the cards.

I tugged my black sweater around my waist and hurried back to the McMurphy. The streets were lined with pansies and horse-drawn taxis clomped by. There were several bicyclists enjoying the cool spring air. Today the lake was as smooth as glass. It was funny how quickly you became accustomed to the lack of traffic sounds. Instead, the gentle clip-clop of horses filled the air. Unless you were down by the docks. Then you had the sounds of the ferry motors and the crowds of tourists. The shouts of the dock workers.

It's not like the island was completely sleepy. There were gardeners in the yards and painters touching up the cottage exteriors. The trash wagon rumbled by. Carriage drivers talked to their horses as they lined up waiting for fares. Shop owners swept their stoops while women in maids' uniforms hurried off to work.

The island was a fun mix of time and place. The

no-car rule and gorgeous, painted-lady cottages gave it a solid Victorian feel. Meanwhile, people walked by talking on cell phones or sat on Victorian chairs scrolling through their iPads and tablets. Time and place indeed.

Frances waited for me outside the McMurphy. "Where did you go?" she asked. Today she wore a bright red felt coat and matching red felt fedora with navy-blue trim and a peacock feather accent.

"I took a casserole to the Jessops." I unlocked the McMurphy and turned on the chandelier that lit the big lobby. Mal got up from her bed inside her crate and stretched. I walked over and let her out. She ran to Frances.

"You did not." Frances picked Mal up and petted and squeezed her.

"I did so. Joe's daughter Elizabeth brought me a casserole when Papa died. The least I could do was return the sentiment." I took the puppy from Frances and put on Mal's halter and leash. I had read in a dog training book that you were supposed to take them out the moment you let them out of the crate. Since Mal had the unfortunate tendency to piddle, I wasn't taking any chances.

Frances hung her coat and hat up as I went out the back door and across the alley to the tiny patch of grass. While Mal did her figure eights, I studied the back of the McMurphy. If there was really a secret tunnel in the basement, where would it go?

The McMurphy was built in the Victorian era, when storefronts and hotels tended to be attached.

That way there were no fights over property rights. An alley ran down the back of the block allowing access for workers. Across the alley was a pool house that McMurphy guests shared with the Oakton Bed and Breakfast. Papa Liam and Pete Thompson's grandfather Alfred had pooled their money and built a pool house. Sometime in the 1980s Papa had sold his share of the pool house back to the Thompson family with the condition that McMurphy guests had free access.

There had been talk of putting in a walkway from the second floor of the McMurphy to the pool house, which sat farther up the bluff and faced Market Street. But that had never happened.

Mal finished her business, and I cleaned up after her. We both went back inside to find Frances talking to Rex Manning.

"Hello," I said and disappeared into the washroom to wash my hands.

"Why didn't you call me last night?" Frances had her hands on her hips and a frown on her face. "You should not have spent the night alone."

"I was fine." I wiped my hands on a towel. "We boarded up the coal bin. Besides, who knows if there even is an entrance through there."

"It would explain how Joe Jessop was able to come and go at random," Frances said.

"I can't believe there was a secret door in the McMurphy that Papa didn't know about. He lived his entire life here and he did most of the maintenance." I turned to Officer Manning. "Hi Rex, what brings you into the McMurphy?"

He wore his pressed uniform complete with Kevlar vest and gun holster. His hat was in his hand. His blue eyes twinkled. "Hi Allie, I came by to check out the coal bin. I got Judge Astor to agree to ask your permission to check for any egress through the basement. It could explain how a killer got into the McMurphy to kill Joe."

"Or could get in and kill you." Frances picked up Mal and hugged her tight. "Seriously. You should not be staying here alone."

"It's okay, Frances. My friend Jennifer is coming in today. I've hired her for the season. We need the extra help."

"I thought you'd hire some interns like your Papa always did."

"I plan on it, but with the coffee bar and the fudge shop, we'll need another full-time person on board. That way I can concentrate on building the fudge shop back up."

"Humph." Frances snorted. "Can you afford another full-time employee? You still need a new handyman."

"I've got it handled," I said. "Could you watch Mal while I take Officer Manning down to the basement?"

"Fine." Frances turned on her heel. "Come on little dog, let's see what mischief we can get into today."

I rolled my eyes, and Rex stifled a chuckle.

"Thanks for coming back." I led him through the back and down the staircase. "Do you really think we boarded someone inside the coal bin?"

"I don't know," he admitted. "I wanted to come down in the daylight and do a thorough search. I want you to know I didn't get a warrant. This is a voluntary search."

"I understand." I turned on the fluorescent light. There were two window wells in the back, but it was still a bit dark. The light buzzed. The walls held a damp, musty smell. Shadows loomed along the dirt floor. "I'm glad you came. I didn't want to have to search the walls by myself."

He flicked on his flashlight and walked a grid from under the stairs toward the sunlight side. There were wood pallets on the floor that held stacks of boxes. I had no idea what all was in them. I imagined it was over one hundred years of old lamps, doorknobs, and other bits and pieces of junk.

I added a note to my mental list to go through the basement next fall and sell what I could to the scrap man and toss out the rest. It certainly wasn't doing anyone any good sitting in the basement of the McMurphy gathering dust.

Rex nosed through boxes, and I went to Papa's workbench and looked through old Mason jars filled with screws and nuts and bolts and such. Somewhere along the way, Papa had hung up Peg-Board and then created metal holders that raised the glass bottles of metal up on the wall and off the work surface. There was an old band saw, three kinds of hammers, all kinds of saws and wrenches. There was a heavy metal box marked Craftsman. Inside was a wide array of tools.

"That box is worth a fortune," Rex said over my shoulder. "If I were you I'd get the place inventoried sooner rather than later. It's hard to tell if someone is stealing if you don't know what you have."

I closed the lid of the toolbox. "Right." He was, I knew it, but I simply hadn't had time to think about the basement. It took a good two hours of poking around before Rex was satisfied that there was nothing of much use to the investigation in the main part of the basement. We both stood outside the boarded coal bin. It wasn't a bin, really, it was a small room that was maybe nine by nine foot wide.

If anyone were locked in there, I could imagine they'd be pretty claustrophobic fairly fast.

"Hammer?" Rex asked.

I handed him a claw-head hammer, and he gave me his flashlight. Then he dug under the nails with the forked part until it was snagged under tight, then leveraged the nail up and out of the board. In no time at all the boards were in a pile at his feet. The door to the bin was free.

"You two all right down here?" Frances asked from the top of the stairs.

"We're good," I called over. "We just unboarded the coal bin.

Frances came downstairs with Mal tucked under her arm. "I haven't been down here in years."

"Do you know if there is some sort of secret passage in the coal bin?" I asked.

"No." Frances shook her head. "Liam never mentioned any secret passage. I can't imagine what they would need one for . . ."

"We are reasonably close to Canada," Rex said.

"So is Detroit," I said. "It would seem Detroit would be easier than riding on a ferry on and off island."

"Did you find a tunnel?" she asked and peered at the door.

"Not yet," I said and took the hammer from Rex and handed back his flashlight. "After you."

He pulled the gun from his belt and opened the door, careful to check the corners before he stepped in, gun first. "Police," he said loud and clear. "Come out with your hands up."

Chapter 19

I held my breath and listened. Nothing. Not a single sound. All I heard was my own heartbeat.

"I'm doing a sweep of the room," Rex continued. "If I were you, I'd come out with my hands up before I got shot."

"I know I would," Frances said. She petted Mal, who whined.

I took my dog from Frances and snuggled her against my face in the hope of calming her down or maybe I hoped to calm myself down.

"Clear," Rex called. I stepped inside the small room. It looked completely different in the daytime. The metal shelves looked dusty, and the jars that sat on them were empty and covered with dust.

"I thought I told Liam to have this place cleared." Frances tsked. She ran a finger along a metal, gray shelf and lifted it up to show me the dirt. "This is appalling."

"I'll hire someone to clean it out," I told Frances.

"Right after we ensure there isn't some sort of secret passage."

"What makes you think that anyway?"

"I swear someone was down here moving shelves last night," I said. "Rex heard it too."

"There are marks where this shelf has been moved," he said and holstered his gun. He put his shoulder into moving the shelf, but it didn't budge. "There has to be some sort of locking mechanism." He ran his capable, square hands along the underside of the shelf.

I walked the wall, looking for footprints. I felt a definite draft near the back corner and tucked Mal under my arm to take a closer look. On close inspection, there were tiny cracks in the mortar—outlining what looked to be a door about five feet in height and three feet wide.

"I think there's a door." I ran my finger along the edge. "There's a breeze coming through here."

"We need to figure out how to open it." Rex came over to see where the door was. "Try pressing on the rocks of the wall."

On one side of the coal bin was a large metal hook, and a set of heavy chains hung from it. I remember asking Papa about the chains as a kid. He had told me they were from a dark period in the history of Mackinac. I had made up a story in my head about escaped slaves. But the truth was most likely it was used for preparing pigs for slaughter.

We didn't do that now, but my guess was one hundred years ago when they were feeding hotel guests, the meat had to come from somewhere. Ugh, I didn't want to think about it. In fact maybe the first thing I'd do when I hired a new handyman was have him remove the chains.

Side-by-side, Rex and I pressed rock after rock to no avail. Frances held Mal and watched us from beside the shelves. "Wait!" I said and walked over to them. "Rex, didn't you say the shelves were moved last night?"

"Yes." Rex studied the shelving. "I also remember it was too heavy for me to move by myself."

"Then how do you know it was moved?" Frances asked.

"There were scrape marks in the dirt." Rex pointed down and there were indeed marks in the floor that suggested the shelves were swung out and then back into place.

"Maybe the lever is in or on the shelf," I suggested. The shelves themselves were made of metal and stacked high with old bottles and some boxes. Some of the boxes had begun to rot out. It was hard to imagine anything being a lever. "Didn't Papa ever throw anything away?"

"Your grandmother would make him spring clean once a year, but the basement was a bone of contention to them. I don't know why exactly, but she never came down here and he didn't talk about cleaning it."

"Sounds like the old man had a secret," Rex said as he opened and closed boxes on the shelves.

"Whatever the secret was, it died with him," I

muttered. The boxes in front of me were filled with rusted things. Springs and clockwork and old locks. "I need a pair of heavy gloves if I'm going to go through these."

I stopped and studied the shelf. Whoever came down here knew about the wall door, and they knew how to open it. Those boxes looked like they hadn't been touched in decades. I sincerely doubted our mystery killer had gone through them. So what would he have touched?

I ran my hand down the side of the shelf. Nothing but cool metal and flakes of rust met my fingertips. I then ran my fingers under the shelves, and on the second from the bottom shelf I found a lever. It felt like the lever inside the hood of a car. I squeezed it hard and the shelf moved.

"Watch out!" I called. Thank goodness it swung out slowly or it would have run over my foot. The shelf swung out in a slow arc revealing a metal handle with a rubber grip resting lengthwise on the floor. "What is that?"

Rex squeezed out from behind the shelves and examined it. "Looks like an old railroad lever used to switch tracks."

"There isn't a railroad on the island." I liked to state the obvious.

"Pull it," Frances said. Mal barked excitedly as if to agree with her.

Rex looked at me as if asking permission.

"Hey." I shrugged. "You're the man with the gun."

"And no warrant," he reminded me.

"I doubt there's another dead body on the other side of this door." I waved my hand toward the wall.

"And if there is?" he asked, his eyes twinkling.

"I would not let you push that lever. I'm not stupid." I planted my hands on my hips. "So open it or I will."

He reached down and grabbed the lever with one hand, his shirt straining across his shoulders, and pulled. The screeching sound was horrible and exactly what I had heard the night before, only this time it was loud enough to deafen me. I put my hands over my ears. Mal barked up a storm as the wall slid back inside itself revealing a small three-foot-by-five-foot hole.

"Aye, Matey, there be treasure," Rex muttered. I glanced at him, uncertain if I heard him correctly. "What?" he asked. "Have you never seen *Treasure Island*?"

"You know there was some talk about buried treasure on island somewhere," Frances said, petting Mal to calm her down. "When the British took it from the Americans the fort commander was said to have buried the gold and precious items to keep them out of the British hands."

"Are you talking about the War of 1812? The McMurphy wasn't even built yet."

"All the better," Rex said as he turned on his flashlight and approached the door. "This looks like it was done before the hotel was built." He glanced at me. "Do you know what was on the site first?"

"I don't know." I shrugged. "Papa told me that his great-grandfather bought the land from a merchant's daughter. The man himself died in a flu outbreak the winter before. The building was torn down and the McMurphy was built over the top.

"Maybe this is more recent than that," he said as he examined the wall opening. "This mechanism is early twentieth century. It has the look and feel of Art Deco."

"Like the twenties?" I asked, "Or was that the thirties?"

"My best guess it was during Prohibition, but you'd have to research it to find out exactly." He rubbed the hinge. "There's a patent number on here." He took a small pad of paper out of his pocket and copied the number down. "If I had to guess, I'd say it was used during prohibition, even if it was built before that."

"What's inside?" I stuck my head in to see. There was a set of stairs that led down under the basement and the alley behind the McMurphy. "Stairs . . ."

This stairway was cut into the rock, and the ceiling was so low that Rex had to duck his head. The walls were slimy and cold. Water dripped as we descended into the darkness. "Good thing I'm not claustrophobic or anything," I said.

Rex glanced back at me. "You shouldn't be down here in those shoes." His flashlight hit my black pumps. I had not changed since I'd been to the Jessops' for Joe's memorial. I still wore my black sheath dress, dark black sweater, and three-inch heels.

"Hey, if a girl's going to find treasure, she should at least be able to look good doing it."

"Yeah, well, you won't be the one having to carry you out of here if you fall and break something."

The man did have a point.

"I'm not going barefoot," I said. "And I'm not turning around, so unless you're going to lend me your shoes . . ."

"Not likely," Rex said. "These are government issue."

I scrunched up my face as he waved the light over his black shoes. "To begin with, I highly doubt they issue you shoes. And secondly, those soles look slicker than mine."

"I guess if we go down, then, we go down together." He waggled his eyebrows at me.

There was a noise in the distance. "Did you hear that?" I whispered, my fingers wrapped firmly in his shirtsleeve. Funny, but I don't remember moving toward him. He had his hand on my hip, keeping his body in front of mine.

We both held our breath, but no further sound was made.

"Stay here," he said and moved forward.

"Right." I kept pace behind him. I didn't have a flashlight, and I refused to stand in the dark alone. I thought I could take a robber, maybe even a murderer, but if there were rats down here I refused to wait for them to crawl by me in the dark.

The tunnel, if you could call it that, stopped maybe twenty feet from the McMurphy. If I had to guess I'd say it was the length of the alley. There were two doors at the end, one on the left and one straight ahead.

Rex shone his flashlight on the doors. One looked as if the hinges were rusted and the wood planks on the door were black with rot and dampness. The door straight ahead had fresh hinges. Both doors had old wrought-iron handles.

"Door number one or door number two?" Rex asked, both hands wrapped around his gun, his flashlight balanced on top of the revolver.

"Door number two," I whispered. My fingers were still clutching his shirt. If we were going to be shot, I was smart enough to use his Kevlar-protected chest as a shield. If that made me selfish, well, I could live with that.

He reached down and checked the door handle. It didn't appear to be locked. "Police!" Rex put his shoulder into the door, and it creaked open with a terrible screech.

I held my breath as he stepped into a darkened room. The sound of mechanical humming filled the air. The musty, dusty smell was infused with the sharp scent of chlorine. His light bounced off thick pipes, thin pipes, and barrels of chemicals.

"Hello?"

There was no answer as he checked the corners of the warm, wide room. If I had to say how big it was, I'd guess the size of a swimming pool. I searched the wall next to the door and found an old-fashioned push-button switch. I pushed the top button, and two bare lightbulbs burst to light.

"I think we're under the pool house." I relaxed a bit and studied the door. "Papa and Mr. Thompson must have connected the buildings."

"Which could be how your killer got into the McMurphy." Rex holstered his revolver and turned off his flashlight. "Who would know about the tunnel?"

"I have no idea." I shook my head. "Whoever Pete hires to work on the pool. Whoever helped build the tunnel and the pool house. It could be anyone, really."

"Pete Thompson knows about the tunnel, but you don't?"

"I'm guessing." I hugged my waist. "Papa Liam sold his rights to the pool house after Grammy died. He said it made more sense to work out a gentlemen's agreement on use instead of worrying about who would be responsible for insurance and maintenance and such. I agreed. I mean, I was more interested in fudge making than pool houses."

"I suggest you get a lock on your side of this door," he said.

"As soon as I hire a locksmith to do that the entire

island will know about this tunnel. Sally will want to bring folks down for her haunted tours." I shook my head. "I can't afford that kind of insurance."

"Add it to your list. I don't like the idea of anyone having that kind of access to the McMurphy." His face had that serious cop look.

"You and me both." I blew out a breath. "I'll talk to Pete." I didn't want to talk to Pete. The man was a creepy jerk. But if I were going to be a business-woman, I'd have to suck it up and learn to talk to creepy jerks. It was all part of life.

"Let's close the door and go up through the pool house," Rex said. "I need to see what sort of security the Thompsons have."

I closed the door and noted that it did have a skeleton key lock. There wasn't any key. "What about the other door?"

"I wouldn't worry. It didn't look as if it'd been used in decades," Rex said. "The door would probably fall off if you tried to open it."

He was right of course. Besides, I'd solve the whole problem by walling off the hidden door in the McMurphy.

"Wait," I said as he opened the door on the other side of the room. I could see that it led to stairs going up. "What if there's really treasure behind the other door?"

Rex tilted his head and gave me a look that said I was being silly. "Do you think your grandfather or the Thompsons for that matter would be sitting on a treasure?"

I worried my bottom lip to hide my disappointment. "I suppose not." I closed the door and crossed the room, dodging pipes and barrels. The stairs led straight up to another door, which was locked.

"Step back."

I went down a couple of stairs and watched as Rex kicked open the door. "Wow, do they teach you how to do that in cop school?"

Rex shrugged. "If I told you all my secrets, then I'd have to . . ."

"Kill me, I know." I rolled my eyes and followed him through the door. It did indeed lead into the pool house. The door he kicked open was marked UTILITIES and EMPLOYEE ACCESS ONLY.

Luckily it was off-season and no one was in the pool house. The water itself was still as glass. The pool was built in the 1920s. It was made of poured concrete. In the 1970s they had added a small room on the end and put in a raised hot tub. The cedar hot tub had a blue fiberglass interior, which sat empty waiting on the season. It was in strange and stark contrast to the concrete and tile style of the pool. Beside the utility-room door were two bath-house doors. The entire building was made of cedar and smelled of chlorine and age. Old windows lined three of the four walls. They still had storm windows on them. The screens had yet to be put in place. In the summer months, the pool house was screened. The cedar board roof would reflect the water from the bottom of the pool.

I had spent days in the pool house as a kid, floating on the surface, imagining who else had looked at the cedar ceiling over the years. I would wonder what it might have been like when the pool was first poured. Papa had lined the pool house with framed old photos of guests through the decades. Those pictures still hung on the walls. It had been years since I'd looked at them.

"There aren't any cameras in here," Rex said as he walked around the pool. He checked the doors. "Unlocked."

"Well, yes, it's against the fire code to lock people inside a building. Besides, it's the weekend and this close to the season they may have guests already," I said.

"Is the pool house kept open year-round?"

I turned myself away from the pictures. "Not that I'm aware of. Papa used to have the pool drained in October and then refilled in April. The pool house is open from April first until October thirtieth. That's what we have posted on our Web site and our information, but I can ask Frances. She'd know for sure."

Pete Thompson walked up the deck and stopped and stared at us. Then he opened the pool-house door. "How'd you two get in here?"

Fuzzy Navel Fudge

4 cups dark chocolate chips
4 tablespoons butter
1 can sweetened condensed milk
1 teaspoon vanilla
1 can mandarin oranges
4 ounces peach schnapps (to taste)

Soak oranges in Schnapps for at least 1 hour—drain just before use. Discard Schnapps.

Butter an 8" x 8" x 2" pan, then line with wax paper or plastic wrap. (I prefer wax paper.)

In a double boiler, fill the bottom with water and place on high until it reaches a rolling boil then turn to low. In the top pan, melt chocolate, sweetened condensed milk, and butter until smooth and thick.

Remove from heat. Add vanilla and stir until combined. Add drained oranges. Pour into pan. Cool. Tip: let cool outside of the refrigerator for 30 minutes so that no condensation mars the top. Refrigerate overnight. Remove from pan. Cut into pieces. Store in a covered container.

Chapter 20

"What did you tell him?" Jennifer sat on one of two bar stools that allowed guests to look into the apartment's tiny galley kitchen without getting in the way.

"I didn't tell him anything. Rex asked Pete if he knew about the tunnel connecting our two hotels." I poured chocolatinis into martini glasses and handed her one. "It took him a minute to answer."

"Seriously?"

"I know, right? He looked at me first as if wondering how much I knew." I pulled down all the ingredients for fudge. I wanted to try a new recipe. My idea was to base fudge flavors on different cocktail drinks. They would be part of my 21-and-up flavors. Fudge shouldn't be only for kids.

"Creep. He did know about the tunnel. Oh, yuck, he might have been sneaking over here spying on you."

"I thought of that. I think that's worse than

finding a dead body in my closet." I mixed the sugar, coconut milk, spiced rum, and white chocolate chunks and placed them in the top of a double boiler. Stirring was my favorite part; most people hated how long it took to stir and carefully heat chocolate, but I loved it. There was a certain anticipation of watching for the moment when the mixture thickened and plopped like little volcanoes.

"I'm here now," she said with satisfaction and sipped her drink. "Let him try to sneak in and scare you now."

I laughed. "I hired a new handyman. He starts tomorrow and the first thing on his list is to wall off the basement door."

"Wait, so the tunnel is still open? Can I see it?"

I stirred the melting ingredients with a wooden spoon. "No, Rex sent his cousin over to board up the coal bin. But I want it walled off. I need to inventory Papa's things on the shelves in there."

"Darn, it might be kind of fun to check out a tunnel with a cute policeman." She waggled her eyebrows at me.

"Not as much fun as you might think," I said and checked the temperature of the fudge with the candy thermometer.

"We don't believe you," Jennifer said in a falsetto voice. She had picked up Mal and moved the puppy's front paws as if she were talking.

"I'm a person of interest in an ongoing murder investigation." I stirred the fudge.

"And he's a hot cop," Jenn said. "We like him, don't we, Mal?" She snuggled the puppy. "Yes, we do."

"You haven't even met him." I rolled my eyes and removed the fudge from the stove and poured it on to the small marble candy slab I kept on my countertop.

"He has to be hot if he's been married twice." Jenn played with the puppy. "Isn't that right?"

Mal answered with a bark of agreement.

"See?" Jenn's blue eyes twinkled.

"Don't you think married twice means something bad?" I asked as I scraped and turned the fudge, waiting for it to cool into a solid mass.

"Only that he has baggage." Jenn put the puppy down and picked up her drink. "Didn't you say his first wife was his high school sweetheart? Those kinds of marriages rarely last. I mean, would you have wanted to marry anyone you dated in high school?"

I frowned at the thought of marrying Mike Beisterfield. He'd been a cute boy with a shock of black hair and sweet green eyes who'd gone on to run for state representative with dramatically opposed political views from me.

"And didn't his second wife decide she didn't like the isolation of island living in the winter?"

"That's what Frances said." I added chunks of pineapple and pecans and continued to mix the fudge as it cooled into the perfect texture. "For that matter, I've never spent a winter on island either. So who knows if I will like it?"

"It doesn't mean you can't have a little fun with a local. How long has it been since you dated anyone, hmm?"

I finished up the fudge and left it to cool. "Two years." I winced at the length of time. "In my own defense, I didn't have time to date in culinary school. That place was cutthroat."

"I'm here now," Jenn said again, her eyes twinkling. "We'll have this place running like a well-oiled machine and you'll have your pick of hot cops and, hey, maybe even some rich dude from Chicago with a family cottage on island." She grinned. "Then you'll never have to know what it's like to live on island during the winter."

"That's your idea of the perfect life." I raised my martini glass to her. "This run-down place is mine."

"Then here's to being happy in our personal perfect lives." Jenn lifted her glass and we toasted. "Now, how far is the yacht club from here and when does the season open?"

I laughed. "First things first, let's make sure the McMurphy doesn't go out of business."

Chapter 21

"I'm here." Mr. Devaney arrived the next morning. His bushy eyebrows pushed together in a scowl. "I expect a fifteen-minute break in the morning, a half-hour lunch, and a fifteen-minute break in the afternoon."

I smiled. He was the same grumpy man in jeans and a cotton work shirt as he had been in corduroy pants and a dress shirt when he'd taught me how to use the microfiche at the library.

"Of course," I said. "There's coffee on the back of the coffee bar. Feel free to help yourself."

"I bring my own."

"Okay, well if you ever forget it, I offer my employees free coffee."

"I won't forget."

"There's a fridge in the break room if you want to bring your own lunch."

"I make my own lunch, have for years. I don't

need a fridge. I need a list of expectations and tools to do the work."

"Let's start in the basement." I took him through the lobby.

"Good morning." Frances sailed through the door. "Looks like the sun is out today." She wore a pale green fedora with matching wool coat. "A great day to sell some room space." She stopped short at the sight of Mr. Devaney. "Hello, who's this?"

"Frances Wentworth, this is Mr. Devaney. He's our new handyman starting today. Frances is my front-desk manager. She handles all the hotel reservations and manages the housekeeping staff."

Frances gave his hand a firm shake. "Nice to meet you, Mr. Devaney."

"Pleasure is mine," Mr. Devaney said, his gruff voice suddenly smooth. I swear there was a moment between them. It was kind of strange. I liked Mr. Devaney for his gruff, no-nonsense demeanor. But his gruffness completely disappeared the moment Frances walked in the door. "Excuse me. I've got work to do. Okay, young lady, show me where the tools are."

"Right. The basement is through here." I took him down into the bowels of the McMurphy, but not before noticing how Frances watched us leave. "The workbench and tools are all over here. Make a list of anything you think you need that you can't find. Also, anything that is worn out or no longer of any use. I'll have them replaced."

"What's going on over there?" He pointed at the coal bin with his chin.

I winced at the sloppy job of boarding. "That's the first thing I need you to do." I explained the tunnel and the need to have it mortared off.

"What was wrong with using a sturdy lock?" he asked.

"Officer Manning was concerned it would be too easy to take the door off its hinges." I pointed out the ancient hinges on the coal bin. "The door was meant for access, not for keeping people in or out. Can you fix it?"

"I can fix anything." He scowled at me. "If I couldn't, you shouldn't have hired me."

"Right, well, I'll leave you to it," I said. "I'll be in the office on the third floor or in the fudge shop. If you need something and can't find me, ask Frances or call my cell phone."

"Got it." He studied the door to the coal bin. I stood for a moment watching him. "What? Don't you trust me to do my job?" he groused.

"No, no." I hightailed it upstairs with a smile on my face. The man did so remind me of Papa in his younger days. I hoped that he was as good as he seemed. The McMurphy needed someone good with their hands to love it as much as I did.

"Oh, my, this spiced-rum fudge is to die for." Jenn came down the stairs with one hand holding a piece of fudge and the other cupped under to catch crumbs. Mal followed her down the stairs, her little tail wagging with glee.

"Spiced-rum fudge?" Frances looked up from the reception desk where she sat working on her computer. She wore purple glasses on the edge of her nose with rhinestones on the frames. A beaded necklace held the ends of the glasses so that she could take them off and let them hang. Her soft lilac sweater had a V-neck and went well with her full navy skirt and jeweled belt.

"Yes, try this." Jenn had never met a person who wasn't an instant friend. My friend was a curvy size six with long black hair and bright blue eyes. At five foot nine in bare feet, she stood out in any crowd. Today she wore jeans and a pale blue long-sleeved T-shirt. Her feet were bare, but her toenails were painted a bright sparkly blue.

"Wow," Frances said after tasting the fudge. "Did you make that?"

"Oh, no." Jenn laughed. "I'm a hotelier, not a candy maker. She held out her hand. "I'm Jennifer Christensen."

"Jenn is a dear friend from college. We both majored in hospitality. I went to get my culinary degree and Jenn worked as an event planner."

"Well, hello, Jennifer," Frances said. "Are you staying for a few days?"

Jenn's laugh floated through the air. "Nope, I'm here for the season and longer if I have my way."

"Jenn's the friend I was telling you about. She's going to stay with me in the apartment and help us get our first season off the ground."

"Good," Frances said. "We need more hands and I'm glad to hear you're not staying here alone."

"Did she tell you about the tunnel in the basement?" Jenn went over to the coffee bar and poured herself a cup.

"Yes, I was there when they figured out how it opened," Frances said. "So strange that I've worked here for twenty years and never knew it was there."

"Perhaps the guys who built it had a reason for keeping it secret." Jenn sipped her coffee.

"What kind of reason?" I asked. Mal jumped up on me and I picked her up. She snuggled under my chin and gave me a kiss.

"I did some research on the patent number Officer Manning wrote down. According to the patent, the tunnel was built in the 20s," Frances said. "Before my time even."

"Papa would have been a little kid, so it must have been his father who had the tunnel built," I said.

"Then we may never know." Jenn sipped coffee.

"Maybe Mr. Devaney would know," I mused and gave Mal a kiss and set her down to go play with her puppy toys. "He was an American history teacher."

"Mr. Devaney?" Jenn asked.

"The new handyman," I said at the same time Frances did.

"He was a teacher?" Frances asked thoughtfully.

"Yes." I looked at her carefully. "So were you, right?"

Frances blushed. "Yes, English." She went back to working on her computer.

I gave Jenn a look, letting her know that something was up there. Jenn picked up on it right away.

"Did you two work together?"

"No, I never met Mr. Devaney until this morning," Frances said, her expression carefully composed as she studied her computer screen. "It is merely a coincidence."

"Maybe," Jenn said and sipped her coffee. "Or maybe Allie likes to hire teachers."

"Have you ever been on island?" I asked Jenn, changing the subject.

"No." She wandered to the front windows that looked out onto Main Street. "If you don't mind I'm going to take a bicycle tour today. I want to get a feel for the place from the tourist point of view. I think it will help me develop a sweet Web site."

"There's a bike in the back utility shed," Frances said. "Two actually, cruisers."

"Sounds perfect. Allie, want to come along?"

"You go." I smiled. "I've got to open the guest rooms, air them out, and make a list of things that need fixing."

"I'll be back by lunch," Jenn said. "I'll let you know if I see any hot yacht club members." She winked at me.

"Take a jacket," Frances said. "It's sixty-eight degrees outside."

"Right," Jenn said and looked at me quizzically.

"There's a hoodie hanging next to the back door of the apartment."

"Thanks." Jenn ran up the stairs. "See ya!"

Frances studied me. "Hot yacht clubbers?"

I shrugged. "Jenn's from Chicago." As if that explained anything, but Frances seemed to accept my answer. I grabbed the clipboard I had left on the reception desk. "I'm going up to go through the guest rooms."

"Before you go, you'd better answer the door," Frances said, her eyes not leaving the computer screen.

I frowned and looked from her to the front door. Standing in the doorway, scowling, was Trent Jessop. A pretty brunette stood beside him, wearing black cropped pants, a black blouse, and black pumps. She had the well-groomed look of money and in her manicured hands was my lasagna pan. Thankfully it was empty.

I unlocked the front doors and opened them. "Hello, can I help you?"

"Hi, I'm Paige Jessop," the young woman said warmly. "My brother and I came to return your dish. May we come in?"

"Certainly." I opened the door wide and she came inside. I noticed that Trent shoved his hands into the pockets of his jeans and refused to smile as he entered.

"You've done a wonderful job redecorating," Paige said as she looked around. "Seriously, it looks like a whole new place."

"Thank you." I took my dish from her. "Would you like coffee?"

"Oh, no, thank you," Paige said. "I wanted to meet you and thank you for the lasagna. It was very good."

"Allie is a chef and candy maker," Frances said from her perch behind the receptionist desk.

Paige looked from Frances to me, her eyes wide. "Really?"

"Yes, I graduated with my master's degree from the Culinary Institute."

"See, I told you this was the best lasagna I have ever tasted. My silly brother was afraid to try it. He had some silly idea you were trying to poison us."

"What?!"

"I told him he was way off base and that he had to come and apologize to you for not letting you into the memorial. Grandpa Joe would have been happy to have you there." She nudged Trent. "Apologize."

"I'm sorry I didn't make you feel welcome," he said, his voice gruff and his eyes narrowed slightly. "That was rude of me and it won't happen again."

"I didn't hurt your grandfather," I said. "I just

lost mine a few weeks ago. I would never put anyone through that kind of pain."

"See? I told you she was nice," Paige said to her brother. "Well, we'll be going now. Thank you for the lasagna and for thinking of our family."

"You're welcome." I opened the door. Paige stepped out and I held my breath as Trent stopped beside me. He was one of those handsome men that made your brains fall out if he stood too close to you. I swear he smelled of expensive cologne, warm starch, and a tiny bit of horse. The man did own the island stables.

"Contrary to what my sister said, I did try the lasagna. It was very good," he said, his voice low, and it vibrated through me. "Thank you."

"You're welcome," I squeaked. The man was hot. I don't know, did I shiver when he came near because he was such wonderful eye candy? Or, was I insanely crazy attracted to him because he didn't like me? I mean, everyone liked me. I'm likable. Why wouldn't he like me?

Well, okay, so I wasn't pretty like his sister or beautiful like Jennifer. But darn it, people usually liked me right off.

"Who was that piece of man candy?" Jenn stood next to the door. She had her hands on a beach cruiser bike that looked as old as it probably was.

"That is Trent Jessop." I stepped outside, using the excuse that my friend stood on the sidewalk, when in reality I wanted to watch Trent walk away.

"The guy who thinks you killed his grandpa?"

"Yes," I said with a sigh. "He owns the local stables."

"Is she his girlfriend?"

"No, his sister, Paige," I said. "They brought back my lasagna pan."

"You took them lasagna?"

I sent her a look. "Did you see the man?"

Jenn laughed. "Let me guess, he lives on island year-round."

"I'm not sure." I frowned. "I think the horses go on one or two of the last ferries. So he may live in St. Ignace or Mackinaw City."

"I wonder if he belongs to the yacht club?" Jenn's eyes twinkled.

"Is that one of the bikes from the shed?" I changed the subject. I wasn't ready to admit that Trent hated me and I didn't have a chance in hell with him.

"Yes, I pumped up the tires and it could probably use some chain oil, but I think it will do for my purposes." She patted the seat. "Want to come along?"

"No, thanks, I've been around the island every summer. You should know that bikes aren't allowed in front of the Grand Hotel. They have people stationed at the road that will stop you before you get too close."

"Seriously? It's not even open yet."

"Park the bike and walk," I said. "That way you won't make a bad first impression should there be anyone from the yacht club up there."

"Right," she said and winked at me. "I'll be back."

I watched her hop on the bike and head off down Main Street. Jenn would know everything and everyone by the end of the week. I bet no one would call her a fudgie.

Chapter 22

"Your boy, Manning, was over at my place asking questions." Pete Thompson watched me haul out trash from Papa's apartment. "Thanks a lot for siccing him on me. I had nothing to do with Joe Jessop's death."

"I didn't sic him on you, Pete." I lifted the lid on the Dumpster and tossed in the two garbage bags. "He followed through on an intruder alert call."

"What, you saw someone in the pool house?"

Mal pulled to the end of her leash and growled at Pete. I reached down and picked her up. 'No, someone tried to break into the McMurphy."

"Through the pool house? That's ridiculous." Pete snorted.

Mal barked at him.

"Look, I don't care what you believe. I'm still shocked that you knew about the tunnel and didn't tell me."

"It's an old maintenance tunnel for God's sake,'

Pete said. The man wore baggy blue jeans and a ridiculous sweatshirt. His cheeks were pink from the cold wind and his nose shone bright red. "I thought everyone knew about it. It's probably in the city planning drawings. Anyone with any brains could go down to the courthouse and look at the old plans."

"Wait, so Joe Jessop probably knew about the tunnel all along?"

"Sure, why?" He crossed his arms, but didn't step closer. I got the distinct impression he was nervous around my puppy. Good. Maybe Mal really could put some distance between undesirables and the McMurphy. In fact, I might have to reward her with a treat when we went back inside.

"Frances tells me Joe and Papa Liam used to play tricks on each other. If Papa knew that Joe knew about the tunnel, then he should have bricked off the entrance long ago." I put Mal down and walked her over to her patch of grass. Pete stepped back away from the fence.

Mal growled at him, then stuck her leg out and peed. I tried not to laugh.

"That's what I was trying to tell you. Those old coots had some sort of secret society going. My grandfather and yours would meet down there twice a year. When the meeting was over, granddad would always come back with a wad of cash in his pocket. I used to think there was some sort of pirate's treasure down there."

"Did you ever look in there?" I had to ask because my own mind had gone to buried treasure.

"There's nothing down there but rocks, dirt, and probably old photos Granddad had of your papa doing something illegal."

"Papa would never do anything illegal. Grammy would have killed him."

"Anyway, I came to tell you that I put a new lock on the pool house utility-room door. If someone is going down through that tunnel, it's not my fault, so don't try to pin any insurance claims on me."

"Insurance claims? I would never."

"You say that now. Wait until that money pit eats away all your cash. You'll be looking for any way to make money, just like your precious papa did."

Mal sniffed and wiped her feet in Pete's direction, kicking up particles of grass and dirt.

"Hey." he stepped back. "Control your mutt."

"Don't be ridiculous," I said and picked Mal up. "She's just a puppy."

I turned my back on Pete and walked back into the McMurphy fuming. I was glad Rex searched Pete's place. Maybe he'd find a clue that would exonerate me from the investigation. Not that he would tell me, of course, it was a police matter and all. But darn it would be nice to know.

"We have a problem," Frances said from her perch on the receptionist desk.

"Okay." I took off Mal's halter and leash and put

her down. She ran off to get a drink from the downstairs dishes Frances had for her behind the desk. "Is it a good problem or a bad problem?"

She looked at me over the top of her glasses. "Is there such a thing as a good problem?"

"Sure." I sat in the chair next to her. "Overbooking is a good problem."

"Perhaps, but we have the opposite problem."

"Oh. I thought you said we were booked solid from Memorial Day to the Fourth of July."

"The key words being *were booked*." Frances sighed. "Word has gotten out about Joe Jessop's murder. People don't come to Mackinac for the excitement, they come to relax. I've had five regulars cancel this morning alone."

"Oh, no." I frowned. "How do they find these things out?"

"Regulars have a subscription to the *Town Crier*, and then there's this whole social media business . . ."

"Jenn is a wizard at social media spin. She'll be able to help with that."

"She'd better get on it right away because Paige Jessop just announced that she will be building a brand-new hotel just north of the Grand. It's slated to open Fourth-of-July weekend."

"What? Wait, there's no way she can have a hotel built and operational in ten weeks."

"Her press release says she has a Chicago firm designing a Victorian hotel built with modern materials and methods. They build it off-site in a factory and put it together on island." Frances clicked her mouse and brought up the news story on her computer along with artist's renderings. "I've had two customers cancel their July reservations. They want modern and new."

"But they come to the island for the back-in-time feel," I argued.

"Not this new generation," Frances said. "And there's more news."

"All right." I sat back. "Tell me."

"The historical society is demanding a tour of the place before you open to ensure your renovations are within the latest historical standards."

"Well, that's an oxymoron, isn't it? I mean, new historical standards?"

"It's not a joke." Frances's expression was grave. "They can demand changes to paint schemes, etc., and they can fine you up to ten thousand dollars."

"What? But Papa had the paint approved by the committee last fall."

"That was before Liam and Joe died. The committee has no connection to you."

"Because I'm not an islander," I said. "Susan Goodfoot called me a fudgie. I tried to explain that I'm a McMurphy. That I spent my childhood summers on island with my grandparents, that I'm heir to the McMurphy, and that my family has been on island for one hundred and fifty years."

"Honey, it's a tight-knit community. You have to give them time to accept you. If they ever do."

Mal whined and jumped up, begging to be let in my lap. I picked her up and snuggled into her soft fur. "There is only enough money in the funds Papa left me to go a full season if we are fully booked. There's no room for fines or new paint schemes."

"Then you need to get to work," Frances said.

"Who's the creeper nosing around the back of the McMurphy?" Jenn walked into the lobby from the back. Her checks were pink and her eyes sparkled. Her hair was still perfect and I envied her a bit. I mean, if I had just biked around the island my hair would be a tangled mess and my nose would be running.

"That's Pete Thompson," I said. "He owns the B and B behind us."

"Oh, the guy with the pool house?" She poured herself coffee.

"Yes, he wants to buy the McMurphy."

"Well, that's not going to happen." Jenn added cream and sugar. "This island is beautiful."

"You biked the entire eight miles around?" Frances asked.

"I saw Arch Rock and the woods and all of Main and Market Streets. I even parked my bike and did a sneak peak around the Grand Hotel. Those lawns are impressive. Several of the hotels with lawns have fire pits scattered around with lawn chairs and blankets. I can imagine sitting around a warm fire and toasting marshmallows."

Mal let up a loud whine. I covered her puppy ears. "Don't say that in front of the puppy."

"Why not?"

"Her full name is Marshmallow," Frances said with a twitch around her mouth.

"Yikes, my bad," Jenn said. "Sorry, pup."

I took my hands off Mal's ears and patted her. "She forgives you."

"Did you know they're setting a foundation for someplace huge above the Grand?"

I sighed. "Yes, Paige Jessop is building a new hotel with a Victorian theme."

"It's going to have great views." Jenn sipped her coffee.

"And one hundred and fifty rooms." Frances read from her computer screen. "A salon and spa, lawn tennis courts, Olympic-size pool, high-end restaurant with world-renowned chef Armond Calvarez."

"There's no competing with that." Jenn sipped.

"Right?" I laughed at the absurdity of it all. "We have ten rooms, no lawn, but views of the harbor and Main Street."

"We have the world's best candy maker in the lobby," Jenn said. "Period décor that is actual vintage." She waved her hand. "Fireplaces in all ten rooms, cool creaky floors, and access to a pool house where twentieth-century vacationers actually swam."

"Wow, you make it sound great."

"Because it is great," Jenn said. "It's all how you spin it."

"Tell that to the regulars who are cancelling bookings left and right."

"What? Why?"

"They heard about Joe Jessop's murder."

"How?" Jenn drew her eyebrows together, marring her perfect skin.

"The *Town Crier* has an Internet subscription service," Frances said.

The phone rang. "The McMurphy Hotel and Fudge Shoppe. This is Frances speaking, how can I help you?"

"Hello, Mrs. Zeiland." Frances's fingers clicked over her keyboard. "How are you? Uh-huh, and how's Emily? Doesn't she graduate from Northwestern? In two weeks? Wonderful, please tell her congratulations from us." Frances made a note in the file to send a graduation card. "You're most welcome. How can I help you today? Uh-huh, oh, I'm so sorry to hear that." Frances shot me a look. "Is there anything we can do to change your mind? Okay, did you know we added Wi-Fi this year along with a coffee bar free of charge to our valued customers. Of course, we understand. I hope you do stop by when you're on island and purchase some of our fudge."

I wrote a quick note and slid it to Frances.

"Allie McMurphy is our new owner and is continuing the McMurphy fudge tradition with old favorites and a new line of fudges for adults based on the latest cocktail recipes."

Frances hung up the phone and typed in silence. My heart was heavy. The Zeilands were long-standing clients who usually booked a weekend a month during the high season.

"How bad is it?" I asked.

"They cancelled all four weekends," Frances said. "They're worried for the safety of their family and . . ."

"And they want to try out the new Grander Hotel," I finished.

"Yes," Frances said.

"How much is that going to cost us?"

"You don't want to know."

Chapter 23

"It's going to cost twenty-five hundred dollars for materials to shore up the basement so that we can wall off the tunnel entrance," Mr. Devaney said. "I will need to order the materials today to get them in next week."

"Can you have the project finished before Memorial Day?" I asked.

"As long as I don't put any time into any other projects." His brown eyes were serious. "Unless you want to hire brick layers."

"How much would that be?"

"I could get a few quotes, but they usually run fifty dollars an hour."

I tried not to wince. "We need to expand our security system to include the basement and possibly add cameras for all the public areas. Any idea how much that would cost?"

"I'll quote it, but my guess is at least two thousand dollars for an advanced system."

"Don't forget the historical society," Frances said. "They will want you to show them plans before you install anything. You can't have anything that is too terribly obvious in a historical building."

"How long will that take?"

"Depends on how many friends you have on the historical society committee," Frances said.

"Really?"

"Really."

"Well, I know how to help with that," Jenn said. "Let's plan a huge party for them. Maybe even a fund-raiser." She rubbed her hands together. "We'll serve cocktails and your new 21-and-over fudge flavors will be given as take-home treats."

"That's certainly a start," Frances said.

"We'll have to get all new plumbing before the party," Mr. Devaney stated flatly.

"Okay," I said. "Plumbing, fudge, what else?"

"Take an advert out in the *Town Crier*," Jenn said. "Send a press release and let the local reporter get a preview tour."

"Advertising, right. What else?"

"It never hurts to do things for the community," Frances added.

"Like what?"

"Donate new park equipment."

"Help clean up park trails."

"Get involved in local societies."

They all spoke at once, and I tried to write it all down. "Okay." I held up my hand to stop them.

"And where am I supposed to get the time and money to do any of these?"

"If you don't make an effort, there won't be a McMurphy," Frances groused. "Is that what you really want?"

"No." I slumped in my chair. "Fine. I'll take ideas on how to stretch our time and money resources."

There was a long drawn-out silence in my office. Mal stood up and stretched, then trotted over and licked my ankle under the flowing skirt of the shirt dress I wore.

"You need a silent partner," Frances said. "Someone who will help financially without taking over management of the McMurphy."

"Wouldn't that be nice," I said and put my chin in my palm, resting my elbow on my desk.

"There is one person." Jenn looked me straight in the eye.

I sat up. "No, no, I said I wouldn't, not unless I was in dire straits."

"Straits don't get much more dire," Jenn said. "I mean, there is only so much we can do without capital."

Frances and Mr. Devaney looked at us back and forth as if watching a tennis match.

"No."

"Yes. You have to." Jenn was firm.

I closed my eyes. "Fine."

"Is there someone I should call?" Frances asked.

"No," I said. "This is something I need to do by myself."

"Good." Jenn stood. "While you do that, we'll make a plan. Frances, you make a list of things we can do for the community. Mr. Devaney, you make a list of things that must be done to ensure the remodel is completed and the extra security is installed and ready. I'm going to plan out the party and the Web site and social media." Jenn gently shepherded the others out of the office. She grabbed the door handle, and as she closed the door she gave me a thumbs-up sign.

I sighed and hit the speed dial on my phone.

"Hello?"

"Hi, Mom, can I speak to Dad?"

A Clockwork Tangerine Fudge

- 4 cups dark chocolate chips
- 4 tablespoons butter
- 1 can sweetened condensed milk
- 1 teaspoon vanilla
- 1 packet Kool-Aid Tangerine Mix
- 1 ounce rum
- 1 ounce vodka

Butter an 8" x 8" x 2" pan, then line with wax paper or plastic wrap. (I prefer wax paper.)

Using a double boiler fill ⅓ of the bottom pan with water and heat on medium high until the water is boiling. Then you can turn the heat down to low and in the top section, melt chocolate, sweetened condensed milk, and butter until smooth and thick.

Remove from heat. Add vanilla and Kool-Aid mix and stir until combined. Add rum and vodka 1 tablespoon at a time (to taste). Mix well. Pour into pan. Cool. Tip: let cool outside of the refrigerator for 30 minutes so that no condensation mars the top. Refrigerate overnight. Remove from pan. Cut into pieces. Store in a covered container.

Chapter 24

"Well?"

"I don't want to talk about it." I grabbed the coffeepot and poured myself fresh coffee. I turned and faced three people staring at me: Frances from her normal perch on the receptionist desk, Mr. Devaney from the chair beside her, and Jenn on the floor, playing with Mal. "What?"

"Do we move forward or are you planning to sell to creepy Mr. Creeper next door?" Jenn sat back on her heels.

"We move forward, of course." I rolled my eyes.

"What did you do?" Frances asked.

"I called my father." I winced—it was hard to think that I did indeed need his help and his money. I wanted to believe I didn't, but at this point it was simply stubbornness on my part. "I convinced him to give me the money he has stashed for my wedding. Goodness knows if that will ever happen anyway.

We now have an extra twenty thousand dollars. Will that help?"

"It's a start," Frances said with a nod.

"A good start." Jenn got up and hugged me. "I know how hard that was. Good job."

"I don't know how good." I ran a hand through my hair and tugged. "But it was definitely a job."

"Why didn't you just get a bank loan?" Mr. Devaney asked, drawing his bushy brows together. "You've got collateral in the building."

"That's what I thought," I said. "But it turns out banks are much pickier with loans these days. I didn't have enough credit even with the collateral and my solid business plan."

"Did you try off-island banks?" Frances asked.

"Everything from here to Chicago, including a few credit unions." It was embarrassing to let my staff know how dire our straits really were, but if they were going to be part of my team, then they needed to know just how good or bad things were.

"Well, you don't need to pay me," Jenn said. "All I need is a place to crash for the summer and a good reference."

"They do a lot of weddings on island," Frances said. "If you're serious about event planning, that would be a great angle to start."

"Wait! That's awesome. We could use the McMurphy to book wedding parties. We could set up a plan where for a discount, parties could buy out the entire hotel. We'll become a destination wedding hotel."

"And fudge shop," I said.

"And fudge shop," Jenn added.

"I don't know about the rest of you, but I expect to get paid for my work," Mr. Devaney said firmly.

"And you will be," I said. "I have funds now to get us through a season even if we don't book all the rooms."

"What did you have to do in exchange?" Frances blinked through her glasses.

"Besides give up my dream of a big wedding?" Okay so sarcasm didn't really work on people who were contemplating working without pay. "I promised to spend the holidays in Detroit with Mom and Dad."

"The holidays as in Christmas Day and New Year's?"

"As in, one weekend a month and the entire months of December and January," I said. Three pairs of eyes looked at me, stunned. "I know it sounds like a lot, but I'll use the time to craft new fudge recipes and drum up business. Besides, lots of business owners aren't here on the off-season."

"What weekend a month?" Jenn asked. "When does that start?"

"The second weekend of the month and it starts in June. So I'll be here for the rest of the new opening prep and then for Memorial Day, Independence Day, and Labor Day."

"What about the lilac festival and the horse festival and all the other festivals?" Frances asked. "Those are not acceptable terms."

"We turn a big enough profit this season and I'll pay my parents off. Once I've done that, then I don't have to continue with the visits."

"Incentive," Jenn said. "I like that. Come on then, let's get our plans together. We have work to do, people."

"I don't understand it." I looked up from the accounting books. It was late at night. Jenn was in her nightgown, her hair wrapped in a towel. She painted her toenails grape while Mal curled up beside her on Papa's old couch.

"What?"

"Pete is right. The McMurphy hasn't made a profit in decades."

"But your Papa Liam had no problem keeping it going and even left you money when he died." Jenn looked up from her work.

"I know, and it shows at least one solid entry every month in the bank account."

"What kind of solid are we talking about?"

"Ten grand," I said.

"That's pretty solid. Was your grandfather into something illegal?"

"I highly doubt it." I frowned. "Seriously, Grammy would have killed him."

"I think I would have loved your grandmother. She certainly sounds like a strong woman."

"She had to be to keep Papa in line." I pursed my

mouth and scrunched it to one side. "So where do you think he got the money?"

"Maybe there really is buried treasure in that tunnel," Jenn said. "Didn't you say there was another door down there?"

"Yes, but it didn't look like it had been opened in years."

Jenn went back to painting her nails. "Did you ever figure out what that tunnel might have been built for? I mean, the twenties were well past the need for an underground railroad, right?"

"Right." I turned to my computer and did a search for keywords of "Mackinac" and "tunnels." It popped up a story of a little boy who was killed when a snow tunnel fell in on him. "Tragic."

"What?"

"Some poor kid lost his life five years ago when he tried to make a snow tunnel. It wasn't stable and it fell in on him."

"Sad."

I continued to peruse the articles that popped up. Nothing was earlier than 1995. So I tried again, searching with the words "historical" and "1920s." There it was plain as day. "Oh, I would never have guessed," I said.

"What?"

"I bet that tunnel was created to move smuggled goods onto and off the island."

"What kind of goods would someone want to smuggle here?"

"It was the nineteen twenties and thirties . . ."

"Wait—Prohibition." Jenn pointed at me and I smiled.

"Yes, I bet Papa's father was in the business of rum-running. Especially since we are so close to the port and there are so many wealthy vacationers who come to Mackinac for the summers." I felt so proud of myself.

"What we need is proof," Jenn mused.

"Well, there wouldn't be any liquor left down there," I said. "It's been legal since 1933."

"Still, it makes a great story," Jenn said. "I know, we can have a costume party. Let's say a Great Gatsby party. It goes nicely with your cocktail-inspired fudges. Oh, we totally have to get flapper costumes."

Jenn was so excited she got Mal worked up. Both hopped off the couch, Jenn racing around with cotton between her newly polished toes and Mal running circles around her and barking. It made me laugh.

"Stop laughing," Jenn muttered as she grabbed a pad of paper from my desk and a pen. "I'm being flooded with cool ideas and I need to get them down. This is awesome. It fits the entire theme of the McMurphy."

"Wait, I thought we were Victorian . . ."

"Well, you are, but the twenties weren't too far off that. Too bad you don't have a lovely lawn where we could set out lawn games."

"If you need a lawn you'll have to stay at the

Jessop Grander Hotel," I grumbled. "We have fudge and easy access to downtown."

"Oh, honey, I didn't mean anything by that. I was only saying how cool it would be with our theme. Besides, your guests don't need a lawn. The grassy plaza at the foot of the fort is merely blocks away. Practically right next to the yacht club, too." She grinned at me.

I shook my head.

"Now, I'll have to plan this just right. With any luck, we can showcase the improvements to the McMurphy and I can show off my party-planning skills. Kill two birds with one stone."

"Do you think Papa knew about his father's rum-running? I mean, Papa was just a small boy when Prohibition was over. Did he know how or why they built the tunnel?"

"We will never know unless you uncover diaries in those bazillion or so boxes he left," Jenn said. She sat back down on the couch and flung her feet and arms wide. "I'm exhausted."

Mal took a flying leap and landed square onto Jenn's stomach. My friend gave a solid umph and laughed, grabbing the puppy and planting kisses on her. Then she made Mal stand on her hind legs and dance. "We're going to have a Great Gatsby party, Marshmallow," Jenn said with glee. "We're going to be flappers and drink from martini glasses and eat finger foods. Oh, we should see if we can have the pool house for the party. Then we can bring everyone through the tunnel as if they are going to a speakeasy."

I stood. "I'm not having anything to do with Pete Thompson, and unless you want to pay for the insurance to have party guests crawling through tunnels in their party dresses, I think neither are you."

"True." Jenn pursed her lips and looked at Mal. "We're going to be flappers right here in our newly remodeled lobby and showcase our complete twenty-first-century security system to boot."

They both turned toward me, and Jenn made Mal do a little dance standing on her hind legs. "We're so happy we could just die!"

"I'm glad you're happy, but please don't die. I have enough trouble with finding only one corpse in the McMurphy. The last thing we need is two."

Chapter 25

"I can't believe she got everyone on the historical committee to agree to coming to a party this Friday." I washed the front windows in the fudge shop area of the McMurphy. "That leaves me three days to make the new cocktail fudge recipes and box them up as take-home gifts."

"You don't have to make the entire series," Frances said as she cleaned out the candy counter. "Just a representative few."

"It takes weeks to perfect a recipe."

"And you've been working on yours for two years." Frances straightened. "Don't worry. You're ready. You'll blow them away."

"And if I don't?"

"Then I'll give up my summer salary to pay the difference in the repair costs they require."

"I don't want you to have to do that," I said.

"Then make good fudge," Frances replied.

It was early morning, and I noticed that Paige

Jessop walked down the sidewalk across the street from the McMurphy. She was with someone who looked familiar. "Who is that walking with Paige?" The man looked to be in his thirties, he wore a pale blue polo shirt, khaki pants, and boat shoes with no socks. His Windbreaker had an Izod emblem on it. His brown hair rustled in the wind and his hawk-like nose was tinged in red from the chill in the air.

"That's Emerson Todd. The guy you took the picture of," Frances said. "He sold his family land to Paige. It's the only way she could have gotten the plot of land big enough to build her new hotel."

"I thought he went broke in the real-estate bust."

"All the more reason to sell out to the Jessops," Frances said with scorn. "Do you know they rail-roaded the project through the zoning commission by promising to pay higher taxes?"

"Wow, it must be nice to be so sure of success that you would offer to pay higher taxes."

"Oh, she won't pay higher taxes. Her uncle is on the county commission. He'll make sure the taxes are delayed for seven years. By then she'll sell off that hotel and walk away with a tidy profit."

"Who thinks like that?" I asked, shaking my head. "I'm surprised she got them to okay a new building. I mean, the beauty of the island is its age. Its old-time appeal."

"You know as well as I do life is about who you know." Frances handed me her cleaning cloth. "Speaking of people you know, I need to get back to checking the RSVPs."

"Wait, you invited Paige and Emerson, right? I mean, if they have that kind of pull with the society, then I want them here."

"Yes, they are both invited, but I advise you not to put all your eggs in one basket, so to speak. I heard that the money Paige gave Emerson for his family's land was well over a million. I doubt he'll be wearing anything but a purple ribbon on his lapel."

"Right." I watched them walk down the street and go into the Parrot's Head Restaurant and Pub. It would be hard to compete with a woman who looked like Paige, even if I had a million dollars, which I most definitely did not.

"I scored insurance." Jenn rushed into the office, her cheeks pink with excitement. Mal jumped up and raced to her.

"What?"

"I scored liability insurance so we can take everyone on a tour of the tunnel." Jenn picked up Mal and gave the fluffy puppy a squeeze. Mal licked Jenn's face and my friend chuckled. "She is the sweetest puppy."

"She's smart, too," I said. "She's almost completely house trained and she will sit for a treat." I was such a proud doggie mommy.

"You should teach her tricks to entertain your guests."

I got up and took Mal from Jenn. "I will. We're going to go to obedience class next month. Frances got me in with the local vet. Now, what is this about insurance and why do I feel as if I should be worried?"

"I called in a few favors and I got liability insurance for the night of the party. Douglas won't have the materials to wall off the tunnel until next week."

"Wait, who's Douglas?"

"Your new handyman, silly." Jenn rolled her eyes at me. "You just hired him."

"Mr. Devaney lets you call him Douglas?" I sat down and squeezed Mal. You couldn't help but squeeze her—she was soft and warm and fluffy.

"Yes, he was telling Frances and me the most amazing stories today."

"Where was I?" I wondered out loud.

"You're the boss, silly, you were up here doing paperwork or something. Anyway, Douglas reassured me that he would not have the materials to wall off the tunnel until after the party. And, since I got liability insurance, I sent a note around that the party would begin in the McMurphy and we would tour the smuggler's tunnel to the pool house. I'm hiring a couple of actors from Mackinaw City to come in and act out a murder mystery. It will be fantastic. Trust me, when people leave with your 21-and-older cocktail fudges, they will do nothing but rave."

"I'm not sure a murder mystery is in the best taste," I mused. "Considering that I want to make a good impression on the Jessops."

"Oh, I'm sure they'll be fine with it. Everyone will

be in costume and it will be completely staged, far from the second floor and any reference to their grandfather. In fact, I've even scheduled a séance for later that night for anyone who wants to get in touch with the ghosts of McMurphy past."

"I don't know," I said and put a squirming Mal down. "Check with Frances."

"Oh, she is totally on board with the idea. Now, how do you feel about an advertisement in the *Town Crier*? We could call it Fudge, Flappers, and Femme Fatales." She drew the title across the air. "It's sure to get everyone who is anyone to come."

"Why would they come? They all hate me."

"Because, silly, I have also hooked us up with a local charity. There will be a fifty-dollar cover fee and all proceeds go to the children's clinic on island. Brilliant, isn't it?"

I slouched. It wasn't a bad idea, but how were we going to pull it off in three days?

"Don't worry." She winked as if reading my mind. "You make the fudge and I'll do the rest. I'm nothing if not brilliant at event planning."

"It's not you that I'm worried about as much as Murphy's Law." I frowned. "Anything that can go wrong will go wrong."

"That's why we make it a murder mystery. Everyone will be thinking murder anyway. This gets it out there and gets them actively looking to solve it. Trust me, the party's going to be killer."

"That's what I'm afraid of . . ."

Chapter 26

"I knew you were brilliant." I studied the lobby of the McMurphy. "But I had no idea how brilliant. This place looks awesome."

Every bit of glass sparkled and shone, the wood trim was polished to a honey glow. The wood floors gleamed. There were round tables of various heights—some bar height, some table height with chairs—all covered with white linen tablecloths. Jenn had brought in potted palms to fill in the corners and add interest to the walls. The fireplace was filled with stacks of white candles that put off a soft glow. The two chandeliers gleamed and sparkled, dimmed to half their usual daytime brightness.

A three-piece orchestra played on the left-side stair landing. The fudge shop area held fifty gift-wrapped boxes, each containing four quarter-pound cuts of different cocktail fudges.

Mr. Devaney wore a 1920s-style tuxedo and prepped the four waiters Jenn had hired to serve coffee, cocktails, and fingers foods. Frances wore a sparkling red flapper outfit complete with beading, flapper headband, and an elegant white purse.

Jenn had done my hair for me, braiding my long wavy locks into a soft style that might pass for short at first glance. After nearly emptying a bottle of hair spray in it, she had pronounced my hair perfect. Then we attached a pearl headband into it with hairpins and added another coat of hair spray for good measure. I swear I wouldn't be able to taste anything but hair spray the rest of the night.

I had on a white drop-waist sleeveless dress and long strands of pearls. The big find was a second-hand pair of shoes that fit perfectly and appeared to be right out of a 1920s catalog.

"Where on earth did you find these shoes?" I asked.

"I have my secrets," Jenn had said with a twinkle in her eye. She wore a peacock-blue flapper dress with sparkling beads and a peacock-feathered hat. Her hair was perfect. She looked like she stepped out of an old-time photograph.

Even Mal had gotten into the party spirit. She wore a flapper costume and did her best to rub off the headband Jenn had secured in her puppy hair.

"No sense in fighting it, ducky," I told her. "Jenn knows how to make clothes stick."

To which Mal snorted and stopped rubbing. She sat down and eyed me with her black button eyes.

"Everyone, I want you to meet Madame Evelyn." Jenn sailed across the lobby with a turban-wearing woman behind her. "Madame Evelyn is from St. Ignace and she has graciously agreed to run a séance tonight to try to reach any spirits hanging around the McMurphy."

"Hello," I said and stuck out my hand. "I'm—"

"Allie McMurphy." She took my hand in both of hers. I noted that her hands were warm and her fingernails were filed into near points and painted blood-red. "You have some really good energy." She tilted her head and studied me with brown eyes until I grew uncomfortable and withdrew my hand.

"Thank you," I said. "Jenn has set you up a table in front of the elevators. They have been blocked off for the night as we really want to keep everyone in the main lobby."

"Perfect." She floated off. "Is that an open bar?"

I watched her as she crossed the floor. She wore a red-and-gold caftan and a gold turban. I figured she might have been Grammy's age. Tiny tufts of gray and white hair slipped out behind her turban.

"Where did you get her?" I asked in a low whisper.

"She runs a little psychic shop at the far end of Merchant Street. I thought it would be good to hire people from the community." Jenn shrugged. "She came highly recommended."

"Well, then we had to have her," I quipped.

"Ah, here are Russell Haver and Angie Knight. They're tonight's actors."

A twentysomething girl and guy walked in dressed in full-on costume. Russ was dressed as Sherlock

Holmes and Angie looked like a dame right out of
the movie *Chicago*.

"Kids, over here. I want you to meet Allie." Jenn
waved them over.

"Hello." I shook their hands. "I'm Allie McMurphy,
proprietor."

"What a cool place," Angie said as she shook my
hand. "I can't wait to see the tunnel. Jenn tells me
it's awesome."

"Right." I said and turned to Russ. "I'm Allie."

"Russ." His grip was firm and his dark black eyes
and high cheekbones showed he had a bit of native
in him. "We've rehearsed the script Jenn sent over,"
he said. "But do know that we are also good at im-
provising. Once the guests arrive we will not break
character until the last guest leaves. We work to give
the partygoers the feeling they are part of the
story."

"Great," I said. "It's important that we impress
the people here tonight. They have all paid good
money toward the cause and I want them to feel as
if they are getting their money's worth in entertainment."

"They will, don't worry," Jenn said and put her
arms through Angie's and Russ's. "Come on, kids,
I'll show you around the lobby and the basement
and such so that you are familiar with the layout."

"Here." Frances handed me a glass. "Have a
highball. You look like you need it."

I winced and took the glass from her hand.
"What's in it?"

"Bathtub gin, of course." She laughed. "Oh, and some tonic and a squeeze of lime."

"Perfect." I took a sip and found I actually liked it. "Not bad."

"The bartender is as pretty to look at as he is talented." Frances winked. "Relax, have a good time tonight. Your friend Jenn is a miracle worker when it comes to a party. I can't believe she set this all up in a matter of days."

"I knew she was brilliant." I sipped more gin. "Are we good to go? Do you have the scrapbook display out and ready for the historical society members to look through? I think if they can see that we have kept within the spirit of the original building they will sign off on the changes."

"A few free drinks and they should be more than happy to sign." Frances agreed. "Too bad we can't have the paperwork out and ready."

"It would be too obvious." I looked around. "We want to wine and dine them first. Hopefully it will be enough if, by the end of the night, they leave with yummy fudge and a memory of a good time."

"It should be more than enough." Frances patted my arm. "I want you to know that I prepared the rooms upstairs in case anyone feels the need to stay the night. If they ask, send them to me, and I'll walk them up and let them in a room."

"You are brilliant," I said.

"Of course, that's why you love me." Frances winked at me. "Ah, your guests are starting to arrive. Good luck and have fun!"

I watched as a horse-and-carriage taxi pulled up to the front of the building. Men in suits and fedoras helped women in wool and fur coats down out of the taxi. It was dark, but the street light shone on them, giving them the odd appearance of stepping through time.

"Welcome," I said when they entered. Frances stood beside me and introduced the couples. "A pleasure to meet you. I'm so glad you could come."

"The place looks wonderful," Mrs. Cunningham stated. "I do so like the pink on the walls. Oh, whose adorable puppy?"

I bent down and picked up Mal. "This is Marshmallow. She's here to ensure you are safe from any gangsters."

The crowd laughed and Mrs. Cunningham, a senior member of the historical society, cooed at Mal. She did her job and nuzzled her way into Mrs. Cunningham's heart.

The door opened again and another group entered. This one included Paige and Trent Jessop, along with their mother and her husband.

"Thanks for coming," I said and greeted them all as warmly as possible. I noted the purple ribbons on their lapels. Tonight I didn't wear my ribbon. It was time to show the community that we were here for the best of everyone involved. But how could I blame the Jessops for their purple ribbons? Joe was their patriarch.

"We can't stay long," Karen Jessop said as she took my hands. "But you were so kind to us that we felt we should come out and support a worthy cause."

"I agree. The children need access to good health care," I said. "Please, before you go, make sure you get some food. I know how difficult it is to eat properly when you're grieving."

"You're very kind," Karen said. She was about my mother's age but her hair was that perfect champagne blond that wealthy women wore. The tone played off her flawless skin and brown eyes. I realized that Karen Jessop was a beautiful woman. Trent had her eyes and Paige had her sense of style and grace.

"Frances will show you where the most comfortable seats are," I said. Mal wiggled in my arms. Her nose twitched at Trent. My nose twitched as well. The man wore a tux and it looked breathtaking on him.

I tore myself away from him before I looked too foolish and turned to Paige. "Congratulations on your new hotel plans," I said. "I understand it is going to be the biggest one on island when it's finished."

"Oh, yes." She gushed. "I had my architect work up plans based on designs from the 1870s. The paint scheme, wallpapers, and flooring are all going to be vintage Victorian."

"As an event designer I'm curious to see the work that went into it," Jenn said as she slid up beside me. "Hi, I'm Jennifer Christensen." She held out her hand to Paige. "I'm working with Allie this summer on all of her events."

"Nice to meet you," Paige said. 'Allie, I didn't know you hired a designer."

"Jenn and I went to school together," I said. "She has worked with some of the best families in Chicago on their parties. If you ever need a party planner, I'm sure she'd be happy to help."

"I most certainly would," Jenn said. "I'm seriously considering starting up an event planning business on island. So if you know of anyone with a wedding or a party they want planned, why, look around. My business cards are on the stand by the door."

"I will keep that in mind," Paige said. "Good help is hard to find on island. Most of the staff are young college kids or interns. It would be nice to actually work with a professional wanting to stay on island."

Jenn turned to Trent. "Jennifer Christensen." She held out her hand and he shook it. "Is Paige your date?"

I had to work at not rolling my eyes. Jenn knew perfectly well that Paige was his sister.

"Paige is my sister," Trent said smoothly. "Since my grandfather just died I didn't feel it was appropriate to bring a date."

"Oh, dear, yes, of course, my condolences on your loss," Jenn said. She slid her arm through his and walked him away from me. "So tell me, Mr. Jessop, what do you do for a living?"

"Oh, she's good," Paige said as we watched Jenn walk off with Trent.

I laughed. It came out a short bark and made Paige smile. "Yes, she is good. Please feel free to use her services. She's been known to even plan wakes that people talk about for days on end."

"I'll have to remember that," Paige said. The doorbells jangled and more couples came in and Paige moved on to join her mother at the bar.

I took the next wave and was happy when Frances returned to my side and continued to introduce me.

One of the last people to enter was Emerson Todd. He came alone, wearing an Oxford baggy suit, complete with waistcoat and pocket watch. It glistened with damp. He took off his fedora and brushed the tiny sparkles of water off himself.

"Hello, welcome to the McMurphy," I said. "I'm Allie, is it raining out?"

"Emerson Todd." He shook my hand. "It's just spitting out."

"Let me take your coat." Frances held out her hand. "Almost everyone is here. I'm glad you could make it."

"The pleasure is mine." He had light brown eyes that were almost tan with a ring of black around the irises. "Wow, you've done a lot with the place."

"Thank you. Have you been in the McMurphy often?"

"My folks used to come for the fudge and on

Tuesday nights they would play cards with your grandparents and the Thompsons."

"Just the three couples?" I tilted my head. "Wouldn't it take four?"

"You are quite right." He yanked on his waist-coat. "I forget who else was there. I was, after all, just a child and more interested in the video games."

"Of course, I'm sorry." I lifted one corner of my mouth. "I don't remember who they played cards with. I would come in the summers and it was usually too busy for too many card nights."

"It's the trouble with your livelihood relying on tourists," he said. His tone was matter-of-fact, but while he didn't seem to purposely insult me, I came away feeling a little bit like trailer trash.

"I understand you sold your family land to build a tourist hotel." I tilted my head. "A brand-new hotel."

"In the style of the old." He nodded and his mouth turned up. "There is very little use for dilapidated buildings and empty grounds. I actually did the island a favor."

"I'm sure you did. Thank you for coming. The children's clinic appreciates your help." I watched the arrogant man walk off. He gave Paige Jessop a nod and went to speak to the Birdwells. Frances had introduced me to Mr. and Mrs. Birdwell, explaining that they lived in Chicago but had ties to the island that went back to the days of the fur trade. It was Mrs. Birdwell who was the head of the historical committee and the one I needed to impress tonight.

So I bit my tongue and held back my dislike of Emerson. If Frances was right and he had lost all of his family money in the real-estate crash, then maybe he really had had no choice but to sell to the Jessops. You never know what truly drives a person—even an arrogant person.

"The place really does look good," Pete Thompson said. The man stood a hair too close. He wore a suit, waistcoat, and jacket. Cream-colored spats covered his dark shoes. "I know you have an asking price in mind. How much is it? I'll give you ten percent less."

I grabbed a cocktail off the tray of the passing waitress. "The McMurphy is not for sale, Pete."

"Having this party instead of an open house was a great idea. People can see the possibility in the old place." He sipped his drink. "Don't waste your time walling off the tunnel, though. When I buy the McMurphy, I'm going to use it to link the two hotels."

"Don't be ridiculous," I said. "First off, I'm not selling. Secondly, no one will want to go through the mechanical room under the pool."

"Sally tells me differently. She says the ghost tours will double when I open the tunnel to the public."

"Please, if it were really such a big moneymaker,

then why didn't your grandfather and my Papa open it up before now?"

He shrugged. "There used to be shame in rum-running. Now it's ancient history and everyone likes history."

"I'm not selling, Pete, so get over the notion. The McMurphys are here to stay."

Chapter 27

"We should take everyone through the tunnel now," Jenn said as she came up beside me. "The pool area is where most of the food will be served and Russ and Angie are ready to start the mystery portion of tonight's entertainment."

The lobby was a bustling mass of costumed people. All of them drinking and eating finger foods. Mal was running around from person to person, waiting for pets or to see if they dropped anything. My tiny white puppy was a real hit with people, but she did look tired from the crowd.

"Come here, Mal." I snatched her up and put her in her crate behind the receptionist desk. She whined for a moment but then walked around three times and plopped down with a comfortable sigh.

The band played jazz as I picked up a martini glass off the waiter's tray and clanged it with a silver fork. Jenn waved the band to a stop and the room grew silent. "Good evening, everyone. I want to thank you again for coming out tonight and supporting a good cause. Again, all proceeds from tonight's event will go to the Mackinac Island Children's Clinic to provide year-round care for the children who are growing up on this beautiful island."

There was a polite round of applause. "Tonight's theme was inspired by the discovery of a rum-runner's tunnel in the basement of the McMurphy. And so I'd like to invite you all now to follow me downstairs and through the tunnel. The other side of which ends up in the Oakton pool house where the party will continue with a 'Play It Again Sam' mystery production staring Russ Haver and Angie Knight."

The two actors took their bows. "And now, follow me into the depths of history." I opened the basement door and the band fell in line playing marching jazz.

The basement had been cleaned and lit with strings of fat white bulbs and beads. The door to the coal bin was removed and the secret lever to the tunnel revealed with many oohs and aahs. The partygoers grew solemn as they entered the tunnel, whispering at the work that had been done to carve it out, right under the alley. The door to the pool mechanical room was left open and the room itself was well lit to the code set down by the insurance company. The stairs to the pool house seemed anti-climactic.

The pool house itself was lit with strings of white

fairy lights running along the rafters. White tables laden with a buffet lined the edges of the pool. The band played "When the Saints Go Marching In" as people spilled into the pool house laughing and giggling over the adventure of the rum-runners tunnel.

There was a sudden scream and the band stopped as everyone took note of the water and the old man floating facedown, wearing nothing but boxers covered in red hearts.

A Crow Left of the Murder Fudge

5 cups white chocolate chips
4 tablespoons butter
1 can sweetened condensed milk
2 ounces cranberry juice
2 ounces pineapple juice
2 ounces bourbon (Old Crow) to taste

Butter an 8" x 8" x 2" pan, then line with wax paper or plastic wrap. (I prefer wax paper.)

Using a double boiler fill ⅓ of the bottom pan with water and heat on medium high until the water is boiling. Then you can turn the heat down to low and in the top section, melt chocolate, sweetened condensed milk, and butter until smooth and thick. Add cranberry juice and pineapple juice—heat and stir until reduced.

Remove from heat. Add bourbon 1 tablespoon at a time (to taste). Mix well. Pour into pan. Cool. Tip: let cool outside of the refrigerator for 30 minutes so that no condensation mars the top. Refrigerate overnight. Remove from pan. Cut into pieces. Store in a covered container.

Chapter 28

"So much for our murder mystery play," Russ said as he sat dejectedly on one of the pool chairs.

"All that lovely food gone to waste," Frances said as she looked at the untouched buffet. "Not that I blame anyone. Who could eat knowing a dead man was in the room?"

"They do it all the time at funerals." Jenn could be so matter-of-fact. "That was twelve-dollars-a-plate service. I'd like to get my hands on that old man."

"Or whoever pushed him," I muttered. They all stared at me. "What? There seems to be a rash of old men dying on island. It doesn't take too big a leap of faith to think he was murdered."

"People die, dear." Frances patted my hand. "It's a fact of life."

The ambulance came quick. George Marron hurried in, carrying his bag of equipment. A younger man, tall and thin with sandy-brown hair, accompanied him. Both were damp from the rain outside.

The wind had picked up and a regular howl was brewing.

When we'd seen the weather we hadn't worried because everyone would be traveling from the pool house to the McMurphy via the tunnel. Now it merely added a strange atmosphere to the scene.

Two of the bigger men had ripped off their suit coats and hauled the old man out of the water and up onto the gray concrete. CPR was started. In the five minutes it took for the ambulance to arrive, the old man hadn't budged. His skin was as blue as Joe's had been. I was beginning to tell a hopeless cause when I saw it.

Officer Brown had arrived on scene first and asked everyone to stay put. Another younger officer fresh on island for the summer season took down people's names and what they saw. It was all the same story. We came up through the tunnel. No one had been aware of anyone unusual in the tunnel or the mechanical room. No, the pool house was not locked. Yes, the catering staff had been the only ones who were supposed to be on the premises, as the pool house was officially closed to any early guests at the Oakton.

George went to work, took the man's vitals, tried to shock his heart into action, and when that didn't work he called the clinic and the man was pronounced dead.

"Do you know who he is?" I asked Frances.

"I didn't get a good look at his face." She shrugged. "Hang on, I'll see what I can find out."

I had stayed as far from the scene as possible. The last thing I needed was to be associated with another dead man.

"I've been told this is your party." The young officer looked at me warily. "You're Allie McMurphy?"

"Yes." I tried not to sigh. "I'm Allie McMurphy and this is my party. It is a benefit for the children's clinic on island."

The officer, whose name tag read "Wright," wrote in his notebook. "And you are a person of interest in the murder of Joe Jessop, is that right?" He looked at me with crystal-blue eyes.

"If, by person of interest, you mean that I found Joe Jessop dead at the McMurphy, then that would be correct."

"Hi." Jenn interceded. "I'm Jennifer Christensen. I planned the entire party for Allie." She walked the officer away from me. "I can get you a list of guests and the publicity plans. That way you'll know who was involved, although I'm certain this was merely a strange coincidence."

"The dead man was Theodore Finley," Frances said.

"Who?"

"Theodore Finley." Frances pulled me closer to the wall. "He was the town mayor for twelve years back in the early 1980s."

"Oh, no, please tell me he wasn't on the guest list."

"Sorry, he was on the guest list and the historical committee."

I cringed. "Did he have family at the party? I don't remember you introducing me to any Finleys."

"His wife died last year and his daughter is in New York."

"Good, I'd hate to have had them see him that way."

Rex came through the pool-house door wearing his uniform covered by a plastic rain poncho. He held the door for the EMTs as they took the body away on a stretcher. The wind howled and the rain blasted the glass walls of the pool house.

Rex consulted with Officer Brown and Officer Wright, then turned to the waiting partygoers. "You'll be allowed to leave, but the weather is not conducive to walking from the pool house to Main Street. We're going to walk you through the tunnel in groups of four. That way you can pick up your things at the McMurphy and head home. Taxis have been contacted and are currently lined up on the street."

I went straight to Rex. "Do you want me to stay here or to go to the McMurphy first?"

"I would prefer you were at the McMurphy," he said. "Is there someone who can stay at the pool house while we walk people through the tunnel?"

"I'll stay," Mr. Devaney volunteered.

"I'll stay with him as well," Frances said. "That way you have two witnesses."

"All right." Rex nodded, his mouth a firm line and his gaze flat. "I'm going to lock the pool-house door and I want you to make sure it stays locked."

"Done." Mr. Devaney took Frances by the arm. "Come on, let's get you a seat near the door."

"What's going on?" I asked Rex. "This makes two dead men since Papa died."

"If I were a conspiracy theorist, I'd be worried about that," Rex said as he opened the door to the mechanical room. "But I'm a realist. The only murder is Joe. There is no evidence of murder in this case."

I frowned. "I don't know, this looks pretty suspicious to me."

Chapter 29

"Nothing like death to put a damper on the night, no pun intended," Frances said.

"At least this time someone had the sense to scream at the sight of a dead body." I rubbed my bare arms. The band packed up and the last of the guests had been escorted through the tunnel and out to waiting cabs.

"What are you going to do with all that food?"

"I had Jenn contact the soup kitchen in St. Ignace. They are more than willing to take it and will have two guys here in the morning to pick it up. In the meantime, we're putting it in the fudge shop refrigerators."

"Noble of you." Trent Jessop walked into the lobby. He wore a dark raincoat over his suit.

"I wouldn't say noble." I studied him. "I'd say practical."

"It's sure to get you in good with the locals."

"Have you come back to bait me?" I could not

believe the nerve of the guy. Really, he had been part of the first group to leave. Don't get me wrong, I get it. He had just lost his grandfather in the McMurphy. The last thing he would want is to subject his family to more mayhem.

"I came back because I'm worried." He shook off his coat. "Too many good men are dying around you."

"And you came to keep an eye on me?" I put my hands on my hips. "Because I really think you should go home and keep an eye on your family. Let me worry about me and mine."

"I came back because I know that Rex and Charles need some help. And because I don't like the idea of a couple of women staying alone in a building where two men were murdered." He put his hands on his hips and stood toe-to-toe with me.

Darn, the man did look good in a suit. "I'm a grown woman and I'm perfectly capable of handling myself in my own home."

"I'm sure you are," he said, his tone low. "But this is not your home, not yet. And you may be full grown, but so were my grandfather and Mr. Finley. If this turns out to be a serial killer, I don't like the fact that you are living in the killer's hunting grounds."

Okay, that sounded kind of creepy. "There's no one here but my staff and I. I walk the halls every night and check each room."

"What would you do if you found a killer? Call Rex Manning? Run? Or worse, try to detain him.

Think about it. This guy has killed two grown men.
Did you ever stop to think about what you'd do if
you found him?"

Okay, so he had me there. I winced.

"That's what I thought."

"Mr. Devaney is here," I said.

"That man is sixty-two years old."

"And every bit as wise," I stated. "Like I said, I've
got it covered."

Trent raised a dark eyebrow. "I don't like how
you've got it covered."

"What is that supposed to mean?"

"It means that he is going to help us out by
taking a shift and patrolling the grounds," Rex said
as he walked up from the tunnel. "I'm serious, Allie.
The summer officers won't be here for another two
weeks. Now, having four or five officers on island
during the off-season usually isn't a big deal, but
in times of crisis . . ."

"Are you saying I'm in crisis?"

"I'm saying the island is in crisis. I've got an
entire island to patrol—not just the McMurphy and
the Oakton."

"Well, I know that. I'm fine, really."

"In times of crisis," Rex repeated, "it's tradition
to call on the men in the community to pitch in.
Think of it as your neighborhood watch."

"How sexist is that? This is the twenty-first century.
Women are perfectly capable . . ."

"And they have the day shift," Rex cut me off.
"I fully expect you and your staff to patrol the area

during the day, but you have to rest. That's why Trent is here. He's going to be staying the night and ensuring you're safe to take the morning patrol. I expect you to report anything out of the ordinary. Have I made myself clear?"

"Fine." I gave him the stink eye. "It doesn't mean I have to like it. I'm from Chicago for goodness' sake. I know what it's like to live in a sketchy neighborhood. Mackinac Island's not sketchy."

"Allie, two men have died within one hundred yards of your home. I think you need to let us watch out for you. It's what neighbors do."

"Think of it this way," Frances said. "You're now a part of the community." She held Mal tight against her. "That was what you wanted, right?"

"Yes, of course." I felt deflated. I had this grand idea that I could take over the family business and continue the McMurphy tradition of fudge and family. I looked from one handsome man to the other and suddenly realized that some things a person simply couldn't do on their own.

"I thought you hated me," I said to Trent.

"Why would you think that?" He looked affronted.

"Because of the purple ribbons and everything." I waved my hand at the ribbon clearly pinned to his suit coat.

"My sister Paige bought that. I completely forgot it was there."

"Listen Allie, I'm going to walk Mr. Devaney and

Frances home. Are you okay to stay here with Trent, because if you're not you need to say so right now."

"I'm fine," I said. "Officer Brown is still processing the pool house. Jenn and I have cleaning up to do."

"And I'll be here as well," Trent said. "I've got your cell-phone number in my phone."

"Fine, I'll see these good people home then."

"Oh, dear, what are you going to do with all that fudge?" Frances looked into the fudge shop window at the stacks of pretty wrapped presents.

"Do you think it would be awful to send it out to the partygoers?" I asked. "They did pay for their tickets and should at the very least get some fudge out of it."

"We'll send it out with a nice thank-you note," Jenn said. "A personal touch will go a long way to helping everyone heal from tonight's shock."

"Don't worry, Frances," I said. "Jenn's right. We'll send it out with thank-you notes in the morning. Go on home. We've all had quite a day."

"All right, if you insist." Frances looked exhausted. Mr. Devaney and Rex escorted her out into the storm.

Jenn smiled at Trent. "Do you mind helping us move the furniture and take down the strings of lights?"

"Not at all." He actually smiled. I tried really hard not to roll my eyes.

"Great, I'll go get a stepladder." I headed to the

basement, where I found Officer Brown studying the mechanism for the doorway to the tunnel.

"Oh, hello, I didn't know you were down here," I said.

"I'm doing my best attempt at being a crime-scene investigator." His green eyes sparkled. "There really isn't a whole lot of evidence. I'm snapping a few photos of things I find interesting. I hope you don't mind."

"I don't mind." The stepladder hung from two hooks that were screwed into the wood joists. I grabbed a wooden box from the piles and dragged it over to the ladder. Pulling it down was no problem, the ladder was aluminum and light, but bulky.

Officer Brown reached up and helped me.

"Thanks," I said.

"No problem." He tilted his head. "What's in the box you're standing on?"

"I don't know, why?" I looked down at the box.

"It seems to be bleeding." He snapped a photo as red liquid oozed out from beneath my feet.

This time I did scream.

Chapter 30

Okay, so I never climbed off a box so fast in my life. I have no idea how the ladder got tossed across the basement or how I managed to put Officer Brown between me and the oozing box. Sheer terror can make stuff happen.

"What happened?" Trent came tearing down the stairs.

"Are you okay?" Jenn was right behind him.

"It's not blood." Officer Brown squatted down and put his fingers in the liquid. "It's too thin." He sniffed it, then licked his fingers.

I felt the blood drain out of my head.

"Sit down!" Trent commanded and pushed on my shoulder until I did as he said. "Head between your knees."

"I think I've done this before," I muttered.

"It's wine," Officer Brown said and I heard his camera take a few shots. "Do you have a hammer? I'll open up the box."

I kept my head down and pointed. "It's on the workbench."

Jenn rubbed my back. "Are you okay? What happened?"

I sat up and concentrated on her face and making the room stop spinning. "I pulled a box over to get the ladder when Officer Brown asked me what was in the box. I said, 'I don't know. Why?' He said 'It seems to be bleeding.'"

"It's not bleeding," he said, his tone calm. He had a claw-backed hammer in his hand and bent down. "It tastes like alcohol."

"Probably left over from a New Year's party or something," Trent said.

The men took turns cranking on the top of the box. It creaked and moaned as the nails strained and suddenly it popped open.

We all looked inside.

There was what remained of twelve dark bottles. Only two were intact. Officer Brown pulled them out and wiped the dust off. "*Châteauneuf-du-Pape* 1933."

"Damn, that's an old vintage," Trent said and took the bottle from Officer Brown. He held it up in the lamplight. "The cork's not brittle so it had to have been stored properly." He drew his eyebrows together in a frown. "Why is the box full of broken bottles? Did you roll it on its side?"

"I didn't roll it." I got up and looked at the box. "I pulled it from over there." I pointed to the spot near the other boxes where this box had been.

"I was here when she did it and I didn't hear

glass break." Officer Brown pulled out the second unbroken bottle. "These were broken not too long ago or the dirt floor would have absorbed the liquid and it wouldn't still be oozing."

"True." It was my turn to frown. "Do you think the box was dropped?"

"It could account for all the broken bottles," Trent said.

"Who would drop it?" I wondered out loud.

"Didn't you say, Mr. Devany has been cleaning down here? It might have been heavier than he thought," Trent suggested.

"Wait, the box has some old papers in it.label." I knelt down to look at the paper advertisement on the side of the wooden box. "Someone used this paper to wrap the wine." I pulled it out and looked at it closely. "It's fudge wrapping paper and it says, 'Agatha's Fudge voted best on island 1945.'"

"Mabel Showorthy owns Agatha's," Trent said.

"She was here the other day commenting on the renovations," I added. "But this box is heavy. There is no way she could have come down and tried to carry it off."

Officer Brown took some snapshots of the box and the label on the side. "For all we know the box could have been in the basement since 1945. Its use might have been out of convenience."

I bit my bottom lip. "Papa does have a lot of old stuff down here."

"Do you remember the box?" Trent asked.

"No." I shook my head. "We were down here

most of the day yesterday taking inventory and making a list of necessary purchases to wall off the tunnel."

"Don't wall off the tunnel," Trent said.

"Why not?"

"People love a good ghost story."

"Besides," Officer Brown said, "the opening mechanism is really unique."

"It's not safe for me or my guests," I said and meant it.

"Then lock it off, but don't wall it," Trent said. "For all we know, there could be an entire network of smugglers' tunnels under the island."

"What? No, there is only the passage from here to the pool house, remember?" I was still feeling a bit fuzzy-headed from my scare.

"There is that other old door," Officer Brown said. "Did you check that out?"

"What other door?" Jenn asked as she squeezed my arm between her palms. I think she meant to hold me up, but had somehow forgotten. I could feel the excitement in her palms.

"There's a second door near the pool house." I shrugged and gently dislodged her from my arm.

"I didn't notice it," Jenn said.

"Because it hadn't been opened in years and years," I said. "Rex and I decided it was not an issue with this investigation."

"You can't know that for sure unless you check

it out," Officer Brown said gently. His dark eyes sparkled with excitement and hope.

"Fine, it's probably nothing more than a broom closet," I said. "But you have a gun so I imagine it's safe to go check it out."

I hoped those weren't going to be famous last words.

Chapter 31

"I see chivalry isn't dead," Jenn said in a stage whisper as the two men took off toward the door, leaving us behind.

"You would think I said there was a pot of gold behind door number one."

"There might be," Jenn said as she waved me through the door first. "You never know. We could use a miracle right about now."

"Right," I agreed. We got to the end of the tunnel to find Trent and Officer Brown wrestling with the old door frame. It seemed to have swollen up in the damp tunnel. The lock worked well but the key appeared to be permanently in the lock, having rusted into the mechanism. The hinges were tarnished as well and refused to budge even when the door was knocked upwards in an attempt to dislodge the door from its hinges.

"Can you get that hammer?" Officer Brown asked me.

"I can't believe you two left it behind." I went back to get the hammer. The basement was cool and quiet compared to the warmer, wetter tunnel. I suspect that the number of people traipsing through there tonight made a difference.

I grabbed the hammer off the top of the box and when I straightened a big hand covered my mouth and arms locked around me like a vise.

My first instinct was to scream, but I couldn't. I hadn't had time to catch a deep enough breath.

"Make a sound and I will kill you with my bare hands," said a raspy voice. His hot breath bathed my ear and had creepers running down my spine.

I tried to silence the screaming in my head and pay attention to things. Whoever held me was definitely a man. Besides the deep tone of the thick, raspy voice, he wore a black suit coat and no jewelry.

I was pulled up against a solid wall of heat. The man was a little taller than me and definitely wider. My hands were free and I still had the hammer. There were a number of things I could do. I tried to remember self-defense.

SING, right? What did that stand for? Solar plexus, Instep, Groin, Nose . . . Was that right? It didn't seem like the right order. Darn it, it all seemed so easy in the movies. I tried to step on his instep with my pumps, but he shifted and I stumbled backward. He grabbed my hand with the hammer and squeezed hard enough to bruise it.

I grabbed his thumb and he was forced to let go.

"Bitch!" Something hard hit the side of my head and knocked me sideways.

I made a small sound as I stumbled back into the boxes. Look up! I thought as I worked to catch my balance. My hair hung in my eyes and I clenched the hammer like a wild thing as I dug my hair out of my eyes.

But he had snagged the bottles of wine and rushed up the stairs in a blur of footfalls and black suit.

"No!" I thought I shouted the word, but it came out more of a squeak as I scrambled to follow him up the stairs. He had slammed the door behind him.

The gang from the tunnel rushed through into the basement and up the stairs.

"What happened?" Trent asked.

"There was a man," I could barely get the words out as I threw open the door, holding the hammer high. The McMurphy lobby sat empty and quiet. The lights had been dimmed and in the distance the grandfather clock chimed twelve. I rushed to the door, yanked it open, and nearly beaned Emerson Todd with my hammer.

"Whoa." He raised both hands and stepped back. "I'm not doing anything."

"I'm sorry," I managed to squeeze out. I glanced around him. But there was no one else on the street. "Did you see a guy run out of the McMurphy?"

"No, why?"

"I was just attacked in my basement," I said

and turned on my heel to run straight into Trent Jessop.

"We have to quit running into each other," Trent said as he gently pulled me off him.

"Seriously," I agreed.

"What's going on?"

"She says she was attacked in her basement," Emerson said. He shoved his hands in his pants pockets. "I swear, I didn't see anyone run out of the McMurphy." He made me sound like a crazy woman.

I gave him the stink eye. "I was attacked. The man ran off with the two unbroken bottles of wine."

"I believe you," Trent said. "If Emerson didn't see anyone run out, then your attacker may still be inside the McMurphy."

"Exactly!"

Officer Brown and Jenn crowded the doorway.

"I didn't see anyone in the lobby," I said. "He had to have gone upstairs."

"Oh, I certainly hope not," Jenn said. "I'll have nightmares the rest of the night if he did."

"I'll clear the place." Officer Brown had his gun out and pointed toward the floor. "You guys stay here and watch the front door. If anything happens, make sure it's safe before you pursue. Do I make myself clear?"

"Yes," I said.

"I'll go with you," Trent said. "Two sets of eyes are better than one."

"I only came to get my coat. I forgot it in all the excitement," Emerson said.

"Your coat?" I drew my eyebrows together.

"Yes, you took it from me when I came in to the party." He crossed his arms.

Mal barked and startled me. In all the excitement I forgot she was around. She stood near the door of her crate and looked at me with big round eyes.

"Hold on." I opened the crate and let Mal out. She jumped up on me, coming only to my knee. I reached down and patted her head. "You didn't see the bad guy, did you? Maybe you can tell me where he went?"

"Hello, my coat please? I want to get home sometime tonight." He tapped his foot.

Mal sniffed in his direction and growled.

"Mal," I admonished her. "No growling!" It was only the second time I had ever heard her growl at a person. I didn't want her to make a habit of growling. Luckily she quit as soon as I said something. "I'm sorry. Your coat must be in the fudge shop. I'll get it."

I found his coat hanging on a coat rack in the corner of the fudge shop. I usually used the rack for hanging aprons and such, but when the lobby closet had filled, I used the rack to store the last coat or two.

"Here you go." I handed him the wool coat. It was thin and heavy. Black in color, it had a thick notched collar and large pockets. The man's coat

must have been a real period piece as I hadn't seen
anything like it before. "Nice coat. Kind of heavy,
though. Is there something in the pockets?"

"No, nothing in the pockets. It's my grandfather's.
He bought it in the late twenties. It's a sentimental
heirloom." Emerson slipped his coat on. The
motion caused Mal to bark at him again.

"Mal, no!" I picked up my puppy. She snuggled
against me, but watched Emerson warily. "I'm so
sorry. She is usually so good with people."

"It's been a long night." Emerson shrugged.
"I'm sure she is tired and mixing me up with someone else."

"Of course." I wasn't sure who Mal could be
mixing Emerson up with, but it didn't matter. What
really mattered was to get the man to understand
that I have a good business—as good or better than
Paige Jessop would ever have. "Let me get you your
fudge." I carried Mal into the kitchen and grabbed
one of the colorfully wrapped gifts off the counter.
"The price of tonight's ticket included a free
sampling of my latest fudge. This series is based on
alcoholic drinks like piña colada and tropical rum."

"Thanks." He took the box from me and stepped
outside into the darkness.

The sky still misted, and the wind blew cold off
the lake. I watched as Emerson walked down the
street. The coat was not only heavy but oversized
and made him look bigger than normal. Who
would wear a coat that made them look larger?

"Was that Mal barking?" Jenn asked as she came down the stairs.

"Yes, weird right?" I snuggled with my puppy. "She doesn't seem to like Emerson."

"I kind of agree with Mal, there's nothing much to like." Jenn patted Mal on the head. "Listen, I ran upstairs to see if I could find a guest list for Officer Brown." She waved a paper in her hand. "I knew I had one in my computer, so I printed out a copy."

"Was Mr. Finley on the list?"

"No, I had invited him, but he had declined. He said he was going to be out of town for the evening."

"You don't think that was code for spending time with a mistress, do you?" I asked and put Mal down.

"Really, a mistress? I hadn't thought of that."

"Think about it," I said and locked the front door. "He told you he was going to be out of town. Then we find him floating face-first in a pool wearing only boxers covered in red hearts. If he were having a fling, he could tell everyone he was going out of town and no one would suspect he was slipping away for a weekend of fun."

"Wouldn't they expect him to go out by ferry?" Jenn pondered.

"There's also the airport. He could have taken the ferry out and then a private jet back onto island. Met his lover with the intention of taking a plane back to the mainland and then coming back in the ferry where everyone could see him."

"You have a suspicious mind." Jenn shook her

head at me. "What if he did have plans to be out of town and then came back and surprised his killer?"

"Well, yes, I guess that could be possible as well." I gave in, picked up a box of decorations, and took it to the first-floor utility closet. "I suppose I might tend to think the worst."

"Besides." Jenn followed me. "No one has found the girlfriend."

"So you did think that, too." I put the box on the shelf and stepped out to see the two guys coming down the stairs. Mal ran up and jumped on Trent, who tousled her head and kept on going. Mal followed him as if he were her favorite person in the world.

"The place is clear," Officer Brown said. "Whoever attacked you had to have gone out the front door. The back is all locked up."

"Emerson said he didn't see anyone," I said. "I don't know how that can be."

"Did Mal bark or carry on at all when your attacker ran up the stairs?" Jenn asked.

"She was in her crate." I shrugged. "I don't remember her barking before I let her out and she growled at Emerson."

"This little baby growled at Emerson?" Trent reached down and picked my puppy up and gave her strong pets.

My heart melted more than I'll admit to even you. Seeing him hold my puppy like she was a baby made me think of babies and all the wonderful sexy things that went with them.

"I know, right? She hasn't met a person she didn't love. Maybe it was his coat. He said it was an authentic period piece." I shrugged. "I'm simply not sure."

"Hey, we all have people we don't like, so do dogs. It doesn't mean anything," Jenn said.

"It wouldn't hold up in a court of law," Officer Brown said and winked at Jenn.

"Did you get the tunnel door off the hinges?" I asked. "I sort of forgot about it in the heat of my attack."

"No, we needed the hammer," Officer Brown said. "Its badly rusted hinges and warped materials mean we'll have to break it down."

"It can't be that important to your investigation," I said. "No one must have opened it in years. I'll have Mr. Devaney open it up in the morning. If it's okay with you all, I'm not going back down to the basement tonight."

"It's fine with us," Officer Brown said.

"Here." Trent handed me my dog. "Why don't you and Jenn go on upstairs and lock yourselves in the apartment. It's been a hell of a night. Brown and I will stand watch down here."

"Do you think it's safe?" I asked and bit my bottom lip. "Do you need to check with the others investigating the pool house?"

"Yes, but one of us will be down here all night," Officer Brown said. "Someone is terrorizing you and the people of Mackinac Island. It's time we got to the bottom of things."

"Before the season starts," Jenn added.

"Exactly." Trent nodded. "Do you want me to walk you two up?"

"I think we're fine," I said and looked at Jenn, who nodded. "Thanks. I'm sorry I misjudged you."

"Maybe when this is all done, we can get a drink and get to know each other better."

He was so sincere that it made a shiver go through me. "Sure."

"Good. Good night, ladies."

"Good night." Jenn pushed me up the stairs. I unlocked the apartment with shaking hands and put Mal down the moment we got inside.

Jenn turned the dead bolt and leaned against the door. "Well, that certainly turned out different than I imagined."

"I know." I sat down on my couch. It was then that I noticed the bruise on my knee. "Yikes." I poked at it.

"Ouch." Jenn said. "Let me get some ice for that."

I leaned my head back and listened to her in the kitchen dumping ice from the ice tray into a cloth. Suddenly, I was very, very tired. It must have been the adrenaline drop.

"You look exhausted." Jenn handed me a towel with ice in it. I placed it on my knee and only winced a little. "Was it scary?"

"Was what scary?"

"When the guy attacked you?" she asked and sat on the arm of the couch. Her flapper dress sparkled in the lamplight.

"It's scarier now than when it was happening," I said. "It all happened so fast."

"What exactly did happen? I mean, we heard a commotion and a short scream and we went running only to find you scrambling up the stairs with a hammer in your hand."

I closed my eyes and rested my head against the back of the couch, trying to remember exactly what happened. "I grabbed the hammer off Papa's tool bench, then this guy grabbed me from behind."

"Where did he come from?" Jenn asked. "He wasn't in the tunnel with us."

"I have no idea. He was behind me and put his hand over my mouth and pulled me against him."

"Okay, now that's scary." She sat on the couch and patted my hand. "What did you do?"

"I tried to remember what you're supposed to do—you know, in self-defense."

"Yes."

"I tried to step on his instep, but he anticipated that and stepped back. So I realized I had a hammer in my hands and I swung back, thinking I could hit his groin."

"And?"

"I grabbed his thumb when he tried to make me drop the hammer. I must have hit his thigh somehow because he cursed and let go of me. But he didn't double over or anything."

"You said he ran up the stairs?"

"Yes, but first he grabbed the two unbroken bottles of wine from the box." I made a face. "Don't you think that's weird?"

"Really weird," she said. "What's the big deal about some wine?"

"I have no idea. Let's research it." I hobbled over to my desk and started up my computer. Mal jumped up, licked my face, and curled up in my lap. "Yes," I cooed. "You're my big guard doggie. It's my fault you were stuck in your crate."

The search engine came up and I entered the name from the wine bottle. "Oooh," I said and pursed my lips.

"What?" Jenn looked over my shoulder.

"It's a very rare wine. It looks like most of the great vintage was lost in a massive storm that sunk the cargo freighter it was shipped on. The ship went down during Prohibition and the vintage was being smuggled from France through Canada. The vintage was lost except for a few rare bottles." I read on in silence. "Check this out. The last bottle sold at auction went for a whopping five hundred thousand dollars."

"Holy shit!" Jenn cursed. "That means your attacker potentially stole a million dollars from your basement."

"No wonder he ran off with it." I sat back. "Pete

Thompson told me that Papa had a source of income other than the McMurphy. Do you think he was referring to this wine? Where did Papa get it? Who else knew about it?"

"You'd better call Officer Manning," Jenn said. "I think we cracked his case wide open."

Key Lime Island Fudge

5 cups white chocolate chips
4 tablespoons cream cheese
1 can sweetened condensed milk
1 lime—squeeze juice and grate peel
1 teaspoon vanilla

Butter an 8" x 8" x 2" pan. Line with wax paper or plastic wrap. Squeeze juice from lime, save juice, and grate the peel. Set aside. Using a double boiler fill ⅓ of the bottom pan with water and heat on medium high until the water is boiling. Then you can turn the heat down to low and in the top section, place sweetened condensed milk, white chocolate chips, and cream cheese. Stir constantly until chips and cream cheese are melted. Remove from heat. Add vanilla, lime juice and rind bits and stir until combined. Pour into pan or crust. Cool completely. Cut and serve in colorful cupcake papers. Store in covered container.

If you want, you can prepare a graham-cracker crust:

1½ cups finely ground graham-cracker
    crumbs.
⅓ cup sugar
6 tablespoons butter, melted

Mix until well blended. Pat into pan. Bake at 375°F for 7 minutes—cool completely.

Chapter 32

"A half a million dollars a bottle?" Rex whistled. "That's a whole lot of motive."

"Do you think Joe was killed over the wine?" I asked. It was after midnight and Rex stood in my living room looking at my computer screen. He was every inch the police officer in his full uniform with a gun on his hip. There was something predatory about him that made a girl feel protected and nervous at the same time.

Jenn lounged in Papa's easy chair. We had both changed out of our flapper gowns. Jenn wore leopard-spotted leggings and a black tunic. I wore jeans and a purple T-shirt. My hair was still in the braid that Jenn had woven for the cocktail party.

"If he was, it still doesn't disprove you as a suspect." He glanced at me.

"Why not?" I drew my brows together.

"The wine was in the basement of the McMurphy

and everyone is aware of your dwindling resources as you remodel." He was dead serious.

"I have enough money for the season," I argued.

"I imagine that a million dollars would give you more than one season. People have killed for less."

"I know of someone who was killed for a carton of cigarettes," I reasoned. "If you think of it that way, then everyone on island has motive to be a killer."

"Not everyone had a million dollars stolen from their basement."

I stood. I have to admit that my nerves were more than a little raw. "I didn't kill anyone. Someone tried to kill me."

"And Mr. Finley," he added. "George told me that Mr. Finley didn't have any water in his lungs."

"So it wasn't an accidental drowning in the pool tonight?" Jenn sat up.

"It doesn't look like it." Rex's jaw clenched.

"But he could have had a heart attack and fell in the pool, right?" I asked.

"That's for the coroner to determine " Rex had the best poker face ever.

"We have two dead men—both of the same age—and a box of expensive wine, all but two bottles broken. The two that remain were stolen when a man attacked me. I don't understand how you could think I might even remotely be a person of interest."

"This isn't about what I think. This is about the facts. The facts are that no one saw this person who attacked you. Two bottles of wine worth a cool million disappeared and you were the only one in the room. Two men are dead. One in your utility closet and the other in a pool house during a party you hosted."

"You are only saying that because you don't have a clue who's really doing this or why." Yes, I was defensive. I liked this guy. Why did he continue to blame these terrible things on me?

"For all I know your Papa smuggled that wine into the McMurphy. He told you where he kept his treasure and Joe Jessop found out about it. He confronted you and you killed him."

I rolled my eyes. "I'm not talking to you."

"You shouldn't," Jenn said. "You should go through your lawyer."

"We don't need to get all hasty," Rex said, his eyes twinkling for the first time as his cop persona slipped. "I do have another theory."

"Are you going to let us in on it?" Jenn asked.

"Now, that wouldn't be very professional of me," he said. "For now, I'm going to keep a security patrol on the McMurphy. We'll come through every four hours."

"Is that because you think we're in danger or because we're under lock and key?"

"You may leave anytime you want. In fact, I'd prefer you stayed elsewhere—"

"I will not!"

"And that is why we'll be doing security checks

until we have someone in custody or at the very least an answer to who attacked you."

"Fine." I refused to budge from where I stood, which was basically toe-to-toe with the man. I didn't want to admit that my heart raced and my skin flushed. He was infuriating and he thought I was some kind of serial killer.

All I wanted was to be a successful fudge shop/hotel owner. I wanted to fit into the community and maybe someday see as many green ribbons as purple.

"Good. Thank you for your cooperation." He nodded at us. "If you find more of those wine bottles, I expect you to let me know. Whoever is killing may be killing for them and I don't want you harboring anything that might get you killed— even if it's worth two million dollars. It's not worth your life."

"If we find it in the McMurphy, it belongs to the McMurphy, right?" Jenn asked.

"Unless someone can prove otherwise, yes. I'm not calling you thieves. I'm trying to look out for your safety."

I let him out the apartment door.

"Lock it behind me," Rex said. "Dead bolt."

"No problem." I slammed the door closed and threw the dead bolt. I turned to see Jenn grinning at me from the couch. Mal chewed on a toy and glanced at me, wagging her tail.

"That guy is hot for you," Jenn said.

"He thinks I'm a murderer," I pointed out.

"Which makes you off-limits and even hotter."
Jenn waggled her eyebrows. "He's a local, right?"

"And twice divorced."

"Even better, he doesn't strike me as a man who
makes the same mistake twice."

"Wait . . ."

"You said that he married two different women
and divorced them for two different reasons . . ."

"True."

"Then he knows for sure what he wants now. It
looks to me like he plans to go after it as soon as he
solves this case."

I rolled my eyes and picked up my puppy. "He
wants someone who will remain on island. I'm not
certain I can make it beyond the first season."

Chapter 33

The next day I left Frances and Jenn to cross-reference the guest list with the packages of fudge while I searched the office files. If Papa Liam knew anything about the expensive wine, he didn't tell me. The best part was he never threw anything away.

It was family tradition.

We kept anything and everything about the McMurphy we thought might even remotely become interesting in the next couple of hundred years. This meant that the office had rows of file cabinets with files dating back to the grand opening of the McMurphy fudge shop in 1865. It's how we were able to prove to the historical committee that fat pink stripes were authentic to the time period.

"All right. If there is any logic to these files, then the earliest files would be on the lower left and the newest files on the upper right," I told Mal as she sat on her haunches and studied me with blinky, black button eyes. "Let's test that theory." I went to the top right-most cabinet and opened it. Sure enough, it was dated from last year. "Thank you Papa Liam for making sense."

Now all I had to do was figure out where the 1930s were and go through the files one by one until I hit present day. If those bottles of wine had been smuggled in, there was some record of it—no matter how slight. If there was a record, perhaps it would help me discover who else might know about the wine.

"Let's start with the year the wine was labeled." I found the appropriate file cabinet and pulled out the folders in that drawer, took them back to Papa's big oak desk, and plopped them down. Mal waited for me to sit before she jumped up and curled up in my lap.

I was about two hours into the files when the phone rang, startling me out of my thoughts. "Hello?"

"Allie?" It was a decidedly male voice and the rumble had the full attention of my nerves.

"Yes."

"Trent Jessop. I've been going through Joe's things and I think we need to talk."

"Will I need my lawyer?" Why was I always such a jerk to this guy? "I'm sorry. I don't know where that comment came from. I've been buried in McMurphy files looking for clues."

"Right. Should we meet in a neutral place?"

"Like where?"

"Let's meet at JL Beanery. Do you know it?"

"The little coffee shop across from the Island House Hotel?"

"Yes. Say in an hour?"

I glanced at the clock on Papa's shelf. It was already one in the afternoon. "Sure."

"Great."

He hung up and I ran my hand along Mal's back. She sighed and tried to curl up tighter on my lap. "I wonder what that was all about?" I picked her up, kissed her on the nose, and set her back in the chair as I replaced the files I had with the next decade full.

Thumbing through the file folders, I noticed a note scrawled in feminine handwriting across a receipt. "Liam and his friends discovered a box. Paper label is wet, but appears to be French. Must look up translation."

Was this what I was looking for? I sat down on the overstuffed green leather couch and put the rest of the decade's files on the floor at my feet. The receipt the note was written on was for laundry. In the 1950s the laundry for the McMurphy was sent out to a service. Most hotels of the time sent their washing out. Even to this day the laundry was done by a service. Papa looked into creating a laundry room, but the basement was too old to be converted. There were plans to add on to the pool house and create a laundry building, but the Thompsons refused to sell Papa the real estate that the laundry would sit on.

Papa had decided that it was no longer in our best interest to co-own things. Instead, he broke off the partnership. The Thompsons built a laundry room for their bed-and-breakfast and the McMurphys sent their laundry out to the Yangs to be washed in professional washers and hung out on long clotheslines to dry in the sun.

"Sunshine is the best antiseptic," Papa would say and point out scientific studies that backed up his theory.

"Besides, sheets simply smell better dried in the sunshine," Grammy would add to the conversation and then wink at me. "All our guests ask where we get our fabric softener. Nothing like fresh air and sunlight to make a bed feel like home."

It was easy for us, of course. The McMurphy had only ten beds. Last count the Thompson's B and B had twice as many beds. Besides, clotheslines weren't allowed in the downtown area.

I dug through the receipts and papers in the folder with the note. It was 1952. There were grocery receipts. The cost of sugar was forty-three cents for five pounds. Candy-grade bulk sugar was a nickel per pound. I was surprised to see another note in the same feminine handwriting concerned about sugar doubling later on that year.

I know that my grandparents kept the cost of fudge low. They considered it more of a draw than a business. The McMurphy was the real business. Fudge was a luxury more than a necessity. Perhaps Papa's mother had been contemplating getting out of the fudge shop business.

It made one wonder if they had a price point where they would decide to get out. If so, did that hit it? And what made them continue? ?

I continued looking through the paperwork for clues. There was no further mention of the box or French translation. All I could do was hope that whatever Trent had found in Joe's papers was more significant than a cryptic note.

I stopped by the general store on my way to the coffee shop. I needed to make a photocopy of the handwritten note I'd found. "Always have a backup," Papa used to say.

"I heard you donated your party plates to the St. Ignace soup kitchen." Susan Goodfoot stepped out from behind the store counter. "That was thoughtful."

"I couldn't throw them away," I said.

"Others would have." She looked at me thoughtfully. "They are calling it a feast day at the kitchen."

"Really?" I winced. "But it's leftovers."

"Most people never get a chance to taste chicken marsala or grilled veggie and steak skewers, let alone the cheesecakes. Trust me, they don't care if the food is a day old."

"Then I'm glad." I made my photocopy.

Susan sat behind the counter reading a gossip rag when I turned to leave.

"I didn't know you worked here."

"I substitute for Mary sometimes," she said.

I drew my brows together. "Is Mary sick?"

"She's in mourning."

"Really? Why?"

"Finley was her lover," Susan said. "They'd been seeing each other for years."

"Seriously?"

"Everyone on island knows." Her brown eyes sparkled at me. I swear she was silently calling me a fudgie. This time I took it all in stride.

"Was she there when he died?" I had to ask.

"Word is they didn't realize the party was setting up in the pool house. When the catering company showed up, she and Finley slipped into the dressing rooms. She heard Mr. Finley arguing with someone in the men's room. Scared, she gathered up her stuff and snuck out."

"She didn't see anything at all?" I clutched my purse.

"She waited in the dark for Finley to come out of the pool house, but he never did."

"That poor girl, what must she think?"

"She thinks if she had stayed in the pool house she might have saved her lover's life."

"Or lost hers as well," I pointed out.

"There was one thing," Susan said and leaned in close.

"What's that?" I asked.

"She said Colin Ferber was hanging around outside the pool house just before she and Finley met up for their rendezvous."

Chapter 34

"Did you notice that we're the only ones not wearing ribbons?" I sat across from Trent Jessop in a sun-filled coffee shop on the end of the marina. The shop itself was painted yellow with white trim. It boasted of lunch favorites and tea-time specials.

There were a handful of baristas and waitstaff. They had whispered when I walked in and the stares and whispers grew frantic as I approached Trent at his table. The entire place went quiet when I sat down.

Trent looked up from his menu. His dark hair shimmered where the sun hit it. The man was ridiculously handsome. His skin had the bronze look of a man comfortable in the sun. Today he wore a light blue denim shirt, the sleeves rolled up halfway. His broad hands were clean and well-groomed, but the air around him smelled rich, of expensive cologne and leather with just the right amount of sun-warmed skin.

"People are still wearing those silly ribbons?" He glanced over at the staff, who had gathered at opposite ends of the counter. The purple ribbon group grinned at him. The one waitress wearing a green ribbon glared at him. He muttered something this side of dark, then looked at me. "Let's dispel this whole feud idea right now, shall we?"

What happened next, I swear happened in slow motion. You know when certain moments of your life are played out in slow motion as if they have more meaning than other normal moments?

Putting down his menu, Trent got halfway out of his chair and leaned across the table, his lovely face a mere breath away. "Ready?"

He kissed me. It wasn't a peck either. The kiss involved lips, hands caressing my hair, my jawline, and the right amount of tongue.

The man took his time and I felt it right down to my toes. When we broke contact, he sat back in his chair, looked over at the staff, who had scattered, then picked up his menu as if nothing happened.

Meanwhile, I sat frozen, leaning halfway over the table. Seriously, who does that?

"The key lime pie is good here." He had the good grace to give me a moment to come back to earth before he lowered his menu.

"I'm an apple fan." Thank goodness my mouth worked even while my brain was still lost in the sensation of that stupid kiss. By the time he lowered his menu, I sat back and studied my menu.

"It's not time for fresh apples." He motioned

with his hand for the waitress and she hurried over. "If you like fruit, I'd suggest the strawberry."

"Are you ready to order?" The waitress had a name tag that said "Tiffany." She was cute with her light brown hair pulled up into a ponytail. Her eyes were lined with black in a cat eye and there was a tiny crystal piercing on the side of her nose.

"I'll have a large coffee and a slice of your strawberry-and-cream-cheese pie." Okay, I was not doing what he said, but it did sound good.

"I'll have the same," Trent said as if he hadn't just manhandled me in public.

I did notice that Tiffany had the good grace to take her ribbon off before she got to the table. She poured coffee and left. I added cream and sugar to mine. Trent drank his black.

"What did you find in Joe's papers?" I cut to the chase as I stirred.

He raised a dark eyebrow. "Not good at small talk, are you?"

"I figure we're kind of beyond that." I sipped my coffee and noticed that his eyes glittered. Maybe he wasn't cool about the kiss either.

"Right." He mirrored me and tasted his coffee as well. "Grandfather Joe was a regular journaler."

"Seriously?"

"Wrote down what happened every day of his life from the time he was ten. I have to say some things are best not known about your grandfather." Trent winked at me.

I tried not to blush, but some things are beyond control. "Are you trying to distract me?"

"Maybe." He grinned.

Tiffany stopped by the table and delivered two plates of the most beautiful pie I'd seen in a long time. Really, my mom wasn't into cooking or baking. When I was in school, I'd been concentrating on candy. It was rare to see good pie. I dug in.

"You were going through Joe's journals . . ." I said between bites.

"It turns out he and your grandfather were fast friends. They did everything together."

"Let me guess, a girl got between them." I noticed that I was more than halfway through the pie. Okay, I eat when I'm nervous. I put my fork down and picked up my coffee cup.

"Actually, no."

"No?" I drew my eyebrows together. "What caused the rivalry?"

"There was no rivalry. It was a prank they played that got out of hand."

"But . . . wait, how did it start?" I put my coffee down, drawn into his story. It was strange to think that Papa Liam and Joe Jessop were secretly best buddies.

"There was a falling out between George Thompson and your grandfather."

"Yes, I know about that. Sometime in the seventies, Papa and George got into a tangle over the pool house laundry plans. It was well before I was born so I don't know all the details."

"According to the journals, George got greedy. Liam put his foot down so George bought out the property."

"Okay, what does that have to do with the rivalry?"

"Liam and Joe cooked up the whole falling out so that Joe could mingle with George and keep an eye on things for Liam."

I sat back. It made sense. Papa would never hold a grudge that long unless there was something unforgivable going on. It did make me wonder what George had done. Papa used to say, "Fool me once, shame on you. Fool me twice, well, everyone knows the rest."

"What about the springtime pranks where Joe would sneak into the McMurphy? Frances tells me that Papa would set traps for him but never caught him."

"It was all fake," Trent said and finished his pie. "It was the only way they could get together for the annual season meeting."

"The annual season meeting?" I felt like a parrot, but seriously it was like discovering that the world was not what you thought. Maybe my brains really had fallen out after that kiss.

"Joe and Liam had a secret," Trent said. "I think that secret is what got Joe killed."

Chapter 35

"What secret?"

"There are too many ears in here," Trent said. "Shall we take a walk?"

I glanced outside. The sun was bright. The lake rippled gently, shimmering. The weather was perfect for a walk. "Sure."

We paid the check and Trent put his hand on the small of my back as we walked out. I glanced at him when he touched me.

He leaned in and whispered, "Dispelling rumors of a feud."

Right. We stepped out and instead of walking down Main, we turned in the opposite direction toward the shoreline bike trail that circled the island.

I needed something to do with my hands so I hugged my waist as we walked. It was tough to absorb what he had told me and my mind kept racing to what the secret might have been. Did it have anything to do with the half-a-million-dollar bottles of wine in the basement?

If the wine was so expensive, why didn't Papa's finances mirror that? Wait, he did leave me with one hundred thousand dollars for repairs, but I thought that was his retirement savings.

"The secret is a story straight out of *Treasure Island*." Trent broke the silence.

I glanced at him. "Did it have to do with finding the wine?"

"Yes. What makes the wine so expensive, besides the fact that it was a very good vintage at a very good year during Prohibition, was the rarity."

"Most of the bottles were lost with a ship that went down in a storm," I said, letting him know I had done my homework as well.

"The key being most of the wine," he agreed as we followed the bike trail around the island. "Joe, Liam, George, and Colin Ferber—"

"Wait, my old handyman? That Colin Ferber?"

"Yes." he nodded. "That Colin was part of the foursome."

"Weird, I never thought of him the same way. I mean, Papa had the McMurphy, George had the Oakton, and Joe had the Jessop Stables."

"Colin's father was the police chief here for years before he was transferred downstate. Colin grew up on island and stayed when his folks left."

"I know he married an island girl. Her family was

here, weren't they?" I waved my hand toard the interior of the island.

"Yes. Anyway, one early November night they were all out partying at the other end of the island near Point St. Clair. Liam and Joe found a wood crate washed ashore. They opened it and saw the wine and being high schoolers did what any young guy would do. They pulled out six bottles, stashed the crate, and shared their discovery with George and Colin. George and Colin wanted to drink it all at once, but Joe and Liam convinced them to drink only two. They carried the other four bottles home to figure out what the label said."

"I take it they didn't take French in high school?"

"Joe wasn't that much into school." Trent grinned. "According to the journal it was Liam who discovered the story about the bottles. But not before the two smuggled the rest of the crate into the McMurphy."

"They brought it in through the pool house, didn't they?"

The path bent closer to the water's edge. "Yes, they used the tunnel and stowed it in the back of the coal bin."

"Wait, I read about this in the newspaper archive. There was an article that mentioned that they found the bottles but it was Prohibition time and the bottles were disposed of properly."

I watched as he picked up a rock and skipped it along the water.

"Remember Colin's father was the police chief. They broke one bottle but sold the other three. The money got Joe noticed by my grandmother's wealthy family," Trent said. "Once he married a Wentworth, they were able to really expand and upgrade the stables."

"It must be how Papa was able to keep the fudge shop as part of the McMurphy," I mused. "Before the fifties the fudge shop was more of a luxury than a part of the McMurphy. According to invoices I found, they were in the red two seasons."

"It's how George went to college," Trent said. The trail weaved in and out of tree cover, but never less than five feet from the water's edge.

"What about Colin? How did he end up a handyman?"

"He gambled it away on a venture that didn't work." Trent shoved his hands in his pockets. "Meanwhile, Joe and Liam had twenty more bottles stashed away. They were smart. In fact, it was Liam's idea to keep the find secret. If the bottles remained scarce, they remained profitable."

"George and Colin never knew?"

"George didn't need to know. He had married a trust-fund girl and spent most of the year in Chicago."

"Let me guess, Colin was too mired in his own problems to figure out Papa and Joe had pulled one over on him. But I don't get it," I said. "How were they able to keep the secret when they sold a bottle?" I watched sea birds land on the water in a splish splash.

"They had a connection with an auction house in New York. When the newspaper story ran about the four bottles, they were all approached by Adam Jerkins. Colin and George laughed him off, but Joe kept the contact."

"So Liam hid the goods and Joe hid the connection."

"It was a huge game to them at first. They were careful and smart. Sold a bottle every two or three years and lived as if the money didn't exist."

I frowned. "I've been through Papa's finances— I saw a regular deposit of ten grand. But if they sold a bottle, the money would all come at once, right? So why then deposit only ten grand a month?"

"They were smart with their money, those two," Trent said. "Anything under ten grand does not have to be reported to the IRS."

"If they didn't deposit it all at once, what did they do with the money?"

"Have you checked his safe-deposit box?"

"No, I haven't had the time. I have a key. Papa put it in my name a couple of years ago. He told me it was the fudge recipe. I didn't check it because I have my own recipes from school."

"Also, Joe lost a great deal in the market crash

of 2006," Trent said as we walked back to the trail. "Maybe Liam did as well."

"I'll have to ask Dad," I said thoughtfully. "But Papa did help pay for my graduate degree. How is this linked to Joe's murder?"

"Of the four men, Colin is the only one left alive." As the trail bent closer to the water's edge. Trent selected another stone and skipped it.

"There is no way Colin knew about the wine," I said. "He was penniless. Papa paid for Colin's wife's funeral."

Trent looked at me. "I find it interesting that George, Liam, and Joe are all dead within six months. Then someone breaks into the McMurphy and steals two high-dollar bottles of wine."

"There's no link. Papa died of a heart attack while playing cards at the senior center," I said.

"Did he?" Trent tilted his head and narrowed his eyes. "Or were we all supposed to believe that? Look, George was found dead in his bed. The cause was never officially investigated. Everyone believed it was natural causes. The man was old and seventy pounds overweight. Liam was laughing and playing cards, then went face-first into the table. No one did an autopsy. No one questioned it until Joe died."

"He was murdered for sure."

"The killer got sloppy. Why? Maybe Joe knew who he was and confronted him."

I frowned. "Did he mention anything in his journal?"

"His last entry was only two words."

"Okay, I'll bite, what were his two words?"

"Well, hell."

No-Cook Peanut Butter Chocolate Chip Fudge

½ cup butter
½ cup peanut butter
1 pound powdered sugar
1 cup chocolate chips (you can use mini if
    you prefer)
½ teaspoon vanilla

In saucepan over medium heat, melt butter and peanut butter together, stirring constantly. Once melted, take off the heat and beat in sifted powdered sugar 1 cup at a time until it forms a cookie dough–like ball. Stir in vanilla.

Pat into a buttered 8" x 8" x 2" pan. Press chocolate chips into peanut butter. Run a butter knife through it to form desired piece size. Cover and place in fridge until cool. Once cool, run a knife around the edge of the pan to loosen. Pop out and serve. Note: fudge must be cut before cooled or it will break.

Also, if you prefer swirled chocolate, melt chips in microwave with 2 tablespoons of butter, then mix and pour over fudge in pan. Swirl butter knife through the peanut butter fudge to create a marble effect. Cut into pieces. Cool in fridge.

Chapter 36

"But Liam died in front of witnesses." Frances huffed. "There's no way he was murdered."

"He could have been poisoned," Jenn said. She twirled the stem of her wine glass. The brilliant red of her drink swirled in the light.

My entire team sat around the fireplace in the lobby of the McMurphy. Frances and Mr. Devaney each sat in sturdy wing-backed chairs. The thin striped pattern of the new upholstery was carefully researched. The settee where I sat with Jenn was a cabbage-rose pattern.

The fire popped and snapped in the cool of the night. The light from the two standing lamps was a soft yellow through lampshades with pale pink tassels. The chandeliers sparkled above, remaining unlit as I preferred the gentle light in the evening.

"Isn't poison usually a woman's way of killing?" Mr. Devaney looked up from the book he read. I think the old man never went anywhere without a book.

Between you and me, the only reason he was here now was because Frances was here. They wouldn't admit it, but I think there was something going on between those two. I'd seen the looks that passed between them when they thought no one was looking.

"Think about it, though," Jenn pushed. "Everyone believes that cliché. If I were a smart male killer, I'd use poison to off someone. Everyone would be looking for a woman."

"Who was at the senior center when Papa died?" I asked. "He was playing cards, right?"

"Yes, it was pinochle day. Liam's team had made the semifinal round."

"His team?" I sat up.

"Yes, of course, we would play in teams of two. Liam always played with Mabel Showorthy."

"Why would Mabel kill Liam?" Mr. Devaney said.

"She had no motive." I curled my jean-clad legs under me. "I've known her my whole life. Besides, it wasn't Mabel who attacked me in the basement and ran off with the wine."

"It had to be someone in the room," Jenn insisted. "Someone who could poison his drink or inject him with no one the wiser."

"My, you are a vicious thinker." Frances eyed Jenn.

"I like to watch crime shows on TV." Jenn shrugged. "Who else was at the center that morning?"

"I was at the other semifinalist table." Mr. Devaney looked up from his book. "It was me and Irene Kiaser against Thaddeus Kozicki and Bill Bogdan."

"Who were Papa and Mabel playing?" I asked.

"The team that almost always won these tournaments," Mr. Devaney said. "Eleanor and Henry De Cross."

"Again, where is the motive? If they win all the time there was no need for them to poison Papa."

"People come and go from the center," Frances said. "It was an especially busy day with the card tournament and the March birthday celebrations."

Mr. Devaney nodded. "It could have been anyone."

"Was Colin there?" I asked. I had kept Papa's secret to myself, only telling my friends that Trent suspected Papa was murdered as well as Joe.

Frances pursed her lips. "Colin could have been there," she said. "He did some work around the center when he was sober. If he was particularly down on his luck, he'd come in for a free meal."

"It wasn't unusual to see him there." Mr. Devaney put down his book. "He's one of those people that fades into the background. Why do you ask?"

"Colin was one of Papa's longtime friends," I said and sipped my wine. "He also had access to the McMurphy."

"You think he knew about the tunnel?" Jenn asked.

"He worked at the McMurphy for twenty years," I said.

"The handyman's workshop is in the basement," Mr. Devaney said. "He had to know about the tunnel."

"You are giving him too much credit," Frances

said. "Colin has been a drunk his entire life. I doubt he thought much past where his next bottle would come from."

"Being the town drunk would be a great cover," Jenn mused. "Think about it. He could come and go and no one would really see him. People tend to overlook those down on their luck."

"You got the keys to the McMurphy back when you fired him, right?" Frances asked.

"Actually, I never really fired him. I haven't seen him since Papa's funeral."

"Oh."

"But I don't think Papa trusted him with the master key," I said. "Seriously, Papa would have told me if Colin had one, wouldn't he?"

"Yes," Frances said. "He would have." She patted my hand. "But Colin was here so long it would have been very easy for him to make copies. He could have said he lost the keys and no one would have been the wiser. In fact I can see him making several copies over the years."

"So he had opportunity and he had means. The man had access to all gardening and household chemicals. No one would think a thing if he ordered extra rodent poison."

"The McMurphy does not have rodents," I said.

"You know that," Jenn pointed out. "But others wouldn't think twice."

"The McMurphy is over one hundred years old," Mr. Devaney added.

"Even if we had Liam exhumed and they discovered he was indeed poisoned by some sort of household poison, what in the world would be the motive?" Frances asked.

"A million dollars' worth of wine, hidden in the basement," Mr. Devaney said.

"It's true," Jenn said. "Who else would know it was down there?"

"Pete Thompson had access," I said. "His grandfather could have told him about the tunnel. Or he might have found it when they did the last renovation of the pool house."

"Pete was not at the senior center when Liam died," Frances said. "He's young. He would have stood out."

"What about his father?" I asked.

"Richard died a few years back. Boating accident." Frances shivered. "He went out fishing alone. They found his body washed up on shore the next day."

"Seriously?" Jenn sat up. "Could he have been murdered?"

"Okay, now you are simply seeing murder everywhere," Mr. Devaney scolded.

"The police ruled it out," Frances confirmed.

"There is something else," I said. Everyone looked at me. "I heard that someone saw Colin outside the pool house before Mr. Finley died."

"What is the connection between Finley's death and Joe's murder? Is there even one? Besides the McMurphy?" Mr. Devaney said.

"Wrong place, wrong time?" Frances shrugged.

"So all we have is suspicion." I sighed. "No real proof of anything."

"What has Officer Manning discovered? Anything?" Frances asked.

"Trent took Joe's journals in to the police station, but without any solid evidence we've got nothing."

There was a knock at the front door and Rex stepped into the lobby.

"Speak of the devil," Jenn muttered. I shot her a look and she winked at me.

"Hi, Rex." I stood. "Come on in. We were just talking about you."

"All good I hope." He took off his hat and stepped up to the fire. "How are you all tonight?"

"We were talking about the lack of concrete evidence in Joe's murder and the robbery," Mr. Devaney said. "Anything new on your front?"

"Nothing," Rex said. "I stopped by to do a check of the McMurphy. Until we have a solid suspect in custody, I'd prefer if you kept the front door locked."

"This is a hotel, Rex," I said. "We don't lock our doors until after nine PM, eleven during the season."

"I understand that," Rex said. "But until you have a night clerk on duty, I'd rather see you lock the door."

"Night clerk?" I glanced at Frances.

"We never needed a night clerk," Frances said. "Liam had a call button put in that runs from the front desk to the apartment. It's part of the intercom system."

"You're going to need a night clerk," Mr. Devaney said. "Preferably not a young intern, not with the McMurphy the center of these crimes."

"Right." I ran my hands over my face. Where was I going to find a responsible night clerk? For that matter how was I going to pay a responsible night clerk? I found myself wishing for one of those bottles of wine to auction off.

It occurred to me that I hadn't checked the basement for any more wine. Maybe, just maybe those weren't the last bottles.

"Don't worry." Mr. Devaney winked. "I'm sure Frances and I will know someone who'd like to get paid for his insomnia."

Frances stood and patted my arm. "These things have a way of working themselves out." She grabbed her purple coat from the coat rack and her red fedora from its storage place behind the front desk. "It's late. If you're ready to go, Douglas, I could use an escort home."

"Yes." Mr. Devaney closed his book and stood. "Manning, take care of the girls."

The men shook hands. "Will do, sir," Rex said. "Be careful out there."

I rolled my eyes at Jenn. I mean, I could take care of myself for goodness' sake. I'd spent five years in Chicago. This was Mackinac Island. It didn't get safer than here.

By the time Frances and Mr. Devaney left, Jenn had unfolded her long legs from the settee and headed up the stairs, leaving me alone with Rex.

"You really should get all new locks," he said. His gorgeous blue gaze was serious.

"I know. I have an appointment with the locksmith tomorrow."

"Good." He gave a short nod. The silence between us was awkward. Finally he spit out, "I heard you were seen kissing Trent Jessop at the Beanery this afternoon."

My cheeks flamed instantly. No slow embarrassment for me. "He wanted to dispel the feud rumors."

"He certainly did that." Rex studied me. "Are you seeing him?"

"Why?" I tilted my head. "Is he a suspect?"

Rex's mouth twitched. "No and neither are you." His words were thick with meaning.

My heartbeat sped up. "Oh, good to know."

He stepped into my space, heating it up with all his uniformed-covered muscles. He really had the prettiest eyes.

"You know, I never did search the basement for any more of that wine," I blurted out. I didn't want him to ask me again if I was seeing Trent. "If there's more down there, the thief is sure to come back. We don't want that, do we?"

Chapter 37

"You need better lighting down here," Rex muttered as he used his flashlight to look through the boxes Papa had stacked in the dark corners of the McMurphy.

"If you think this is bad, you should go through the attic." I laughed. We both froze. He looked at me. "No," I answered the unasked question. "I never looked in the attic."

We both headed up the stairs.

"When was the last time you were in the attic?" he asked.

"Not since the elevator was inspected. The attic was full of boxes and things covered by sheets. I didn't have time to do anything but show the inspector the way to the mechanism."

"Where is the access?" Rex asked.

"There's a door and pull-down stairs in the hall of the apartment between the bedrooms." We hurried through the lobby and up to the apartment.

"Is that the only access?"

"The only that I know of," I said, breathless. "But then, I didn't know about the tunnel, either."

"Any access from the second floor? Say the utility closet?"

"You checked that room when you investigated Joe's death."

"Yes, but as you said, we didn't know about the tunnel."

I stopped on the second-floor landing. "The utility room is beside the elevator. At best there's access to the elevator shaft. But the elevator doesn't go up to the third floor."

Rex stepped in front of me and used his flashlight to illuminate the hallway. "Since we're here, let's check it out to be sure."

I followed him down the hall to the utility room. I hadn't done anything with the room since I brought in crime-scene cleanup specialists to erase the tragedy from the McMurphy.

The closet was empty except for the set of shelves along the wall. They were made of walnut and built in. I didn't have the heart to pull them out. A single bulb glared above, throwing the corners into shadow. There was enough room for two people to walk in comfortably.

"I haven't been in here since that night," I mentioned as Rex knocked on the walls. "You don't think the shelves would have the same mechanism . . ." I ran my hands along the bottom of the shelves and discovered a metal lever that matched the one in the basement.

The shelves rotated on a silent pivot, revealing a two-foot opening. A rush of musty attic air blew in. I looked at Rex and he looked at me. "Well . . ."

He stepped into the opening, his flashlight revealing a set of narrow steps going up into the darkness. "Now that's something," he said.

"It looks like it was put in when the elevator was put in," I said. "See how it opens up above the elevator. It must have been there for working access."

"Why hide it?" he asked and went up the stairs. His flashlight illuminated the well-oiled mechanism at the top of the elevator.

"I don't know," I said and pressed a push-button light switch. A light came on above the elevator. "I thought these stairs were only for elevator repairs. It never occurred to me that there might be a door at the bottom."

"The door was well oiled. Who else would know about this?" Rex asked.

"Colin Ferber, of course. Maybe the elevator inspector, but he didn't mention the door to me."

We moved into the attic and I noticed that the attic floor was swept clean. There was no dust to look for prints in. Weird, right? I went around and turned on the lights. The attic ran the full length of the McMurphy and floorboards had been put in with the thought that the space might be used for something other than storage. But no one in the family had done anything more than store things up here.

There was a narrow two-foot walkway. Otherwise the attic was filled to overflowing with boxes, cartons, etc. Who knew what treasures the attic of the McMurphy would hold? Maybe it was worth my time to dig around and find out.

"I bet I could have a giant rummage sale and earn enough to pay a night clerk for a week," I joked.

Rex made a sound as if he were listening to me, but his attention was on the light from his flashlight and the boxes with the least amount of dust. "Someone's been squatting up here."

His words sent a chill down my spine. "What?" Had someone been sleeping above me all these weeks?

He moved a set of two boxes and showed me that someone had indeed been living above me. Behind the boxes on the far side of the attic was what appeared to be a mattress on the floor complete with sheets and blankets. A hot plate rested on the top of a wood box. There was a clean fry pan on it along with a stored pile of dishes.

"They haven't been here in a couple of days," he said as he checked out the bed. "There's a fine layer of dust on the trunk."

"Well, that's a relief," I muttered. Only it wasn't. Not really. I looked up at the sloping roof of the McMurphy. "Do you think it was Colin? I heard he'd lost everything when his wife died."

"Hard to tell," Rex said as he investigated the

well-hidden squatter's nest. "Had to be here when you had the elevator inspected," he said. "There is more than a week's worth of dust on these things."

"Okay, super creepy. There isn't a lock on the attic door to the apartment," I said. "I never thought I needed it."

"There will be one before I leave tonight," he said gravely.

"Right." I opened the attic door to the apartment, lowering the stairs. "Jenn?" I called. "Don't freak, it's me and Rex in the attic."

There was no reply. I drew my brows together. "Jenn?"

"Is she in the bathroom?" Rex asked.

"Maybe she came back downstairs," I said and went down the attic steps to the apartment. It was strangely quiet. "Jenn?"

I checked the bathroom, both bedrooms, and the living area. There was no sign of Jenn. The door to the interior of the hotel was open slightly so I pulled it open. "Jenn?"

"Is she here?" Rex asked as he emerged from the hallway.

"Not in the apartment," I said. "She did say she was coming up here, didn't she?"

"Yes, she did," he agreed.

"I'll check downstairs." I went to move through the door when Rex gently grabbed hold of my arm.

"Let me."

I didn't like the way he was thinking. "Okay, but I'm sure she just went down to the lobby for something."

"It's better if I went." His eyes glittered like a predator who smelled his prey.

"Okay." I hugged my waist and felt very small. Rex went through the door and moved off into the stairwell. I swear it was creepier to stay in the apartment by myself than it would have been if I had run down the stairs with Rex.

I heard barking in the distance. "Mal?" I checked her crate and she was not in it. Anger surged through me. If that creep hurt my puppy he was going to be a dead man. I'd gladly take the rap for that. "Mal? Here, Mal. Marshmallow?" I tried not to sound desperate as I followed the sound of the barking. The barking grew louder as I went toward the kitchen. "Mal?"

Then I noticed the back door was cracked. "Mal!" She was still a tiny puppy. She could easily fall the three stories and hurt herself. Panic whipped through me. My heart rate sped up and my hands trembled as I opened the door.

Mal stood at the edge of the fire escape with her tiny head between the bars, barking up a storm. I bent down and scooped her up quickly. "Oh, my gosh, baby, you scared the heck out of me. How did you get out?"

Mal licked my cheek, then looked out and barked again. The sound was definitely loud and at a tone that made all the hairs on my skin stand up. "Mal!"

She wouldn't stop. I looked out to see that Jenn was being dragged down the alley, kicking and what would have been screaming if the perp didn't have his hands over her face.

"Jenn!" I tucked Mal under my arm and let the fire-escape ladder loose. We scurried down as if my feet were on fire. Mal picked up on my fear and barked her head off. It was as if I had a siren under my arm. I hit the ground as the figure muscling Jenn away glanced back.

It was Colin Ferber. The back door to the McMurphy flew open with a bang and Rex stormed out, gun in hand. Mal and I froze. "Don't shoot!" I raised my free hand. Mal was silent and I swear she had her puppy paws up as well. The sight of a police-issue gun was enough to scare anyone.

Chapter 38

"Damn it, Allie, I told you to stay put." Rex lowered his gun and Mal started barking. "What is wrong with your dog?"

"It's Jenn," I said. "Some guy pulled her down the alley. I think it's Colin Ferber."

"Which way did he go?"

"That way," I said and pointed. Mal squirmed and wiggled, leaping out of my arms. She took off like a shot down the alley. I raced after her. Rex came after me.

There was no sneaking up on the villain. Not with all the noise Mal made. People came around the alley to see what all the commotion was about.

Emily Proctor stuck her head out the back door of her shop. "What's going on?"

"It's Jenn. Someone's kidnapped her. He took her down the alley," I shouted. "Mal went after them."

"Holy moly." Emily closed the door and soon I

heard Mike come running up behind us. Emily herself wasn't far behind.

Mrs. Amerson came around the back of the art gallery. "What is all the noise?"

"Someone kidnapped Allie's friend," Emily said. "The dog is chasing him and we are chasing the dog."

"That's terrible!" Mrs. Amerson took off running with us. "The alley crosses the street up here."

Mal had disappeared down the road as we approached the street that ran perpendicular to Market Street. Mal made a wide circle, barking as if to say, "Hurry, hurry!"

More people poured out of businesses. I let Emily and Mike explain what was going on. I had to keep breathing. I tried not to laugh. I felt as if I were part of the mob chasing Frankenstein's monster. A glance behind me showed that ten or more people had become part of the chase. Mal hit Market Street and did a wide circle, moving left.

"That little puppy is fast!" Emily said.

No kidding, I thought, nearly out of breath. At this rate there was no way the kidnapper could be that far ahead of us. He was dragging Jenn. Mal took off right at the next alley, her barking drawing us on. Suddenly there was a loud bang and a yip.

My heart sank and I screamed out, "No!" and sprinted. I turned the corner to see Mal lying on her side under the light of a streetlamp. The hooded man stood with a gun to Jenn's head. Jenn was very still, her eyes as big as saucers.

"Freeze!" Rex commanded and pointed his gun. His voice was so loud it stopped me in my tracks. In fact, the entire mob stopped as if he were talking to us. Maybe he was.

"Don't come any closer," the man said, his face shadowed by the hoodie he wore. "I'll kill her. I swear I will."

"No one's coming any closer." Rex's voice was deadly calm. I could hear the crowd breathing behind me, but no one moved. It might be interesting to see this in a television show, but let me tell you, in real life it was darn right terrifying.

The man waved his gun at the crowd and I could hear people scatter behind me. "Go away, all of you. Go! Get out of here!"

The sound of a siren could be heard in the distance. Police headquarters wasn't too far from here and in a heartbeat Officer Brown and Officer Lasko entered my peripheral vision.

I kept my hands up. "Don't hurt my friend," I said. My voice trembled and sounded breathy. So much for being a brave hero.

"I will hurt her if you don't get out of here."

"Allie, go," Rex said, his voice low and commanding.

"No." I pulled myself up by my imaginary big-girl panties. "Jenn is on island to help me. I am not going to abandon her."

Jenn had her hands on the arm around her neck. She had sweat rolling down her temple. "Allie, go."

"No." I lowered my hands and took a step forward. "Why don't you tell me why you're doing this?"

"Don't come any farther." The gun wavered dangerously at me.

I stopped. My legs shook. The police had him in their crosshairs. Were they looking for a reason to fire? "Let Jenn go and I'll walk away. We won't even press charges. Will we, Jenn?"

"No, we won't," Jenn said. Her gaze never left my face. I knew she wasn't this passive. She had something up her sleeve. Then I remembered how we used to play the scene from *Miss Congeniality*, the movie, over and over. What was her self-defense advice? SING. "Shut up. I'm not letting anyone go."

"Okay then, Jenn and I will have to sing."

Jenn's eyelid twitched and I knew she caught on. "Go ahead Jenn, sing."

Jenn shoved her elbow into the man's solar plexus. Then she stomped on his instep, slammed her palm into his nose, and kneed him in the groin.

He fell like a pile of bricks. Rex and the other two officers were on him before I could let out a breath. Jenn ran into my arms and I hugged her tight.

"Oh, thank God. Thank God!" I kept saying. Then I felt something bouncing at my knee. "What? Mal! I reached down and picked my puppy up and we did a group hug. "I thought you were dead." Tears filled my eyes. "I thought you were both dead."

"We're good," Jenn said. "We're strong. How did you see me?"

"Mal alerted me," I answered and sat down on the curb, not letting go of my best friend or my puppy. "She chased after you."

People came out of the buildings and from surrounding corners. They surrounded us, slapping our backs and talking loudly. Everyone thought Mal had been shot, but I ran my fingers over her and she was not even grazed.

"How?" I asked.

Jenn laughed. "I've been teaching her tricks. Did you know that bichons were circus dogs?"

"You taught her to play dead?"

"Yes, watch." Jenn made a gun shape with her fingers. "Bang!" Mal fell over and closed her eyes. "Good girl!"

Mal came back to life, wagging her tail and licking my face.

"Oh, you sweet thing." I cried some more and hugged her tight. The crowd helped us up and took us to the bar on the corner. I glanced over my shoulder to see Rex cuffing the man and Officer Brown reading him his rights.

"Who is he?" I had to ask.

"That's Freddy," Emily Proctor replied. "Colin Ferber's boy."

"Everyone knows Colin's a drinker. It's gotten real bad lately." Mike said. "Freddy came home to move his dad into a nursing home."

I drew my brows together as we entered the bar. "I didn't know Colin was sick."

Jenn and I were offered chairs at the bar and we

took them. Cold beers were set out in front of us. I swallowed my portion and took ahold of Mabel's arm, drawing her attention.

"I didn't know Colin was ill. I fired him because he didn't show up for work five days in a row."

"Colin has end-stage liver cancer," Mabel said. "He didn't tell anyone as he wanted to die as he lived. But then Freddy found out six months ago and has been trying to convince Colin to get the hospital care he needs."

"Colin wouldn't think of it," Emily said. "He said he was dead either way so why spend the money."

"Oh, that's so sad. I didn't know. He didn't say."

"It's not your fault," Jenn touched my arm. It was then that I noticed a large bruise forming on her knuckles.

"Oh, my, gosh. Bartender, can we get some ice here?" I raised my voice above the crowd and pointed to Jenn's hand.

"That's what happens when you sing." Jenn grinned and sipped her beer. "He was warned."

I laughed and touched her longneck bottle with mine. "Indeed, he was warned."

Chapter 39

"It was Colin living in the attic?" We were once again gathered in the lobby of the McMurphy. This time the fireplace had grown cold.

Rex and Officer Brown and Officer Lasko sat in chairs, while Jenn and I took the settee. Mr Devaney stood next to Frances who sat on her stool behind the reception desk. Mal curled up warm and sleepy in my lap.

"He sold his house to pay off his doctor bill," Rex said. "Freddy got wind that the property was for sale and came up on island to find out what was going on."

"Was he estranged from Colin?" I asked. "I don't remember Papa ever talking about Colin having any kids. Not even when Colin's wife died two years ago."

"He had a record a mile long," Officer Brown explained. "Freddy had been in jail for the last five years. It was after his parole that he heard about the sale. He had come up to see if he could get any of the money."

"But if Colin used the house to pay his medical bills," I said.

"He didn't have any money," Jenn added.

"Exactly," Rex said. "It pissed Freddy off so he followed his father to the McMurphy."

"He must have been in the process of coming or going from visiting his father in the attic when Joe caught him." I ran my hands along Mal's soft back.

"Freddy claims that Joe attacked him and he fought back, knocking Joe against the shelves and running out," Rex went on.

"Why didn't Colin come to see me?" I asked.

"He was too sick," Rex said. "All that drinking has taken a toll on his liver. The night you stayed with Frances, he slipped out through the apartment. He's been in St. Ignace at his sister's house ever since. His sister tells us that the doctor said Colin doesn't have long to live."

"But Benny saw him at the bar that night and Susan told me that Mary saw him outside the pool house the night Mr. Finley died."

"They must have seen Freddy," Lasko said. "He looks just like his father."

"Neither of them are young men," Mr. Devaney said.

"But who was in the basement?" I asked. "I don't think it was an old man who attacked me and stole the wine."

"Freddy swears he didn't have anything to do with Mr. Finley's demise," Rex said.

"So there is still a killer and a thief out there," Jenn said.

"How did you fall into Freddy's clutches?" Officer Brown asked.

"He was in the attic," Jenn said. "I went upstairs and caught him coming down the attic steps. Scared the pants off me. Before I could protest, he had a gun shoved in my face. He closed up the stairs and dragged me out the back door."

"Why? What did he think he was going to do with you?"

"I'm not sure he knew," Jenn said.

"You must have surprised him," Rex said.

"Do we know why he was in the attic?" Officer Lasko asked.

"He heard about the wine," Rex said. "He thought there might be some stashed in the attic."

"He didn't have any wine," Jenn said.

"There most likely isn't any in the attic," I said and sighed. "Which leads us back to the fact that someone else knew about the wine. Someone was in the basement and attacked me. Someone still could have killed Papa and George and Mr. Finley."

"Which is why I had Devaney stay with Frances and one of us will patrol the McMurphy at night," Rex said.

"That can't go on indefinitely," I said.

"It won't," Rex said. "I've got a plan. We'll discuss it in the morning."

Classic Cooked Chocolate Fudge

2 cups white sugar
½ cup cocoa
1 cup milk
4 tablespoons butter
1 teaspoon vanilla

Butter an 8" x 8" x 2" pan, then line with wax paper or plastic wrap. (I prefer wax paper.)

Using a double boiler fill ⅓ of the bottom pan with water and heat on medium high until the water is boiling. Then you can turn the heat down to low and in the top section, combine sugar, cocoa, and milk—stir until it boils, then stop stirring—cook until it reaches 238°F on a candy thermometer or until the soft-ball stage. Remove from heat, then add butter and vanilla and beat with a wooden spoon until glossy—this is the part where candy makers in most fudge shops scrape and turn the candy with a wooden paddle on a marble board. Do not underbeat. Pour into pan and cool. Cut to preferred size.

Chapter 40

"I saw the trashman was at the McMurphy." Mabel stopped in. Today's tracksuit was gold with lamé accents. She held her hand weights and pumped her arms up and down. "Were those Liam's old boxes he was hauling off?"

"Yes," I said as I made my first batch of fudge in front of the McMurphy's front windows. I stirred the sugar and cocoa and cream in the large copper pot. "I found a bunch of old wine in the basement. Most of the bottles were broken so I tossed the entire crate out. I thought maybe they could recycle the glass bottles."

"You threw out old wine? That was stupid."

"Why was that stupid? The corks were brittle. It wasn't any good. Besides, I think Papa made that batch in the basement. I found some counterfeit labels printed nearby." I shrugged. "I think he made them in French to prank Joe Jessop."

"Counterfeit labels?" Mabel stopped pumping and put her fists on her hips. "Are you sure?"

"Oh, yes, I had them checked out by one of my friends who is a professor in Chicago. They were counterfeit." I poured the liquid fudge onto the marble fudge table. "Good thing we aren't in the business of selling wine."

"Indeed." Mabel studied my face. "Liam loved to prank people, didn't he?"

"He sure did." I smiled at the memory and picked up the paddle to stir my fudge. "Are you sticking around to steal my fudge secrets?"

"Oh, dear. Lord, no." Mabel frowned at me. "I've been out of the fudge business for two years."

"You have?"

"Yes, I sold Agatha's two years ago to Dorothy Todd. I'm retired now and living large." She winked at me. "Have a good day now."

"Oh, I will." I lifted the fudge with the paddle and tossed it in the air. People gathered outside the window to watch. I smiled and performed little tricks, like tossing the fudge so that the ribbons landed making outlines of flowers.

When the fudge got to the right consistency, I added orange pieces that had been soaked in peach schnapps. This was my Fuzzy Navel recipe. I had gotten good comments from the guests on my 21-and-up series.

I glanced outside to see Rex standing near the window. He nodded at me. I smiled back. The plan had worked. The idea was to expose the persons interested in the wine.

Mabel had been the first to take the bait. Our hope was that she would spread the gossip through the town and our thief would show up at the trash site to hunt down any unbroken bottles of wine.

I remained calm. Rex had warned me it could take a full day before anyone took the bait. My part was to make fudge and open the door to the McMurphy for a local tasting before opening weekend.

I wouldn't get to know who they caught at the trash heap. It was safer that way. Jenn and Frances agreed. We planned our day, keeping our roles as normal as possible. It was difficult to stay calm, but somehow I managed.

By 2 PM, the four flavors of fudge I had made were sold out. Jenn had rented a cotton candy machine for the kids since my limited fudges were all soaked in rum, schnapps, and whiskey and were definitely 21-and-older fudges.

Frances paced behind her desk. Mr. Devaney spent the day closing up access to the attic from the second floor. Then he put a large dead bolt on the drop-down door into the apartment.

Mal was aware of the nerves we tried not to show. She was exhausted by the number of neighbors who stopped by to congratulate her for saving Jenn. They brought her treats and toys until she grew spoiled and had to go into her crate for a time-out nap.

"I understand your little dog is a hero." Mr. Beecher walked down the alleyway. He wore a tweed jacket with patches on the sleeves, a matching patterned vest, dress slacks, and soft brown shoes. I had to say one thing for the man. He might be older, but he was always stylish.

"She is," I said as Mal did her figure eights in the patch of grass behind the McMurphy.

"I heard she played dead." He stopped a few feet from us. "I had a pup who could play dead like that. Best dog of my entire life."

"I bet he was."

Mal wiped her feet on the grass and came over to sniff Mr. Beecher. The old man hooked his cane on his arm and bent down to scratch her between the ears.

"My friend Jenn taught her the trick."

"Not every dog can learn it," he said as he straightened with a twinkle in his eye. "Only a good prankster."

"Sort of like Papa Liam," I said.

"Yes." he nodded. "Like Liam. I heard through the grapevine Liam made some counterfeit wine to prank Joe Jessop."

"He did, that's right." I nodded. "There was some story about a rare wine he found as a kid."

"I remember that," Mr. Beecher said. "That wine was destroyed because of Prohibition."

"I guess Papa tried to convince Joe he found some more bottles. So he took some cheap wine and bottled it with counterfeit labels."

"It's against the law, isn't it?"

I shrugged. "As long as he didn't sell it, or claim it was what it wasn't there was no fraud."

"That Liam, always a card." Mr. Beecher chuckled. "You have a good day, young lady."

"Thanks, Mr. Beecher. You, too." Mal and I walked back to the McMurphy when Mal stopped suddenly and started to growl. "What is it?"

Emerson Todd emerged out of the shadows. "So it's true? Your grandfather counterfeited that wine?"

"Yes, I believe so," I said. Mal acted strangely. She was stiff and growling low. "I wouldn't come any closer," I said, drawing my eyebrows together. "Mal doesn't really like you."

"Smart pooch," Mabel said as she stepped out behind Emerson. "Too bad for both of you." It was then that I noticed the gun in Mabel's hands.

"Mabel?" I looked from her to Emerson. "Wait— are you two related?"

"Everyone on island is related in some form or other," Emerson said, "it's a small community."

"I'm starting to understand that," I said. Emerson took a step forward. Mal barked at him.

"Shoot that damn dog," Emerson told Mabel.

I dropped Mal's leash. "Run, Mal!" I shouted. "Go!"

The puppy grabbed up her leash and took off around the building.

"Don't think that will save you," Mabel said. "Liam thought he was clever and that didn't save him."

"You poisoned him, didn't you?"

Emerson grabbed me by the arm. "Don't think you're going to get me with your SING," he said. "Mabel will shoot you the minute you make a wrong move. Now, let's go."

"Where are we going?" I asked. His hands bruised my arm as he dragged me through the alley.

"We're going to the pool house," he said. "I happen to know that wine was not fake."

"We had it tested," Mabel said. "We also know Liam had at least one more bottle in the basement. You're going to tell us where you hid it."

He dragged me through the bushes and into the pool house. It was quiet now, the pool drained. "I haven't found any more," I said. "You got the last two bottles."

Emerson hit me with his fist and stars exploded in front of my left eye. "Don't lie to us."

"I'm not lying," I said when I could breath. "Why would I lie? You have a gun."

"Open the door to the tunnel," Mabel ordered.

"I don't have the key. Pete has the key."

"Nonsense. You co-own the pool house. You have a key," Mabel said.

"Papa Liam sold our shares in the pool house years ago," I said. "I don't have the key."

"Liar!" Emerson hit me again and I fell to my knees.

"Freeze!" Nothing had ever sounded so sweet to me as Rex's voice. "Put the gun down, Mabel."

"Shoot me and you're precious girl gets it," Mabel said.

"I said put the gun down."

"Do it," Officer Brown said from behind her.

"This isn't over," Mabel said as she put down the gun. Officer Brown rushed up and kicked it away. He grabbed Mabel's hands and cuffed them behind her. Rex had Emerson cuffed, and then he holstered his gun and hunkered down to check on me.

"Are you okay?"

"Sure," I said. "Maybe I should put my head down."

The next thing I knew, George Marron was beside me with an ice pack. Mal leapt on me, licking me with warm puppy kisses.

"So it was Emerson and Mabel all along," Jenn said once they got me up and resting in the lobby of the McMurphy.

"Do we know why?" I asked as I held an ice pack to my eye, which had begun to swell. George checked me out and pronounced that I would have a shiner, but my bones were not broken. He recommended ice and a few days of rest. This time I was happy to oblige.

"Mabel's daughter married Emerson. When Emerson lost all their money in the stock market, Mabel sold her business to her daughter. But the tourism hasn't been what it once was."

"How did she find out about the wine?"

"When the last bottle was auctioned off. The auction house sent out a press release to indicate the value of the wine. Mabel saw the news clip on it online. She remembered the boys had found a few bottles in the 1950s and even though they supposedly destroyed the wine, it didn't take much for Mable put two and two together."

"She confronted Liam first, but he laughed her off."

"So, she poisoned him?" I asked.

"In plain sight, too," Frances said. "Brazen."

"And Joe?"

"Joe figured it out, but before he could do anything he ran into Freddy."

"And Mr. Finley?"

"Caught Emerson leaving the tunnel through the mechanical room under the pool," Jenn said. "When Mr. Finley questioned Emerson's reason for being in the mechanical room, Emerson killed Mr. Finley and then hurried over to arrive at the party. It's why his coat was wet. He tossed him in the pool."

"So it was Emerson who attacked me and ran off with two bottles of wine. Where did he put them? I mean, he met me at the lobby door shortly after and he was empty-handed."

"When we searched his things, we discovered that the lining of his coat has two pockets where he hid the wine," Officer Brown said. "In fact the wine was still in the coat. He may have kept them hidden so that he had two bottles of his own that Mabel didn't know about."

"Wow," I said. "I thought the coat was heavy but I didn't even suspect there might be wine bottles in the lining."

"Now, are you ready for the good news?" Frances asked.

I laid my head back against the settee. "There's good news?"

"Oh yes." Jenn's eyes sparkled.

"They recovered the wine bottles," Frances said. "You have enough money to keep the McMurphy going for at least five years."

"Really?"

"Really," Rex said.

"That's the best news." I hugged Mal tight. "It looks like dreams really can come true."

Acknowledgments

Many thanks to the owners, employees and patrons of The Island Bookstore on Mackinac Island. They not only answered the questions from an unknown writer, but they allowed me to run a Facebook Contest to determine what Allie's occupation should be—Fudge Shop owner was number one with Horse Stables a close second. Readers, if you get the chance to visit Mackinac, be sure to stop into the bookstore for a great beach read and friendly and welcoming folks.

Next, I need to thank my own Facebook fans for helping me come up with Mal's name (Marshmallow). It was perfect for a fluffy white dog that lives in a fudge shop.

Thank you to USDTL's Research and Development committee for taste testing my fudge recipes and especially to Mary Jones for suggesting Captain Morgan Fudge—which got me started on my cocktail fudge idea.

I can't thank enough my friends and family and the great community of writers who have supported me every step of the way.

Last but not least, thank you to my editor, Michaela Hamilton, and my agent, Paige Wheeler—your help and encouragement mean a lot.

Turn the page for a preview
of the next Candy-Coated Mystery featuring
Allie and Mal . . .

TO FUDGE OR NOT TO FUDGE

Coming from Kensington in 2014!

Chapter 1

"A lilac by any other name still smells as sweet."

"Mal, get out from under that lilac bush," I called. It was almost time for the lilac festival and my bichon/poodle puppy Marshmallow had fallen in love with the fertilizer that was spread under the lilacs. For some reason she found the bushes next to the *Town Crier*, Mackinac Island's newspaper, to be the most malodorous.

I tugged on her leash. Mal dug in her heels and refused to budge. Like a fisherman fighting a hook, I reeled in the leash. This served to pull on her pink harness and drag one stubborn doggie out from under the bush one inch at a time. "Come on, Mal, let's at least pretend I'm in charge," I muttered and pulled harder.

As the proud yet harried owner of the one-hundred-and-twenty-year-old McMurphy Hotel and Fudge Shoppe, I'd walked down to the newspaper to place a want ad for a part-time maid to help fill in during the busy times. Mackinac Island was known for its quaint Victorian feel. There were no cars. In fact they were banned from the island. Only bicycles and horse-drawn carriages filled the streets.

Mal was a gift from my dear friend and reservation manager, Frances Wentworth. The puppy was supposed to keep me safe from evildoers. She had done her job well last month when I found myself investigating my grandfather's best friend's murder. I kind of had to, as he had been murdered in my utility closet.

Still, on the days when she wasn't protecting me, Mal had a tendency to boss me about. Especially when it came to doing things she was interested in doing . . . like sniffing under lilac bushes—instead of what I was supposed to be doing . . . placing an ad in the paper.

"Come on, Mal, I need to get this errand done before noon." I yanked on the leash. Suddenly she popped out from under the bushes with a bone in her mouth.

I did a double take. Was that a sock hanging from that bone?

Surely not. I mean, on close inspection it had an argyle pattern like a sock. It was knitted like a sock. Okay, so there was a huge hole in what appeared to be a heel like a sock. But then Mal loved socks. Maybe other dogs did too. Maybe, just maybe, some dog buried their bone in their favorite sock. It could happen, right?

I mean, what were the chances that the sock belonged to the bone? Slim to none. Right?

Mal proudly dropped the sock-wrapped bone at my feet and nudged it as if to show me what she found. Her little stubby tail wagged.

"I sure hope that's not what I think it is." I poked it with my white Keds. There was no way I was going to pick it up.

She pushed the bone toward me, wagged her bobbed tail, and darted back under the lilac bush. "Mal, come on, I have work to do." I yanked on her harness only for her to prance out from under the bush. This time she had what looked like part of a shoe in her mouth. She shook the shoe as if to kill it. Dirt and mulch went flying, along with hard pieces that hit my legs with a thump, thud, thump.

Those hard pieces had toenails—painted a neon orange.

The spit dried up in my mouth. Adrenaline washed through me. I did what any sane person would do. I scooped up my dog, yanked the shoe out of her mouth, dropped it next to the sock bone, and ran straight into the *Town Crier*.

There was no way I was going to be alone outside with portions of a dead person. I mean really, what if whoever it had been had been attacked by a wild animal and dragged under the bush to be saved for a later meal? Or worse. What if the animal was a rabid creature using the remains as bait? It could be true. There was no way I was going to hang around and find out.

"Dogs aren't allowed in here," said an older gentleman with a white beard, balding head, and a pair of reading-glasses perched at the edge of his nose.

"Right." I faced him and held the door closed with my body. Mal leapt out of my arms and sat down to stare at the old guy as if to dare him to kick her out.

He stared at me. "The dog . . ."

I found my voice. "Just dug up remains from under your lilac bush."

He drew his bushy white brows together over his dark brown eyes. "Excuse me?"

I swallowed and cleared my throat as I fumbled for my phone. "Call 9-1-1. I think there's a dead guy under your lilac bush."

"A dead . . . what?" He stood and took a step away from me, using his desk as a shield between him and the crazy woman at his door. It would have been funny if I weren't the crazy woman.

"Person," I said. "Well, not a whole person. A part of a person that wears argyle socks and leather shoes . . . oh, and paints their toenails orange."

He picked up the phone and hit a single button. "Hi Charlene," he said. "Get Officer Manning over here, will ya? There's a crazy woman in my office. No, she doesn't appear to have a weapon, just a small white dog. Um, hmm, hold on. Are you the McMurphy girl?"

"Yes," I said, my hands fumbling with my phone.

After last month's trouble I had Officer Rex Manning on speed dial and hit the button.

"The one who found Joe Jessop dead in the McMurphy utility closet?"

"Yes." I put the phone up to my ear and listened to it ring.

"It's the same crazy woman," the man said into his phone. "Right. Okay. Bye." He hung up the phone and sat down slowly, watching me with narrowed eyes as the ringing on my phone dropped me into Rex's voice mail.

"Hey, hi," I said into my cell phone. "I hope you're on your way to the *Town Crier.* I'm pretty sure Mal dug up a dead person." I hit the END CALL button.

The old man studied me and I studied him. He reached into his desk drawer and pulled something out. Then he slapped it down in front of him. It was a rabbit's foot.

Ew. Okay, I'd seen enough disembodied feet for one day, thank you very much. "What is that?"

He raised his right bushy eyebrow. "If you don't know, I bet the dog could tell ya."

I sighed and crossed my arms. "It's a rabbit's foot. I know what it is, I wanted to know why you got it out."

"Because I don't know how to make an evil eye." He tipped back in his chair and it squeaked.

"An evil eye?" I shook my head, dazed. "I don't get it."

"It wards off bad omens and such," he said and

reached over to adjust his placement, ensuring the rabbit's foot sat square between him and me.

"Um, okay. I'd join you behind your rabbit's foot, but I'm currently busy making sure the door stays closed."

"Now why would ya be doing that?"

"Because there is a killer out there. It might be a wild animal. It might be a serial murderer. Either way there is going to be a door between me and it." I hated to sound smug, but really, a strong wooden door was a lot better at keeping a rabid animal away than a rabbit's foot.

"Well, there, see, that's where we disagree."

"We do?" I scrunched up my eyebrows.

"As far as I can tell the bad luck is already inside with me."

"What? Where?" I glanced around but there were only three of us inside: me, him, and Mal.

"I'm looking at it." His gaze was steady on me.

"You mean me?" I pointed to my pink polo shirt.

"You're the only one in this room that finds old men dead and seeing as how I'm an old man . . ."

"But you're not dead." I tried to reason with him.

"Thus the rabbit's foot."

"Okay, seriously, I don't know what you heard, but I did not murder anyone."

"I didn't say you did."

"But you just said . . ."

"That you have been known to be alone when you find old men dead." He shrugged. "I'm hedging my bets."

I didn't know what to say to that so I simply glared at him. He glared back. Mal sneezed and we both jumped.

"Does the dog bite?" The man finally broke the silence.

"Mal? No, she's a puppy." I picked her up and decided to play nice. I stuck out my hand. "I didn't properly introduce myself. I'm Allie. I run the McMurphy."

"I know." He sat back carefully, still wary. "Charlene told me."

"Right." I pulled my empty hand back.

"Besides, I'm a reporter. Not much escapes my notice." He crossed his arms over his wide chest.

"Except a dead body under your bushes."

"I thought you said it was a sock and shoe."

"With bones and toenails." I hugged Mal until she squeaked.

"Orange-painted toenails." He pursed his mouth. "Yep, you told me that part, Ms. McMurphy."

"I'm not crazy," I said in my own defense.

"There are people on this island who would disagree with that." He watched me from over the top of his eyeglasses.

"There are people on this island who think we should allow cars. Everything people think is not always right."

"Well, you have me there." He leaned back. "I'm Angus MacElroy."

"I'd say it's very nice to meet you, but right now

I'm not so sure." Mal wiggled, but I held her tight. Her fluffy fur was a comfort.

"Why'd you come here, Ms. McMurphy?" Angus asked.

"I came over to place a want ad, but instead it seems I've uncovered a dead body or possibly a murder victim." I tilted my head and studied him as if he were the perfect suspect. For all I knew he was. "Being a reporter, you probably have seen a million dead bodies."

"Only ten and they were open-casket funerals," he admitted, his brown eyes twinkling. "A murder victim? Isn't that jumping to conclusions?" he asked in a calm manner—too calm if you ask me.

"It looks like murder to me unless you purpose-fully buried someone under your lilac bushes."

He leaned back and the squeak of his chair echoed around the room. "I didn't bury anyone under the lilacs. There's a law against that, you know."

"Grandpa, are you scaring away customers?" A woman about my age stepped out of the back room. She had dark black hair, a heart-shaped face, and soft blue eyes. She wore cargo pants and boots and a pale blue tank top under a red, white, and blue plaid shirt.

"She's not a customer." He glanced at me. "She's a crazy woman who won't leave the door. She has some ridiculous notion that holding the door will keep a wild animal from bursting in and killing us."

"Don't be silly." She buzzed a kiss on his grizzled cheek. "It's more likely she's afraid to get near you."

She stepped around the desk. "Hi, I'm Elizabeth MacElroy. Everyone calls me Liz."

I shook her hand. She had a nice firm grip. "Allie."

"Hi Allie, who's this sweet puppy?" She leaned in and Mal jumped into her arms and kissed her. Liz laughed and stood holding Mal. "Aren't you the sweetest?"

"Oh, no." I tried not to panic. "Don't let her kiss you."

"Why not? I love doggies." Her blue eyes twinkled in delight as Mal proceeded to wash her face.

I winced. "She may have dead body breath."

"What?" Liz froze.

"That's what I told you." Angus leaned back with a smug smile. "Ms. McMurphy seems to think she found a murder victim hidden in the lilacs. Anyone you know missing?"

GREAT BOOKS, GREAT SAVINGS!

When You Visit Our Website:
www.kensingtonbooks.com
You Can Save Money Off The Retail Price
Of Any Book You Purchase!

- **All Your Favorite Kensington Authors**
- **New Releases & Timeless Classics**
- **Overnight Shipping Available**
- **eBooks Available For Many Titles**
- **All Major Credit Cards Accepted**

Visit Us Today To Start Saving!
www.kensingtonbooks.com

All Orders Are Subject To Availability.
Shipping and Handling Charges Apply.
Offers and Prices Subject To Change Without Notice.